Leaving Reality

James Wollrab and Rob Collette

iUniverse LLC
Bloomington

LEAVING REALITY

iUniverse books may be ordered through booksellers or by contacting:

iUniverse LLC
1663 Liberty Drive
Bloomington, IN 47403
www.iuniverse.com
1-800-Authors (1-800-288-4677)

ISBN: 978-1-4917-3644-9 (sc)
ISBN: 978-1-4917-3645-6 (e)

Printed in the United States of America.

iUniverse rev. date: 06/04/2014

Acknowledgements

Many thanks to Stephen McRae for
His great help in editing the text,

And

Many thanks to Mads Buus Jacobsen for
His artistic work on the cover graphic.

This book is dedicated to the members of
THE FLORIDA PANTHERS' BOOSTER CLUB

1

What's a Puck, Anyway?

I recall my fifth grade teacher,
Missus Stupka, telling me...well,
telling our entire class, how life is
just a crazy dream surrounded by a
deep sleep, and in the end we will all
just disappear into space which is where we
all came from in the first place! Somehow
that all makes perfect sense to me right
now, but I'm not exactly sure why that is.
I'm certainly not a philosopher of any kind,
but her magic words keep marching through
my brain like little wooden soldiers. Shakespeare's
Macbeth and Hamlet always appear to me
at the most unexpected moments in my life.
And, on top of all that, you know what?
I didn't ask to be here in the first place!

Jean-Luc

Who the heck are you anyway? I don't remember you introducing
yourself to me. But, then again, I really don't remember much of anything.
For some strange reason I know that I should remember a lot, but I can't
recall a thing right now. Is that normal for someone my age? How old am
I anyway?

And why in the world are you continuing to stare at me like that? Your eyes are huge and brown...or blue? Maybe that color is green? I can't tell from way down here. Are they circular or elliptical? Does it really make any difference?

And where the heck am I...are we anyway? Am I still on Earth? For some reason I do know that I should be on a planet called Earth, and I'm probably there because the air I'm breathing seems normal...whatever that is. Can't anybody give me some answers to my most pressing questions in my greatest time of need? Or is it my time of greatest need? Who knows?

As I try so very hard to say all of those little words out loud so everyone can hear them, I cannot feel my lips move not even one little bit. I feel a lot of pain for sure, but it seems to be coming continuously from everywhere in my body all at one time! Does that even make sense? I can see that you seem to agree with me that it's crazy.

Maybe I'm just trying much too hard to express myself to whoever or whomever or whatever is out there...or maybe I'm just practicing to become a famous ventriloquist for a prime time television show... or more likely than not, I guess I am just thinking those words aloud to myself in my little brain, and I'm the only one hearing them? Is that even remotely possible in this day and age...whatever day and age this is? But, heck, I'll keep trying to express myself and be understood because I want this guy,whoever he is, to hear and understand what I'm trying to say...that's for sure!

Just so the both of you know, I do see both of you fairly easily. I see him quite clearly right now here above me looking straight down... staring down at me through his very glassy bluish-green eyes, but he keeps fading in and out every minute or so. And, funny thing, he doesn't seem to see or notice you at all. And, no, I'm not reciting the lyrics from that fabulous English rock band's great song. You know who I mean, right? It's that great band *The Who*...not to be confused with *The Guess Who*. You now look very confused indeed! I'll try to explain so we can understand each other.

The Guess Who is a Canadian rock'n roll band for sure. One of the very best in the world as far as I'm concerned. I also really like guitar player and singer Neil Young a lot, too. He's not in that band...I can see that you knew that fact already. But, he is a real Canadian for sure, and he absolutely can play that guitar of his really well! So is the band *Rush*, I think? No, come to think of it, I'm absolutely sure they're Canadian, too…all three of them. But my Canadian friends get them mixed up all the time with English and American groups, and believe it or not, I do have plenty of Canadian acquaintances and friends…somewhere around here anyway?

Why in the world am I worried about that stuff right now? It has nothing to do with my current problem or problems for sure, but I am known for going off on tangents all the time especially if I'm telling jokes. I guess it's just my great love for music. I know I should have been a musician instead of whatever I am! But whatever I am, it could never surpass being a great musician…could it?

Oh well, I can see from the weird look in his eyes…the other guy's eyes, not yours…that he is not going to answer me any time soon no matter what I say or how many times I try to say it to him. And, I must tell you that he's definitely getting a little fuzzy around the edges again at that. His hair is pointing up and out in all directions like he's being electrocuted for a crime! Is he one of the Marx Brothers maybe or a relative of John Beluchi?

Do you ever bother to comb your hair? That's the question I want to ask him right now so bad…or maybe ask you the same thing first! But it probably doesn't matter much to either one of you anyway. His friends are probably very used to the untidy look of his fuzzy locks. But that doesn't answer the question as to whether I'm talking to you or to him or to both of you at the same time? Well, if either one of you ever talks back to me, then I will find that out for sure. But it doesn't appear that that's going to happen any time soon.

Anyway, as I indicated before, my little bitty head or what's left of it really hurts like mad right now. No funny stuff or imagination involved with that fact at all. I'm not here looking for your sympathy in any way. For sure, I fully believe that this is definitely not a dream I am having after too much beer or shots of whiskey! That's because this is real physical pain I feel, and I doubt a few aspirins can suppress it no matter how hard they try to do the job for me.

Besides, I rarely if ever drink beer or alcohol of any kind for some very good reasons you might not understand. But the rest of me actually does seem to feel pretty much okay right now. It's just my little head that's throbbing with a thumping noise like Alex Van Halen on the drums, and it sure hurts like hell as if someone hit me with a baseball bat in the very recent past. And I don't even like baseball one bit. It's too slow and much too boring for me! All they do is stand around out there on the baseball field and scratch...oops.

Now that I think about it, it's certainly not the kind of hurt that comes from thinking too hard either, that's for sure. Not that I ever think that hard that often as far as I can remember. At least I don't think so? This hurt isn't even coming from inside my skull where my brain should be...it's on the outside of my head, on the right side of the outside of my skull or maybe the left side of what's left of my skull anyway! But, it is really hard to think clearly and talk at the same time when my head hurts this much so you'll have to bear with me for a while longer.

I'll tell you what's really strange about all this...at least for me right now. It feels just like a large, very hard turnip has been taped to my forehead with duct tape. And, if I could only open my eyes for a moment, I might be able to see what that liquid is that's running all over and down my skin. I suppose it could just be some perspiration because I feel like I'm sweating like mad, but I really doubt that.

Whoops, I just had a really scary thought. Is it...my own blood that's running down across my face? Now that I think about it, I sure hope that it's definitely only my perspiration that I feel. I haven't got that much blood that I can afford to lose right now. It's just got to be perspiration, or is that just my wishful thinking on the loose and running wild again like it always does? I wish that I had a mirror to look into so I could analyze the situation for myself...if I could open my eyes, that is!

I hope you realize that you're not being much help to me in my current tragic moment of need. You just keep staring at me like I'm an old silver coin you found while digging a hole in your yard for a post. A lot of good that does especially with the price of silver being so low these days! Well, gold is down, too, so I guess it doesn't matter at all. Either way, you're not much help and neither of us is getting any wealthier as a result of this.

I'm so tired that I can't get up off the floor or wherever or whatever it is that I happen to be lying on right now. My arms and legs are very, very tired...and really, really weak, and I'm gasping for breath all of the time. Why in the world is this happening to me? This is more than just the relentless pull of the force of gravity as my high school science teacher was known to say all the time. To him life was just photons and neutrons and electrons and tachyons and all kinds of other really small things zooming around so fast that you couldn't see them even if you tried. If you don't know what those things are, go to a science library and look them up. Well, actually, according to him you could see them all clearly in your mind if you just focused your neurons. I always had a little trouble with that concept.

I try, but I can't open my eyes…at least not for very long. But, you know, I can see this fellow's face quite clearly in front of me once again… even with my eyelids closed! Come to think of it, that's pretty amazing. I could never see things with my eyes closed ever before no matter how hard I tried…not even photons unless I was dreaming, of course. Does that mean that he or you are only a vivid dream or a silly ghost or a figment of my imagination? What about an avatar or an apparition? I can see that you like those concepts a lot. This is just like some of the weird movies I've seen lately. Maybe I'll have to stop watching those scary Stephen King movies for a while or at least until I get over this episode. Or maybe I could come up with the plot for a new one and give him a call and be famous and make some money?

Okay, I can tell that you're a bit skeptical about all this stuff I'm letting you in on without much warning. Believe it or not, I do know what an avatar is. Could he be Henry Skutter from Carnivale by any chance? You should know who he is, don't you? He's very scary indeed. Oh, well, if you don't…never mind. It's a very, very long and interesting story, but maybe we'll get into that later once we've solved our current problems.

Let's get back to the guy who is staring at me like I'm a counterfeit hundred dollar bill…or at least a twenty dollar bill. Maybe he can tell me where I am and how it is that I got here in the first place? To say the least, that would be very helpful indeed. If he has an answer, no matter how crazy it is, I'll take his word for it until I can get myself together and figure things out for myself. But getting him to help me will be no easy task to say the least. Besides, all three of us seem to be in the same boat so maybe we should help each other?

Actually, all I really want to do right now is take a quiet nap somewhere where it's nice and warm and soft and comfortable…and safe. It sure is cold right here where I am right now, just like it was almost all the time when I was a little kid. It's easy to nap when it's cold if you have a nice warm blanket and a nice warm fire close by…but I can't feel any blanket or the heat from a fire anywhere nearby right now. But, it really is ice cold to say the least. I sure hope I'm dreaming this whole thing so I don't freeze to death before I figure it out. I know that this is a pun, but that's the cold reality of my situation. Did you get it?

Not to make things worse, but all of the very little I can remember is from when I was a little kid. Am I just a little kid now? Maybe that's the answer except that something in my broken mind keeps telling me that I'm older than that. Maybe some rest will clear all of this up?

Finally, some progress! One eye wants to stay open at least for a short while. Unbelievable! Now I see a rainbow rolling in the air above me, but I don't think that I'm outside because there's a roof up there, too. Am I seeing the rainbow through the roof with x-ray vision? But, like I've said over and over, it is freezing cold in here just as if I…we were on the outside out in some winter weather near the North Pole. I can almost smell frozen water…ice around here somewhere near me. Really, water does have a smell if you are close enough to smell it. But that's not important right now.

Maybe I'm on that river I might have or should have mentioned before? If I am, it must definitely be winter 'cause it's frozen solid. But that raises a really good question. What the heck am I doing on the river while I'm inside a building anyway? As I said several times, I vaguely remember a river somewhere in my past, but I can't recall the name or where it is or was or why I remember it so vaguely…except that it was really cold some of the time! But it didn't have a roof over it back then, of that I am absolutely certain.

You know, if I could lift my arms up just a little bit, I'd pinch myself to see if I am dreaming. But, I can't do either one of those things…lift my arms or pinch myself. I tried to roll over on my side a moment ago, but that's not happening very easily either. Oh, well, dreams can be that way as I remember. You are sure you are awake, but you can't move no matter how hard you try. I'll just wait until I wake up again, and then everything will be fine and dandy once and for all. The first thing I'll do when I do wake up is roll over, that's for sure. Standing up will also have a high priority if that's even really possible.

Now, all of a sudden, some other man in a blue coat and red tie is looking down at me from behind the other guy. Where did he come from anyway? At least his hair isn't all messed up like he's being electrocuted or just been electrocuted! He seems to be asking me a question because he keeps shrugging his shoulders after he speaks as he's pointing at me. I see his lips moving quite a bit, but I can't hear a sound coming out of him. That's probably because it's much too noisy around here right now.

Lucky for me, I think that I might be able to read his lips if I concentrate real hard. That skill comes from my watching TV with the sound turned off. As I remember, I used to do that all the time when my parents thought I was up in my room asleep. I don't think they ever figured it out even though I did it all the time. They thought I was sound asleep up there in my little room, but I was watching John Wayne or Clint Eastwood or Charles Bronson or someone like that in an action movie. Those were the movies I liked best. What fun that was, and they never, ever figured it out!

What's your name? seems to be what he's saying to me over and over. Can you believe it? He wants to know what my name is of all things. Why does he care? Was I in an accident or is he a teacher or a cop? Do we know each other even though we've never met?

What kind of question is that to ask an injured person anyway? But it does seem like he really wants to know. He's asked me three or four times now, but I'm just staring back at him like a dead frog. Mind you, I do want to be cooperative, but I can't figure out why he would ask me such an easy question so many times. Maybe I should just tell him what my name is?

I do remember that my name is…whoops…what is it? I had it there for a moment, but it just slipped away out of my mind like a pickle with grease on it. That always happened to me with other people's names when I tried to remember them, but not my own. I could always remember my own name without any serious problems at least up to now. Well, come to think of it, maybe it's not such an easy question after all. Could it be a trick question? Let me just settle back, take a deep breath and think for a moment. How could I forget?

Robespierre! That's it! My name is Jean-Luc Robespierre.

I don't know why, but I can remember that all of a sudden now that I think about it for a moment or two. I'm definitely Jean-Luc Robespierre and no one else. But the rest of everything connected to my name is still pretty fuzzy right now. Maybe I am really in a dream state or a trance put on me by a hypnotist? Right now it feels like a dream to me, but the other possibilities can't be ruled out just yet. But, I never remember it hurting so much before in any of my dreams or trances. Well, I did know a hypnotist but more about that later.

If I could just lift my arms up off the floor, I'd take a look in my wallet for my driver's license, if I have one that is. Come to think of it, I'm not sure that I have a wallet much less a driver's license But I still can't move my arms an inch, so if he wants to confirm my name and address, he'll have to get my wallet out of my pocket for himself. He should be smart enough to figure that out by now. I don't have to tell him everything, do I? Well, from the confused look on his face, I will probably have to do everything myself.

Now that I think about my wallet and driver's license, you don't think I was in a car accident, do you? I'm not in my car or any car for that matter. I'm not on a street or in an alley, and there are no cars honking and no ambulances speeding up to get me out of here for medical care. Nah, it's a real live dream I'm experiencing for sure. And what's interesting right now is that I don't recall taking any kind of test for my license…if I have one.

What's also very interesting is that my last name is Robespierre just like that fellow in the French Revolution. You remember studying about the French Revolution in school, don't you? My eighth grade teacher, Mr. Webb, told me about the French Revolution in our history class. I don't know how many times he told our class that I might be a relative of the famous Frenchman of the same name. It was getting a little embarrassing for me, I must admit. I think that Robespierre, not me…the other guy, eventually got his head cut off for all his trouble and fame. When I heard that part of the story, that's when I stopped liking the French Revolution very much to be sure. Just think about it for a moment or two! It certainly isn't worth losing your head over just to be famous in the future and to be talked about briefly in an eighth grade history class.

He, Mr. Webb that is, called it 'world history class'. I kept asking myself where else would our history happen except in our world? Outer space history is a possibility, but I think there's no one out there waiting to write it down or remember what just happened, if anything.

Then, he made us read a book entitled *The Count of Monte Cristo*. To say the least it was very difficult reading for us eighth graders… Mr. Webb said it was at least third year high school level reading and understanding, but since we…our class was smarter than the average bear, we could do it.

As a Robespierre, I accepted the obvious challenge and read the whole book. It took me quite a while to get through it, probably a week, but the good guy finally came out on top after a very rough start. I remember how relieved I felt about that! And with a little bit of luck he made a lot of money in the process, too! But that wasn't the most important part of the story from my point of view. It was his great victory over the bad guys that counted most of all. I remember how happy I was for him when he finished polishing them off. Wow, he must have felt good about that!

Am I boring you with all of these trivial thoughts on world history and my possible lineage and reading habits? I hope not because when my body can't work…like right now, it's good to have a brain that can travel over time and space and communicate with others…wow, I'm really way out there right now, aren't I? I can tell by the expression on your face that you think I'm losing it…or have lost it completely. Just give me a little time to collect myself and my thoughts together, and I'll be okay. At least I think that I still have my head on straight even though it doesn't feel that way!

Whoops, he's gone! I must have faded out there for a moment or two. Oh, yeah. Now I remember. He was asking me more questions that I was lip reading as best I could. He asked me where I was from of all things. From what? What the heck did he mean by that? Then he said something about a town somewhere out there. A town? What town was I from? What was my hometown? While I was thinking real hard about it, he must have walked away without waiting for my answer.

"America! I'm an American!" There, I said it aloud twice with a swelling sense of heroic pride rushing through my entire body, at least what's left of it. Well, with as much pride as I can muster under these weird circumstances. For the first time I could actually hear the words my lips were trying to speak with my very own ears. This was a very good thing although the sounds were weak and raspy and didn't come out exactly right or the way I expected them to come out. I just don't sound like my normal self right now. From the look on your face I can see that you agree with me for a change. Well, that's some kind of progress I guess.

But the good news is that it sounded right from a factual point of view at least based on what I remember. When I formed the word 'American' on my lips, it just seemed perfectly natural and sounded right to me. I was…I am an American, all right. None of those stupid *Birthers* who come along and say you're not an American are gonna get me! That is for sure. I'm an American for certain! There is absolutely no denying it except that my name does sound French and I like Canadian rock bands the best! Oh, well, nobody's perfect.

That strange looking guy who was staring at me…he seemed relieved when I told him I was an American. Why shouldn't he be? We Americans are smart and proud and friendly. We're tough and demanding, for sure, but usually quite friendly and polite all the time. Well, except for the stupid political conservatives we have in our government these days. As my dad would say all the time when they were moaning and groaning for no reason, they are just wacko!

Well, the next thing he asked me was what state I was from. What state? What does he want to know that for? I'm from the big one, of course. The cold…big one or the big…cold one, whichever description would you prefer to use. From the look on his face I doubt he knows where that is.

I am from Alaska, goddamn it! The sovereign state of Alaska! And I am proud of it, too. I could see Fairbanks from my bedroom window… not Russia, mind you, just Fairbanks. Come to think of it, I'd rather see Fairbanks than Russia. Russia, that was way too far away for me to be interested.

I seemed to remember that I am from Alaska without any trouble at all. I was definitely from Alaska for sure. It was big and bad, and I was big and bad! Well, anyway, I thought I was big and bad. Whether that's actually true is subject to some question right now. I don't feel real big or real bad at this very moment. But, somehow I think I should be or I would be if everything was normal.

"Alaska" I roared as loud as I could. I wanted to say Alyeska just like the Aleuts do back home. They are the native people living in the area. It means 'The Great Land'. This time I actually heard my voice again and understood the word. "Alaska!" It hurt to say it. I mean it hurt my mouth and my jaw when I moved them. I was proud to be from Alaska but not proud enough to say it aloud a third time. It just hurt too much, and I figured that this guy heard me the first time, and the second, too. No sense repeating myself. There was no point to it.

Before I knew it, the man in the blue coat turned and was talking to someone standing next to him, someone I seemed to know, but I wasn't absolutely sure about that or who he was. They kept talking and laughing and pointing at me. One of them must have been a doctor because they kept on using those meaningless medical terms you hear when you try to talk to a doctor. Well, anyway, when a doctor talks to you its broken this, fractured that, hyper-extended something-or-other. I didn't recognize most of them except that he did say something about my loss of reality.

At that moment a really familiar and noisy bell started ringing from inside my head and with good reason!

Reality? That's very definitely it! It's called Reality! I'm from Reality! That's my one and only hometown for sure. That's the place where I'm from. Reality, Alaska! I felt like grinning from ear to ear and I would smile, but it just hurts much too much to smile right now. I tried real hard to get their attention, but those two guys, whoever they are, seem very intent on ignoring me completely right now and talking to each other instead. So, I decided that it was time to do some very serious thinking on my own. That won't hurt at all as long as I keep it inside my head.

We actually got Alaska from the Russians, didn't we? Actually, I believe I remember that we bought it for cold, hard cash. Was that *Seward's Folly* I'm thinking of? My parents taught me that even before I went to school, and Reality was a major part of the deal. You know where we are, don't you…the small town just down the river from our more famous cousins at Mystery, Alaska? I can remember the town of Mystery because of its strange name, but right now I can't remember why they are so famous. I seem to remember that it had something to do with ice hockey, but, like I said, my memory is a little bit fuzzy right now, and it doesn't seem to be getting any better real fast.

Who are you anyway? A hockey fan? Is that right? A Florida Panthers' fan? I see that you are wearing a Panther hockey jersey. Should that mean something to me right now? Oh, yes, they are my favorite National Hockey League team, too, but they haven't been doing so well lately. Last I remember, we…they lost to the San Jose Sharks in overtime very recently. I remember them playing the Sharks as if I were on the ice with them. But my memory is so fuzzy.

It was a bad penalty call by one of those blind referees. A phantom hooking call it was for sure. I felt like it was called on me at the time it happened. I recall screaming at the referee at the top of my lungs that he needed a seeing-eye dog on skates out there with him! Do they make skates small enough for a German Shepard's feet? I could just picture this dog skating up and down the ice with a whistle in his mouth! One thing is for sure. He'd do a better job than that referee.

All of a sudden I can remember *Istahota*. He was my very own pet dog...actually more of a wolf than a dog as far as he was concerned. We found him outside during that very nasty, cold winter of...I think it was 1985. We named him for his brilliant gray eyes that seemed to be smiling and happy all of the time no matter what. They...his eyes seemed to glow in the dark. And he didn't need any skates on his feet. He could beat all of us kids across the ice on the river with just his bare paws. Sometimes, when he was feeling a bit frisky, he would grab our puck and play a game he called *keep-away*. At least that's what he would have called it if he could talk. Even when we had him completely surrounded, he would zoom past us with great ease, and like I said, he didn't even have any skates on. Now, if I could move like that, I'd be another Bobby Orr or Wayne Gretsky for sure!

I can see that you're having the same trouble I used to have when I tried pronouncing his name out loud. But, if you think about it for a moment, it's really easy to be sure. It's ee-SHTAH-kho-TAH. I think I remember my father telling me that his name means a family dog with gray eyes. But, really, he's a wolf posing as a domesticated dog. I'm sure he does that for the free meals we give him. Whoops, I promised him many times that I wouldn't tell anyone his secret. Keep it under wraps for him, okay? He's a great friend of mine.

Now you're smiling at me again! My head hurts like mad, and you're smiling your toothy smile through the haze. I'm quite sure that you're trying to tell me something, aren't you?

Is there anybody in there? Just nod if you can hear me. Is there anyone at home? Come on now, I hear you're feeling down. Well, I can ease your pain and get you back on your feet again. Relax. I need some information first. Just the basic facts. Can you show me where it hurts?

That's lyrics from Pink Floyd, the English rock group! Roger Waters sings the words much better than me. Oh, I get it. You see my lips moving, and that's why I've got your attention. It was very clever of you to notice the movement, especially under the circumstances. You seem to know that Pink Floyd is one of my favorites even though they're not Canadian.

Here comes another thought into my mind. Let me focus on it.

Who are these people anyway?

No one seemed to say those words, but that very question seemed to echo in my aching head, bouncing from one side to another like a golf ball in a big beer glass. Just like when I was in one of those canyons in the mountains fishing with my dad a while back. I would yell and then listen for the echoes to come back and yell the same words back at me. Even thinking these little crazy thoughts right now is taking a heavy toll on my fragile sanity. My brain does hurt on the inside more and more. I can't ever remember my brain hurting before, but then again, I can't really remember much at all about anything right now. Maybe it did hurt some time in the past, and I just don't remember it happening.

I think I'll stop thinking for a little while and take a little nap to help me recover. I'm very tired all over, everything inside and out hurts, and it definitely feels like it is time for a much needed nap. When I was a boy, a very young boy like I think I am now, my parents would make me take a nap especially if I was feeling crabby. You know what I mean by crabby, don't you? 'Out of sorts, he is', they would always say about me under their breaths. I was a good kid, but once in a while I would just feel a little crabby. And I could hear what they were saying about me.

Hey! Just as I started to doze off into my nap, those two guys put some kind of plastic tube right under my little nose. It certainly snapped me right back to reality in a few seconds. Not to my hometown of Reality, Alaska, mind you, but just plain reality as it exists for us all…I think. Well, consciousness might be a better way to put it. So much for my nap! I'm wide awake now for sure. They stuck that tube in under my nose without even asking if it was okay with me and then they just walked out the door without another word! That wasn't very polite at all. They could have at least warned me about this thing, you know.

Hey, there's a television set up on the wall in the corner. What the heck is going on out there? People are jumping up and down and cheering, screaming. What for? Oh, I see it now. There are four men with a stretcher between them. They are the only ones not cheering. They seem intent on picking someone up off the ground or floor and putting him on the stretcher. I can't see who it is from here. I hope he's all right, but he's not moving at all as far as I can tell.

You know, come to think of it, I sort of remember a big crowd cheering in my recent past. The sound was like an avalanche coming straight down towards me. Somehow I know that I've been around avalanches before. But this time I'm not on a mountain...at least I don't think so? Middle-aged women were screaming at the top of their lungs and dour businessmen laughed and smiled for the first time in their recollection. But why do I know that and remember that?

Hey, you, don't look at me that way! I know what 'dour' means. My Mom taught me that. Don't try to fool me with your vocabulary. It won't work! And 'recollection' is easy, too. My mother didn't want me to be a dummy so she taught me all those big words before I learned them in school. Not bad, eh? My friends and teachers were amazed to say the least. 'Always be prepared' I always say.

Everyone in that crowd on television seems like a child again, dancing, singing and carrying on like it was New Year's Eve or my birthday. That was just a joke if you understand what a joke is?.

What a party! How do I know that? Hey, they are carrying away that man on the stretcher and the crowd is cheering for him to beat the band...I think. He must be some kind of hero to all these folks. They are probably taking him to the hospital to fix whatever ails him.

I wonder who he is anyway? Maybe he's dead or is he just unconscious? Maybe they are glad that he's hurt? Who knows? Nah, that wouldn't make sense. I wish someone would explain these things to me because it's driving me pretty crazy right now for sure.

"How do you feel, Jean-Luc?"

Where did that...those words come from? Oh, there he is. He snuck right in without me seeing him come back. There must be another door to this room somewhere behind me. Where am I anyway?

"Do you remember me, Jean-Luc?"

I'm nodding my head, but I really don't know this guy at all. He has a white medical coat on for starters. Now he's opening a supply cabinet at the far end of the room. I know that because I can hear the cabinet door squeak just like mine does at home.

He must be a doctor, too. He's got some kind of small plastic cylinder with pills in it in his hand. He's coming back over here. I'd better be careful. Who knows what he might do with that stuff?

"This should help you a little, Jean-Luc."

He's twisting the end off of the ampoule with his right hand and waving the cylinder under my nose. Those aren't pills in there. Wow! I've smelled that smell before. More ammonia for sure! As I roll my head to the side I see two other people standing near me looking interested. One is smiling; the other has a concerned look on his face. Which one should I believe?

"You remember your old pal...the trainer and equipment manager, don't you, Jean-Luc?"

Is he kidding me? Maybe this is some sort of test to see if my brain and memory are working? I've never seen these two guys before in my entire... Well, wait. The heavy-set guy looks like someone I might know. And, the other guy, ah, not sure. Maybe he does look a little bit familiar. But then, after a while everyone starts to look the same around here. Some are skinny and some are over-weight. Some have double chins and some have triple chins. You know what I mean, don't you?

"You were out cold as a cucumber on the ice, Jean-Luc. Where does it hurt? Besides your head, that is."

It was the trainer talking to me. He does know my name for sure. That's interesting. Out like a cucumber, huh. Just like the guy on television. We both were out cold, I guess. What a coincidence! Do you think we ran into each other? Whatever or whoever it was that hit me, knocked the living crap out'ta me that's for sure. I mean I don't remember a thing about what happened or how I got here. Maybe he'll tell me what really happened if I give him enough time? Can't he tell that I'm completely confused about everything?

"Everything's normal Jean-Luc...pulse, temperature, blood pressure, reflexes. You've just got a small memory problem that will hopefully... most probably go away after a short while and with some rest, but most likely there is no concussion or similar bad thing we hope."

It's the doctor in that white lab coat talking to the other two guys about my situation. Listen to what they're saying.

"I'll check his visual responses once again, and then we can get him to the X-ray machine over at the hospital and get him an M.R.I there, too. From what I can tell now, could probably be some small broken bones in there, a rib or two maybe from when he fell. He has to be alert for us to make any progress so he can tell us where it hurts. Hit him with some more of that ammonia so that he's out here with us. It doesn't seem to bother him too much."

I do remember the ammonia smell for sure? Absolutely! That's because I'm smelling it loud and clear again right now…again, and it's a heavy dose for sure. Those smelling salts sure bring you back to life whether you want to be alive or not. I couldn't move the rest of my body half an inch, but my head shot up like a rocket when he brought that ampoule up to my nose for me to breathe. I can see that wry, wicked smile show up on the doctor's face every time he points that ampoule at my nose. At least he looks like a doctor looks in the movies I've seen and talks like a film doctor, but you never know about these guys in the real world!

Now that I think about it, I believe that I have seen him somewhere other than a movie before, and in a place just like this. This is no hospital, that's for sure. I'm lying on some sort of cart right now even though I don't know how I got up here. And there are no nurses around as far as I can tell. Every hospital I've been in was full of nurses. They would be poking and prodding you with needles and things when you least expected it! I'll try to ask him where I am and who he is and all the other stuff like how did I get on this cart.

Oh, he saw my lips moving, but he just laughed and pointed and then said something about using my head. Using my head? It hurts too much to think to be using my head for anything. Then he whispered that he thought that I was going to be okay and then mumbled something about X-rays and an M.R.I. again. I don't know how he could be so cheerful when my head hurts so much. And the way I feel right now doesn't give me a lot of hope for being A-okay any time soon or in the very near future as my mom would say all the time to shut me up.

And the ceiling up there above me! What's with the ceiling now? It seems to be moving, turning clockwise… no, it's turning counter-clockwise, slowly, very slowly. I guess that depends on which hemisphere you're in, right? You must know what I'm talking about, don't you? My teacher back in math or science class called it a *Coriolis* force or something like that. How is it that I can remember that very obscure fact, and yet I have trouble remembering my own name? Who knows? Maybe this thing, this cart I am now lying on, is moving in a circle…

spinning around very slowly. No, the walls aren't moving around at all. Just the ceiling all by itself! This is very, very strange indeed and even my physics teacher would have difficulty explaining it.

Well, they all just walked away again without saying a word to me and closed the door behind them without even a glance. Maybe they are going to let me sleep for a while for a change so I can gain my strength back. I tried once again to raise my head, but it goes up only a little bit. The pain on my head seems to be coming from right over my left eye. I can see out of my right eye okay, but my left eye must be swollen shut because it won't open to let me see things. Whatever or whoever it was that hit me, smacked me right over my left eyebrow. That wasn't a very nice thing to do to say the least. But once I figure this out, whoever is responsible better watch out!

Ah, now I understand what they did! The doctor must have placed a small bag of ice over my swollen left eye. I can feel the cold now, and it feels really good. What a difference! Just like my home back in Alaska. Reality, Alaska is the place to be exact unless that's where I am now?

For some reason I can't seem to remember much about the details of the town, you know, like where my house is located and stuff like that. For some reason I can't explain I do remember the river that runs nearby real well. Actually, there's a river that runs right through the middle of the place just like the Nile River runs through the middle of Cairo, Egypt. Fishing is fun in the summer, what there is of summer, and skating in the long winter. Winter is nine months long up there, so I did a lot more skating than fishing. To be sure I was a lousy fisherman according to my dad. Too much jumping around in the boat and scaring the fish away! I guess I just didn't want to hurt the fish. They have feelings, too, you know.

Awe, heck! That ice bag hurts like mad and feels good at the same time. Who's this now coming in the door to glare at me? A big fat guy in a green coat just came into the room or wherever I am. He's carrying a big bag of something in his hands. Without hesitation he took the ice off my face and put the big bag in place of it. Oh, it's so cold! It was a bigger bag of ice, I guess. The cold is good for sure. Thankfully, the pain from my forehead is starting to go away, frozen away by the ice, I suppose. I guess that's why I've always liked ice. It takes away life's pains...sometimes.

It's weird, but when that fat guy put the ice back on my head, it reminded me of one of my very favorite songs of all time. It's by the band called *Little Feat*. Now, don't confuse the name with *little feet*. That's a pretty darn clever name for a famous rock band for sure.

Anyway, it's called something like *Fat Man in the Bathtub with the Blues* or something like that as best I can remember. That's the way I feel right now except that I'm not in a bathtub I don't think, not yet anyway, and I don't think I'm very fat at all. I can feel the notes playing in my head, over and over and over again. At least that feels good for a change, especially the great guitar work! I wish I could remember the name of the lead guitar player.

Well, here comes that same old doctor again. Now he's looking at my good eye with a light he's holding in his hand. Damn, that's bright! He's got one of those metal reflectors on his head like you see in the movies. It looks like a miniature TV antenna. This one reminds me of an alien from one of those outer space flicks I've seen lately. I can't seem to remember the name of any of the movies I've seen, but he looks like one of the bad guys from one of those. I wish I could remember who he reminds me of. Doctor Kildare? Ben Casey? Doctor Strangelove?

Ah, finally he's done probing my skull, and he looks somewhat satisfied for a change. I guess my visual responses from my one good eye are still okay, whatever that means. Sure hope so. I really don't want him shining that darn thing in my eye again trying to completely blind me. Can't he see that I'm down to one and only one good eye to see with? What planet do these doctors come from anyway if they're actually from this solar system?

Now somebody is messing with my feet of all things! The funny part is that I can actually feel my feet right now. I couldn't feel anything when I first woke up. They are bending the knee of my right leg, pulling on my…whatever I'm wearing down there. Ah, skates! Hockey skates. He's undoing the boot. Oh, much better. My toes are tingling. I can feel my toes now! Well, only on my right foot, but this is much better. I must have had my boot tied too tightly and cut off the circulation. Good, there goes the other one off my other foot. Much better, for sure!

I hope they take good care of those skates for me. They're damn good ones as I remember! My dad always told me to take very good care of my equipment. He would make me clean the lawn mower and the snow blower after he used them to make sure they would last a long time. He would watch me to make sure I was learning how the machines worked and to make sure I didn't hurt myself in the process. As far as my skates were concerned, he would say that *if you take care of your skates, they will take care of you in the long run.* It was hard to forget because he said it at least a million times. Maybe more!

I can remember my first set of skates. That's amazing. They were wooden ones with two runners on each foot. My dad made them for me when I was just … well, when I was just a little kid. You know, I was three or four years old, I guess. Then I remember that when I fell down in those days, I didn't fall very far to reach the ground or ice. And I could get up pretty easily, too. Less gravity!

Ah, those were the good old days. My dad and my brother would take me to the river to practice skating. The river was usually frozen solid. I guess it was Christmas or New Year's Day that first time we went together. It's all slowly coming back, but I can't quite remember all the details when I really should.

I can remember that there was a green flag flying on the shore when it was safe to skate on the river. Yellow meant you had to be much more careful when you were skating, and you should never be there by yourself. And a red flag meant stay off the river altogether! You could fall through the ice…even a little guy like me could slip through a big crack and disappear.

You know, all of a sudden I can recall that first day with my new skates real clearly right now, but I can't remember exactly when it was or what happened ten minutes ago. And now they're making a big ruckus right next door. Can't they give an injured man a little peace and quiet? What they're screaming about, I don't know. I'd get up and find out first hand and tell them to quiet down, but that would require too much movement of my head. Ouch! I just felt my back. It hurts, too. I must have fallen down hard…real hard!

No, wait! It's my ribs! My ribs hurt like hell. When I roll to the right, my ribs on my right side burn like they are on fire! If I roll left a little way, it's okay. Something must have hit me in the ribs, too, or I fell on my side. I can't tell which. I don't remember. Ah, what difference does it make, anyway?

Well, forget the pain. My dad was a good skater, but I saw him fall a few times on his butt, and he'd be limping home afterwards. Not me. I was a natural from the beginning. That's except when that bully Schultz would push me from behind into a snow bank when I wasn't looking. He was a rotten kid and one, maybe two years older than me. I can still see his face, and his really large head, and those huge, goofy Alfred E. Neuman ears, towering over me while I was buried in the snow. He was laughing his butt off. He had a really big butt, too.

He didn't always laugh though, and I somehow know that he isn't laughing now, but I don't know why. I can't quite remember now what I did to him back then, but there were at least several serious payback times, that's for sure. The first one was a big payback, it was; I just can't remember what I did to him. Ah, it'll come back to me. All I can remember is that I made him say 'Uncle' three times. Yes, it's true! That was the way it was then. Make a kid say 'Uncle' three times, and he was yours forever or at least he was supposed to be. You could get his lunch money at school or make him wash your bike or your sled, stuff like that. I remember Schultz washing and waxing my bike one summer. I don't know what I did to him, but he must have said 'Uncle' three times, that's for sure.

So, I showed him good. Not right away, of course. I was four, maybe four and a half years old. That Schultz kid was at least six. Good thing they were his first set of front teeth or his mother would have whooped up on me and on my dad, too, that's for sure. His mother was gigantic! All the kids would call her 'Moose', but not to her face, of course. You wouldn't live much longer if you did that!

Suddenly, a bunch of people came into the room. Just to be sure, I looked around the room as best I could to see if my old nemesis Schultz was anywhere around. A certain sense of relief settled over me when I finally realized that none of the faces I saw were his. But then it happened. A loud bang just like the sound of my Uncle's shotgun rang through the air. I must have jumped a foot in the air…horizontally. Was some deranged person firing a gun? Was he firing it at me?

Then I saw the bottle. Then one of these people put what looked like a cork on my chest. It was a bottle of Champagne! In rapid succession three more bottles where coming open. We were celebrating something for sure. One of my new friends offered me a glass, but the man who was the doctor said no to the proposal. I could read his lips. I was a little thirsty so I must have seemed a little miffed.

Now what are they doing? They're squirting the stuff into the air all over the place. Here comes some guy in a uniform over here with a paper cup. He's got a 'C' on his uniform. Ah, the team captain. His face looks familiar to me, but I can't place him, can't remember his name. Maybe he'll turn around so I can see his name and number. Could be a famous guy? He sure is happy as hell. Now he's putting a straw in the cup and … ah, tastes good! What is it? Champaign! Good stuff. It says 'Dom Perig…' something on the bottle. He sees that I like it, and he's giving me more. Ah, great.

Oh, heck, here comes that doctor or whoever he is again. He's telling the captain not to give me any more to drink. Why not? There, I yelled at him. I could hear myself do it. But it sounded more like a groan than a shout. More like a frog or something like that. He's turning over the ice bag on my head. Ah, that feels good anyway. Later, when I can get up, I'll have to go get some of that stuff, the *Dom* whatever.

And, look, up there. Do you see it? The ceiling has stopped moving. Much better! It was making me dizzy. Now, everyone has left the room again. Good! I think I'll take a short nap while it's quiet. Maybe I'll feel better after I take a little snooze. Oh, rats, they're coming back again with more bottles and glasses!

But where am I? This place looks more like a hospital now. The sign on the wall says that this is the Panthers' medical room? You say I got hit in the head? That must be why I don't remember anything very clearly right now.

What hit me anyway? A puck! That would do it all right. All I can tell you is that my head hurts like hell! Like I said, right here above my left eye. I feel like I have a turnip taped to my face. But I think I already told you all that several times. I can see out of my right eye okay. But, as I said, my left eye must be swollen completely shut. I do remember what sounded like a lot of yelling and screaming when I got hit. I can remember lying face down on something cold and then being piled on by a bunch of people. It knocked the wind clean out of me.

Who were those people? The Florida Panthers? All of them at once! I should sue them. My ribs feel broken. What did I do to them to deserve such treatment? Ah, never mind. They're not listening to me anyway. They keep pointing at me and laughing. What is this all about? And the captain is holding something up in his hand and saying it belongs to me. My one good eye tells me that it looks like a puck.

The funny thing is that I seem to recognize most of their faces. No, I recognize all of their faces, but I can't remember the names that go with the faces nor can I remember the numbers on their uniforms. Oh, well.

Here comes that big fat guy again. He says he wants to interview me? For what? I didn't do anything…did I? I try to raise my head, but it goes up only a little. And who's this other guy? The doctor one more time! He's shining that light in my eye again, my one good eye. Stop it! It hurts!

You're talking to me again? Say whatever you said again because I was a bit distracted when you were talking.

Just a little pin prick. You might feel a little sick.

Okay, I see that this doctor or whoever he is, has a needle…a big needle, and he's aiming it at me! Ah, they threw a towel over my face, a wet cool towel, but somehow I can still see the needle.

Hey, that was more than a little pin prick!

Suddenly, I can see that I am wearing what looks like a hockey uniform. Nice one at that, and the jersey has a Panthers logo on it. Ah, oh, there's a little blood on the jersey. Ah, I mean a lot of blood. Must be from my nose! It feels broken.

All of a sudden, several of these people just grabbed the table I was resting on and turned it ninety degrees. After a little discussion, one of them was allowed by the doctor to lift my head after removing the towel. They all started pointing toward a table at the center of the room. All I could see was something that looked like a large trophy. The funny thing was that I knew I had seen that trophy before, but I still wasn't sure exactly what it was.

As I stared at the image, once again the ceiling above me began to spin. This time I took note that the room was spinning clockwise, and I seemed to be standing still. Why this was so important I will probably never know. But it was spinning clockwise and at a slowly increasing rate.

That's the last thing I remember. I must have passed out. Whatever was in that shot the doctor gave me was having its effect on me? Into dreamland I went with no resistance at all. What was unusual about this time was the fact that I was going to be able to remember this dream in its entirety. That would turn out to be really strange because I was almost never able to remember what I dreamed about before. I never had those classic nightmares some people seem to have with ghosts and goblins and vampires. When I awoke from my dreams, I was always at peace and relaxed, but I never knew why because I had no recollection of what my dreams contained. My mind was one complete blank.

This time it would be different. Not bad, just different.

2

Brothers and Sisters

I know you were the one who did it!
I can tell by that obnoxious sneer
Painted on that ugly face of yours.
Just wait 'till my older brother
Arnie gets out of reform school!
He'll teach you a lesson or two!

Schultz

"Hey, Jean-Luc, wake up!"

Somebody's shaking me again. For some reason they seem to enjoy doing that no matter how much I complain or how much I need my sleep and rest.

"This isn't your nap time, Jean-Luc. It's time for you to get up... stand up and enjoy the fruits of your labors and the slaps on your back from your buddies on the team...your teammates! Management wants to see you, too. Think about the next time you want to negotiate your contract! This is no time to be sleepy."

It's the big fat guy once again with the cool ice packs in his fat hands. Who the hell is he anyway, or who does he think he is? If it wasn't for those great ice packs, I'd have to complain. And what management and what contract is he moaning and groaning about? And teammates... what teammates do I have? He's got what must be a cellular telephone in one of his fat grubby mitts, and he's shaking me hard enough to loosen all of my teeth…if I still have any teeth to loosen, that is. What's with the telephone? Is someone out there calling me and for what?

Just to be clear, I hope those are my teeth that are clanking around inside my mouth right now! Can't he see that I'm fully conscious and awake for Pete's sake? The only problem of significance right now is that my lips can move a little when I want them to, but nothing audible is coming out between them as far as I can hear with the ears I have left on my head. I wish someone would give me a little mirror right about now so that I could take a look and see exactly what I look like at this moment. I could see if my head is still intact.

Come to think of it, maybe that isn't the best idea for me right now? I'll just try my voice again without seeing what my face looks like right now because maybe I would start screaming if I could actually see myself in a mirror! Not that I can remember what I look like. I always thought that I was pretty good looking especially when compared to that psycho baboon named Schultz. But that's not much competition to say the least. I can't think of anyone uglier than him.

And why is this clown Schultz so prominent in my memory right now. It's as if I had just encountered him in my life, but I know he's just a dream…I think? But either way, real or imaginary, I know that I don't like him one bit.

"Okay! Let's get out of here!"

Wow, I actually said that with my own mouth, but it really hurt a lot to do it! But I actually heard my real voice or a reasonable facsimile of my voice that time. It was actually a little bit raspy to say the least. Come to think of it, the sound was a lot like the actor Boris Karlov used to discharge through the air in those old horror movies, but at least I heard it in the air with my own ears. Now, my voice works for a change and my ears work, too, but it hurts like hell to talk even if I'm just speaking to myself. I'll try listening much more than speaking.

Whoops, he's trying to tell me something once again, but he's talking without looking at me. As I said, I'd better listen carefully just in case I can understand him and do what he's asking for if it's something helpful to me, especially if it involves more of those ice packs..

"It's your sister on the phone. She wants to talk with you and see if you're okay. Can you talk with her right now, or should I ask her to please call back later when you're feeling a lot better? It's completely up to you, Jean-Luc. Take your time and think about it before you answer. There's no hurry."

Sister? My very own sister? I have a sister out there in the world somewhere? What sister? I don't remember a single solitary thing... Oh, yeah, my sister! Now I do remember having one of those out there somewhere in the universe. But, you know, I have a strong feeling that maybe, just maybe, I have really got two sisters out there somewhere? Indeed, now that I focus on the subject a little more closely with what is left of my puny little brain, I remember pretty clearly that I have actually got two cute sisters out there somewhere in the world! And I love them both for sure.

"Which...which one is it?" I tried to ask. "Give me some help here! Which sister is calling me on that telephone?"

I gasped the words as best I could under the circumstances. I do think he could read my lips real well because he answered my question to him right away with no hesitation at all. Now that's some progress for a change!

"It's your sister, Danielle. Do you want me to have her call you back when you can sit up and hold the phone for yourself?" The man was speaking to me in a really loud voice as if my ears were broken. Maybe they are broken? Who knows?

I can hear him, but when I try to nod my head and say 'yes' at the same time and reach for the phone to take the call now, my voice fails me, and my arms just don't want to work. Whoops, I really meant 'no' because I would like to hear her voice now, not later. That would certainly make me feel much better for sure. But there he goes again. He's talking but not looking at me or listening to me as he's doing it. This is really frustrating for me.

"He's okay, Miss Robespierre, but why don't you give me your telephone number and Jean-Luc will call you back when he feels better and his voice works a lot better. He's taking a half-conscious nap right now, and when he tries to talk, the sounds come out very raspy and disorganized and not understandable. I'm right here next to him, and it is difficult to make out what he is saying or at least trying to say. He's had a real busy and eventful day today as I am sure you must understand and realize."

The big guy wrote something down on a piece of paper which he then folded and stuffed into his pocket. Then he shut the phone off and put it in his pocket, too, and then he walked away without another word to me about my sister or when she might call back. I guess I will have to wait until later to talk with Dani in real time. All he had to do was hold the phone by my ear so I could listen to her voice, and that would have cheered me up quite a bit to be sure. But that would be asking way too much of a chubby dummy like him. Hearing Dani's voice this moment would have really helped my state of mind. She is such a wonderful person.

Now that I think about it, the service around this godforsaken place, wherever I am right now that is, sure sucks. Oh, well, that's life for sure. When I recover from this…whatever it is I'm recovering from, I'll have to have a word with these people on how to properly treat their… visitors or patients or guests or whoever I am. It's all really just plain old common sense to most regular people like me, but these guys don't seem to have much of that around here these days. I'm sure very glad that this isn't some kind of emergency! At least I hope it isn't.

Actually, believe it or not, my memory is starting to clear up a little bit. I actually do have two sisters for certain. And as I rack my brain I realize that they are named Dani and Seal. We…whoever we is, that is, call my other sister Seal because she loves the water so very much. She water-skis all the time and dives and snorkels and does all that other stuff you do in the water when you love being there even if it is darn cold. She goes way down deep under the surface all the time to places I would never have the courage to go, at least not by myself. I swear that she has developed a set of gills somewhere on her body just like the fish have that let her breathe under water for a very long time. As I said, that water is usually…always so cold up in Alaska, too.

I must admit that I went with her once on one of her water projects with some hesitation, but I didn't like it too much at all. I actually didn't think I could do it, but she loves deep water diving, and I tried to humor her because after all she is one of my sisters. Let's face the facts as they are. I definitely like solid ice very, very much, much better than liquid water except when I'm drinking it, but at this moment I'm not sure exactly why that's the case. There is probably a very good reason for that belief which will come to me later as I think about it more.

Dani is a little older than me as I remember. She's more like a regular real girl…whatever that's supposed to be? Everyone, including her best friends, calls Seal a Tomboy. And her real name isn't even Tom!

Well, anyway, she can skate real good, too, but not as good as Dani can skate. As I remember, Dani won lots of trophies in those figure skating competitions when she was a little girl. She's really good at it for sure. She taught me a lot of good and great moves on skates so I could get away from those fore-checkers. You know, I can't quite remember what a fore-checker is, but it must have been important, at least back then. And staying away from them was a primary concern for me even though I can't quite remember why just now.

Hey! I have a brother, too. A big brother! His name is Jean-Paul Robespierre. Wow! I remembered his whole name on my first try. We all called him John-Paul or Paul for short for reasons you can probably understand. Being a big brother certainly wasn't easy when I was a little kid especially in a small town in the middle of nowhere like Reality. Well, somehow I can remember that Reality is a small town, but I can't remember small compared to what. You needed a big brother in circumstances like that to show you how to do things and how to scare off your enemies and how to explain stuff that was confusing. Paul, for sure, was good at all of those things…showing and scaring and explaining and so on.

Well, here comes that fat guy with the phone again probably to harass me some more. Maybe Dani called back again already to talk to me? Let's hope so for sure. Or maybe someone else is trying to call me? You never know about things like that. Don't ask me who that mystery caller might be. Boy, I don't ever remember being anywhere near this popular when I was a little kid. Two calls on the same day would set some kind of personal record for me! I was never very social back in Reality.

"I told him you weren't feeling good right now, and that you needed your rest. I'll have him call back in an hour or so. I just asked him for his phone number so that you could call him back later if you felt good enough to do so."

"Wait!" I yelled, but the sound was much too weak and my arms just shook a little.

Phooie! The fat man just turned around and walked away just like that without any more explanation about the new call! And to think that I could have talked with my brother Paul just at the moment I needed him! But something in my head told me that it wasn't Paul. I don't know why?

Or was it dad who was calling? It could have been dad! I can't remember if he said who it was that was calling me. Like I said before, all he had to do was hold the phone next to my ear for a few seconds. What a dummy that fat guy is! It could have been my brother that's calling for god sakes. He's four years older than me. He's the one who really taught me how to skate in the first place. That should give him the right to talk to me on the phone, and it should give me the right to talk to him! Unless, of course, it was actually my dad, but even so, doesn't my dad have the same rights of free speech as my brother? Life can be so complicated.

I remember feeling sorry for my older brother quite a few times when I was little. Being a big brother isn't all that it's trumped up to be. When I was small, he had to do all the heavy work around the house. You know what I mean, don't you? Move furniture, shovel the snow and go get firewood. These were no small tasks to be sure. Well, I helped with the firewood once in a while, but only by carrying the little pieces that fell off the wagon. Stuff like that. But I don't remember him complaining at all about his many jobs around the house especially in the winter. I remember him calling me his 'little assistant' and his 'little gopher'. I was really proud of those designations for sure. I actually had a job title or two as a toddler!

My mom had a touch of lumbago so she couldn't lift anything real heavy or move big things around the house when she wanted to. And she always was rearranging the furniture in the living room, at least mentally. It was her favorite hobby for sure. Paul had to move the couch over here, over there, tens or hundreds of times. Things were never quite right for mom probably because our living room was much too small in size, for my mom at least. When I was little, I had good intentions and I tried to help him with the big stuff sometimes, but I usually just got in the way and made things worse. Particularly, there was that time when he accidentally dropped the biggest sofa down on my big toe! It got real big after that…my toe, that is. I called it my 'biggest big toe'.

It was Paul who taught me how to play cards, too. For some reason I remember that now very clearly. He showed me how to shuffle the deck of cards and how to deal just like the big kids. He showed me how to deal the regular way and also how to slip a few cards off the bottom of the deck if I needed them. My hands were really small so I had a lot of trouble just holding the deck in my hands at first. When I would do it wrong, he would grab the cards and tell me we were playing 52-pickup.

It took me a while to figure out what he meant by those words. I was ready for his trickery but not ready enough. He would take the cards in his hands and after spreading them a little so I could see the red and black he would throw them on the floor with a flourish and tell me to pick them up! I quickly learned what the 52 stood for, and the experience taught me to count from 1 to 52 really fast.

That was how I learned how to play 52-pickup. I quickly realized that I was the first one in my grade at school to learn how to do it, so, of course, I got to teach all of my friends how to play. I realized that it was my brother who had made this all possible for me. I don't think my classmates appreciated the learning process as much as I did. Still, it was fun to see the looks on their faces as the deck hit the floor and the cards flew all over the place. With stunned faces they quickly learned what I was teaching them. Boy, was that ever fun for me.

My very favorite number is 53 you know. I told you that, right? It's been 53 ever since I played for the Reality Pee Wee Lumberjacks. That was our first hockey team back in Reality. Playing cards is how I got that number. Really! Paul would always tell me to take the deck and add a Joker for good luck. That makes 53 cards in total. Pretty simple concept for sure, yet it was elegant for me at the same time.

He would do amazing things with that Joker when it came up. "Jean-Luc," he would say, "you're one more than a full deck." Wonder if that meant that I was the Joker? Wouldn't I be better with two Jokers? I had so many more questions to ask about the cards, and I still do.

I remember my dad telling me about the day when Paul was born. It was in the month of December, but I can't quite remember the year right now. He told me that it was the coldest day on record in Reality, Alaska. The coldest day ever! And the coldest day ever since! I remember my dad laughing at Paul, telling him how dumb he was to come out on the coldest day in our history. I had to agree with dad about that one. I guess Paul had no way of knowing what he was getting himself into at the time.

I often wondered about that fact myself. Why would he come out from a warm, comfortable place on the coldest day ever? I asked him numerous times to please explain himself to me, but he would never give me a straight answer to that question. He got tired of my questions and would smack me across the face with his gloves whenever I asked too many in a row. He would smack me not real hard, mind you, but I got the idea he was trying to get across so I would shut up at least for a while.

I would stop asking when he would start to look very agitated. I figured it was an older brother's prerogative not to answer questions from his younger brother if he didn't want to do it right then. I remember promising myself that if I ever became an older brother, I would do the same thing to my younger brother. Heck, it's only reasonable and fair. Unfortunately, I don't remember having a younger brother right now. My head just hurts too much.

I remember all my friends in Reality telling me what a great dad I had and how lucky I was because of that. My dad would take us ice fishing in the winter whenever the conditions were right. Ice fishing was very big up in Reality. I often wondered how the fish felt about it when most of the people in the town were trying to catch and eat them. They were probably cold and hungry, more cold and hungry than us, but they weren't big enough to eat us for lunch. And winter was so long that I felt sorry for them. But I couldn't come up with a way to help them.

My brother Paul and I would have to rig a tent out on the ice right after we arrived at the fishing spot dad chose. We wouldn't go to the river to fish in the dead of winter. It wasn't the right place as I just explained. We would go to a lake near Mount Michaelson. Lake Fondulac was the name of the place as I remember. Wow, my memory is coming back to me like a flash! This is a good sign for sure.

All I can remember is that it was uphill all the way from Reality to the lake and that there were bears and moose and other vermin running around everywhere you looked. The moose were generally very friendly to us. I remember that pretty clearly. They would just stand there with their huge antlers looking at us climbing up the hills to the lake. Some of them had big antlers and some just little ones or none at all. I remember that I wanted to ride one, but my dad said they were afraid of humans and that that was a very good thing. He said that bad people would shoot them if they were too tame and came too close. He called them poachers and moochers. He even told me that there was a half-term retarded governor of Alaska named Sarah who used to shoot the defenseless Moose from a helicopter! What a terrible person she must have been! And she was a governor…of our state until she quit? Alaska must have some pretty dumb and drunk voters out there.

How in the world could anyone shoot such a pretty and friendly animal like a moose? That kind of person must be mean and nasty to the core with little or no conscience. But I still would like a ride on one of those beautiful animals. It would have to be a big one if I did that now because I've grown since I was a kid. I just couldn't tell my dad if I actually did it because he would get mad at me for not listening to his very good advice.

The bears were a different story however. They were looking for something to eat all the time, and they probably thought I would make a good snack. My dad would bring bacon and stuff like that and the black and brown bears were always sniffing and following us, at a safe distance though, because my dad always remembered to bring his gun. It was a big rifle, and I'll bet those bears learned about it a few times so they stayed back far enough. It was an eight-gauge shotgun according to him, and he told me he had to fire a few warning shots for the bears to get the idea. My dad called it his *Elephant Gun,* but other times I heard him call it by the name *Big Bertha.* Those bears must have learned real good because he never had to shoot the gun directly at the bears while I was with him. But it was scary, all right. Had I been a bear, I would have given him a wide berth for sure.

Paul would have to shovel the snow off of the ice at the chosen fishing spot on the lake and then cut a fishing hole in the ice so we could reach the fish. That was a big brother's job for sure. It looked like lots of fun to do except when the ice was much too thick.

But we would have fun, too, after our work was done. We brought our ice skates with us to the lake. Then, while my dad sat around the fishing hole smoking his cigars and waiting for the fish that would usually never come, Paul and I would put on our skates and skate around the lake. It was great fun to say the least. We would bring our hockey sticks and practice passing the puck back and forth as we skated around. Sometimes the other fishermen would get mad at us for scaring away the fish so we had to watch where we skated very carefully. We tried to tell the other fishermen that there weren't any fish around for us to scare with our skates, but for some reason they weren't really interested in our wise advice.

The ice was usually much smoother on Lake Fondulac than on the river back in Reality. I guess that makes sense. The only problem was that we would have to shovel the snow off the ice if the wind wasn't strong enough to blow it away for us. When our father wasn't around, that wasn't a big brother job any more according to Paul so I got stuck with the shovel and the job every time we went up there.

It was up on Lake Fondulac that my brother first taught me how to skate backwards. He was an awesome skater back then, that Paul. And, boy, was I proud of myself skating backwards and not falling on my butt every two seconds! None of my friends could do that yet. My dad wasn't so interested, and he just sat there and yawned and puffed on his cigar.

My dad loved to just sit there by that stupid fishing hole in the ice puffing on those enormous Cuban cigars he got from a cousin who lived in Florida, waiting for the fish that weren't there to bite. I think he was really just waiting for Paul and I to get sick and tired of skating all over the place for so long. When we finally did get worn out, we would get together with dad and build a warm and cozy fire.

That was usually a real good thing because by then the sun would start to go down and it would begin getting really cold and much more windy on the lake. My dad would then make great coffee and hot chocolate for us to keep us warm. I remember drinking coffee when I was no more than four years old. Anything hot tasted good out there in winter to be sure. I guess that's why I like coffee so much now. I wonder if the fat guy could bring me a cup of java now? I don't know why I call it java except that it's what my dad called it all the time.

That kid Schultz I haven't told you very much about yet would always tell me that drinking coffee would stunt my growth. Schultz wasn't too smart for sure. You could never believe anything that dummy said to us. Take my word for it! Some of my friends believed him in spite of my warnings to them. Oh, well, that's the way kids are, and eventually they all paid the price for that really big mistake.

Like I said, I could go for a cup of Joe right now. That's what my dad called coffee, too. But someone closed the door again while I wasn't looking, and I'm lying in here in this room with white walls…wherever I am, all by myself again with no coffee in sight. Wouldn't you know, just as I said that, here comes some guy in a suit followed by two other people carrying things that look like cameras. The first guy has some sort of badge on his jacket, but I can't quite read it because his belly shakes too much as he walks.

"Jean-Luc, these fellows with me want to talk to you for a few minutes and maybe take your picture. Are you up to it?"

Talk to me? What did I do now? I don't remember running away or trying to escape from the authorities! Is he a cop?

"I didn't do anything, boss. Not a thing! I never touched her. Not once. You don't need to interview me. I'm innocent." Ah, my darn jaw hurts too much to let me defend myself very well.

What's he laughing about now? The others are laughing, too. What kind of people are these…characters? Here he comes with more accusations!

"I'll tell them to come back in fifteen minutes or so, Jean-Luc. You just rest until you feel a little better. At least your voice is getting better. We can almost understand what you're trying to say."

Now I'm beginning to figure out just who this guy is. He looks just like the Mountie, you know, Royal Canadian Mounted Police, that arrested my dad that time back in Kaktovik. What are these Canadians doing in Alaska with their uniforms on? Ah, must have been an American Mountie? Does America have Mounties? Now I am really confused.

Anyway, it was really scary when that happened to dad. I was only three or four years old, maybe five at the most, and we went up there to Kaktovik to get some supplies. You know where Kaktovik is, right? You should!

It was a bit confusing at the time, but dad got some moonshine from a friend of his up there. He said something about *Tennessee's best hooch*. The first time he said *hooch* I thought he was talking about our dog. I remember that. Our dog wasn't from Tennessee! So naturally I thought he was talking about a dog from Tennessee. At the time I wasn't sure where that was.

Well, my dad got stopped for speeding and his license was expired to boot. You know how those things go. He just forgot to renew it. So, they took him and me to the local jail, and there I was sitting with all those policemen while they tried to get us to confess to our crimes. I remember that I started to sob and cry just like a little baby right in front of everybody. That always worked with my mother so I decided to test it on these folks.

I thought they were going to put me in jail, too, as an accessory after the fact, whatever that is? Conspiracy was another possibility as I learned from watching cop shows on television. And I'd heard about jail first hand from that fellow Schultz. It was something about his older brother doing time up the river? Please don't ask me what river he went up because I have no idea. Well, I must have looked pretty pathetic to them because after a while they gave my dad his license back and took us back out to our car probably just to get rid of me.

I guess they just wanted to get me to stop crying. That's when my dad offered one of the officers some of the Tennessee stuff. You know, *the hooch*. You should have seen that man's eyes light up. My dad gave him a whole bottle full of the stuff! The Mountie guzzled some of the stuff down right there in front of us and was shaking my dad's hand and patting him on the back and telling him he could go as fast as he wanted to in Kaktovik, license or no license. Wow! He promised my dad that he wouldn't ever get stopped again by any of the boys at that station.

When we got back home, my dad didn't say a thing about the incident to my mom as far as I know. Of course, my brother and I had taken a blood oath of total secrecy. I haven't told anyone about that incident to this day! You're the first to learn about it, and I expect you to keep this information to yourself! You understand what I mean, don't you? No squealing!

Next, when we got home to Reality, I saw him hide the other three bottles of the Tennessee stuff he got in Kaktovik in the garage, in an old toolbox he kept out there. Now I wish I hadn't seen that. I told my big brother, Paul, and he snuck out there one evening when my dad was asleep and took a drink or two. At least that's what he said. It didn't help me at all. My dad knew for sure that I was the one who drank it. No pleading for mercy would work on him when it came to the hooch.

When my mom left for the grocery store the next day, he paddled me something fierce for my supposed crime. I cried and my butt was red for a few days, but I didn't squeal on Paul. I'm no tattle-tale or rat or squealer. My older brother was really worried about it for a long time, but I didn't tell on him or even look his way. No, Sir, not me. And I got rewarded for my silence. As a big brother, he's treated me better ever since that incident. That put me in the famed catbird seat for sure.

But that Tennessee moonshine incident wasn't the only one my brother Paul was involved in. There was the time we were coming back from the river where his team had its Friday night practice sessions. I got to come along because they wanted me to be a *gopher* or something like that. I think I mentioned it to you before, but I never could figure out why they called me a gopher. I don't have buckteeth or anything similar to any of the gophers I've seen up in the hills or by the river. As a matter of fact, I don't think I've ever seen a gopher face to face a foot or two away. But I have seen pictures of them in magazines and newspapers. Well, anyway all Paul's friends called me the *gopher* whether I liked it or not.

Here's how it worked. Whenever the puck they were using to practice with would go flying into the snow bank next to the river, I would have to go and get it out of the snow for them. And when they would lose the puck through a crack in the ice and didn't have another to play with, I would have to run all the way back to the Timberline Tavern and get another one from a locker there.

Oh, yeah, the Timberline Tavern had a lot of pucks. They were in the storeroom locker, behind the bar in a cardboard box and even on the walls. My mother worked there part time as a bartender so when she would see me come huffing and puffing in the door, she would immediately grab a puck from the freezer where they also resided and toss it over to me. It was so cold outside I would always wonder why she kept the pucks in the freezer? Why not on the window sill? We'll figure that one out later when we talk to my mom in person.

Well, on one occasion, she tossed me a puck as usual but then told me to wait a minute before going back to the river. She went into the storeroom and came out with a bag and handed it to me, telling me that it was to be given to Ralph. Ralph was one of Paul's friends who played on his team. Mom told me to give it to Ralph and to tell Ralph to take the package home to his mother and father after practice. I didn't see any problem with those instructions and the bag wasn't too big.

Ralph's mother and father were regulars at the Timberline Tavern, but, as it turned out, Ralph's father was recovering from a painful injury he had suffered several days before when his logging crew was working along Birch Creek. Birch Creek, as you probably know, runs just south of Fort Yukon. So I stumbled through the snow back to the river with the puck and the bag in hand. When I got there, Ralph was nowhere to be seen so I gave the bag to Paul. At the time I thought it was the next best thing to do under the circumstances.

I told Paul that the bag was for Ralph and that he was to carry it home to his parents. Paul, being a naturally curious near-teenager, took the bag and dumped the contents out on the ice right in front of me. I knew it was a mistake right from that moment. It was something I never would have done. There, lying on the ice in plain sight, for everyone to see, were two cartons of cigarettes and a box of some things that I had never seen before, much less been able to pronounce.

Before I could express my misgivings to them, Paul and his friends grabbed a carton of cigarettes and quickly skated over to the other side of the river. That's where we had our bonfire, the one we kept going to stay warm between skates. My heart immediately jumped into my throat. They were opening one of the packs from inside the carton and passing the cigarettes around to everyone. The next thing I knew they were lighting them with sticks from the fire. I didn't know that they all smoked cigarettes! That was a really bad thing especially if they wanted to be athletes.

As I stood there pondering my own possible fate from this incident, I remember seeing my life flash before me. I had to act to save myself from the severe adult retribution I knew would be coming from my mom and dad and from Ralph's mom and dad. They would blame me even though I was innocent! Actually, I was the only innocent one of all the kids.

I grabbed the other carton of cigarettes when the kids weren't looking and the box of medical things and ran with all the speed I could muster toward Ralph's house, which wasn't too far away from the practice site. If he wasn't there to deliver the goods, then I would deliver what was left of what I was entrusted with. As I ran, I fell down hard two or three times. It must have been the longest run of my life to that point, maybe half a mile or a little bit more.

Fearful and exhausted, I ran up to Ralph's house and knocked on the door as hard as I could with the little strength I had left after the long run. At first, nothing happened. It was very quiet. Then I knocked again harder and harder as my strength returned. Just as the door began to open, I again dropped the precious cargo I was carrying onto the ground. As I looked up after picking the packages up again, there was Ralph's mother, smiling at me and wondering what I was doing there.

I told her what my mother had said and that I couldn't find Ralph at practice. She laughed a bit under her breath and told me that she had just sent Ralph over to the Timberline Tavern to get the cigarettes and the, ah, she hesitated, then said something like *the other stuff.*

As I carefully dusted off the small box and handed it to her, something made me ask her what was inside. I don't know why I did that. All I remember now is how red her face turned as she looked back at me. She didn't say another word. She just took the box and the cigarettes and gave me a quarter tip for my efforts.

Wow, I thought! I just earned another quarter for my piggy bank. My mom would indeed be proud of me for that.

I was about to leave, convinced that I had saved the day for myself and my brother, when I heard a stern rumbling voice roaring from inside the house. It was Ralph's father, and he was asking about the second carton of cigarettes. In a moment he appeared at the door as Ralph's mom was explaining what had happened. I guess that the look on my face must have said it all. He could tell what had occurred.

"Ralph and his nasty little friends are smoking my cigarettes!" he screamed. I almost passed out. My knees buckled, and I found myself lying face-first on the snow-covered porch.

"It's not your fault, Jean-Luc," I heard Ralph's mother whisper as she picked me up and brushed the snow off of my coat. "Those boys took the cigarettes from you, didn't they?"

I wanted to scream in the affirmative, but my oath of silence prevented me from doing so. I didn't want to be a squealer or a rat as my brother Paul called younger brothers who told on their older brothers. On occasion, he also called them *tattle-tales. I would die before becoming a squealer or a rat or a tattle-tail,* I thought to myself, even as tears came involuntarily streaming down my cheeks.

"Come, Jean-Luc, I'm taking you back to the Timberline to your mother," she whispered as she wiped the tears from my face. "And your secret is safe with us. Don't you worry about those older boys stealing your cargo. There is more than one way to skin a cat, and now appears to be one of those times to use them."

Visions of cats without skin flashed through my mind. I can still see those images today if I think about it for a moment. Why would anyone want to skin a cat anyway? I never particularly liked cats, but skin them, particularly if they were still alive? Not a chance! Those questions are still unanswered.

So, I had dodged the bullet again although after that fateful day my older brother Paul and his friends never did ask me to come along with them to be their gopher. They didn't seem mad at me and no one ever said anything about the cigarettes, but they did say that they didn't need a gopher around anymore. To this day I wonder what it was that my mother or Ralph's mother said to them or did to them. And I've never seen Paul smoke another cigarette either. That was certainly another positive result.

3

My Best Christmas Ever

*Santa doesn't come down your chimney
like people say. It's the elves who do
all the heavy lifting for Santa. So if you
leave some food for him…them, make
it a couple of small donuts and some
hot chocolate with three or four glasses.
The little guys work really hard for you
All year long so you should reward them.*

Uncle Jack from Anchorage

Somehow I can still clearly remember that really great Christmas that occurred in 1974. I was four and a half years old at the time or something like that, and I couldn't sleep the whole night long in anticipation of waiting for Santa Claus to come sliding down our chimney with all those gifts in his big toy bag. I figured that if he was coming down our chimney, some of those gifts certainly would be for me as long as I behaved myself. And there was no way that I would knowingly misbehave near Christmas.

I'd been preparing for that very special night ever since the month of October when the first snow fell in Reality as it usually does. I even checked the famous and very reliable Farmer's Almanac to see if it was supposed to snow near Christmas that year. Of course, I knew that it would snow plenty by that time, but I wanted some confirmation so that Santa would have a fast track for his sleigh full of gifts and other good stuff. I wanted to give him as much help as possible at least around Reality and vicinity. I'm sure most of my friends back then were also hoping for a fast track for Santa's sleigh if you know what I mean.

My reading skills were coming along pretty good…or maybe I should say well at the time as I remember, but actually, it was Dani who had to show me where the weather predictions were listed in the Farmer's Almanac. She showed me how to use the table of contents and the index in the back to find the information you were looking for. Books were something new and wonderful and mysterious to me back then as you might imagine. And charts and graphs with all those bars and curvy lines were almost overwhelming for a youngster who was just starting to learn how to read and interpret them. But, with a little helpful coaching and kind encouragement from her I started to get the idea pretty fast especially when compared to my friends.

These particular skills proved to be very useful knowledge and quite an advantage for me once I got to my regular public school in my home town of Reality. The teacher in first grade liked my positive attitude right away, and she let me know it. But what really blew her mind was when I could do the multiplication tables when I was only in kindergarten. The school taught those skills in third grade back then, and I owed that head start in math skills to my mother, too. She saw it coming and decided that a little head start would help my confidence. Boy, it was great fun to dazzle my friends with 8x9=72! Most of them would just stand there scratching their heads and rolling their eyes. They tried to imagine 72 fish or 72 birds divided into eight groups of nine each. I remember how their eyes would roll back into their heads searching for those flocks of numbers! It was so much fun back then.

Anyway, you can probably imagine just how happy and excited I was to learn that that year was supposed to be a near record year for snowfall in our part of Alaska. How did they…the farmers that is, figure that out? Immediately, I realized that snow was important not only in Reality itself, but all the way back up to Santa's house and workshop at the North Pole. Santa's sleigh ran a lot on the snow or so I was told by those in the know about such things. It could also fly up into the air when it had to like over rivers and mountains and lakes and big cities! But that was a completely separate problem altogether which we can work on at another time.

My first problem with the sleigh flying through the air was the amount of fuel Santa and the elves would have to carry to reach their destinations. Now my know-it-all friends told me that the reindeer made the sleigh fly. I asked them why reindeer weren't used to pull airliners. No answers were forthcoming from either adults or children on that one. I sensed that the sleigh needed fuel and the heavier the fuel, the smaller the load of presents the sleigh could carry. Again, no answers to my questions.

My mother told me that Santa and his loyal team of well-trained elves made our toys in a very elaborate workshop that he had conveniently built right next to his house at the North Pole. She said that they worked all spring and summer and into the fall each year preparing for the upcoming Christmas. He wanted to be absolutely sure that all the toys would be ready. What dedication, I thought to myself! He was working on the problem all year round!

She said that they also had to figure out who got what on that particular Christmas morning when all the deliveries had to be made. My best guess was that that information must have been obtained mostly from each kid's parents during the year, but she wouldn't confirm or deny that for me no matter how many times I asked. How else could they have done it? To me for a long time Christmas was the world's greatest mystery.

My older brother Paul who was also pretty much of an expert on these things like Christmas, said he thought that our teachers were also very important sources of information for Santa for those kids who were in school. Wow, I never thought about that possibility!

He told me that he made absolutely sure that his teacher knew exactly what he wanted for Christmas each and every year. And he would start dropping hints right as school started early in the fall months of September and October. Not a bad idea for sure just to be sure Santa had enough notice to make a particular toy if he didn't already have one in inventory. You can see that Paul was the smart one amongst us, all right, because he was right on top of the problem from the very beginning. And, as you would expect, he would almost always get what he wanted when the big day finally came. He had earned it!

That's when I first confronted the question of exactly where do Santa and Mrs. Claus actually live when he is not out delivering toys to all the children. Oh, I know…you're about to tell me that Santa lives at the North Pole just like I said before. And that his house is next door to his workshop.

My next question to you is…exactly where at the North Pole is his place? As I learned in school, the North Pole encompasses a rather large area of water and ice and ground, and I know right off that there's no pole in the ground sticking up to mark the exact spot! Or at least I don't think so. If there was one, would it look like a barber's pole by a barber shop? Because I had never actually visited the North Pole, there was no way for me to directly observe the answer.

How did I deduce that essential fact? Easy! My big brother told me that there was a barber pole in the ground marking the spot. He said it was put there by Mrs. Claus after she first trimmed Santa's beard. Some of the elves needed quite a bit of trimming, too, so it was the natural thing to do. But I had my suspicions about that particular tale. Big brothers did that sort of thing to little brothers all the time. This might require some research.

Right away, when he told me that detailed story about the pole and the haircuts, alarm bells went off in my head. One of the first things I learned in life was that my older brother was always trying to fool me with his expert explanations. I'm sure that he thought that it was his job, and it was a means of teaching me what to believe. I quickly learned that fact when he told me the story of the headless horseman! He said that his teacher read his class that story in school, and he wanted to pass it on to me.

I detected that total fib right off the bat. I pretended to take it all in with baited breath, and I even nodded my head a bunch of times. But I knew better. No one could ride a horse a long distance without having his or her head screwed on tight! It feels really good to outsmart an older brother like mine once in a while especially on April Fool's Day. Of course, I couldn't tell him that I had outsmarted him. It would have killed all the fun I was having.

Later, I asked my Uncle Jack, who was indeed a pretty smart fellow on most things, and he told me that it's the place magnets point to! Now I'm back to the North Pole thing. My Uncle Jack always told me the truth…at least when he was not drinking that red wine from California that he liked so very much. He still told the truth to me then, but it took him a lot longer and his voice was harder to understand for sure.

And he would keep knocking his glass over which made my mom real mad! You can see the problem there, can't you?

But my main concern from the very beginning was Santa's ability to touch down safely on our flimsy wooden roof with that real heavy sleigh filled with all those toys he had made and all those muscular reindeer and a few tough elves not to mention any fuel he had onboard. It was going to be tough for the old geezer and his entourage because we had a two-story house with big trees sticking up into the sky all around it. My dad said he planted the trees to protect the house from the strong winds that came up once in a while. I figured that Santa and the elves could handle those obstacles with some good luck if he came straight down on the roof. But when I factored in the pitched nature of our roof, I became very concerned all over again. Once again I began to worry about my Christmas presents and their difficult delivery.

I even brought the problem up with a few of my very best and smartest friends, but none of them had a clue as to the answer. I should have realized that fact right off the bat because to start with none of them had any idea what the multiplication tables were. They were still working on the difference between nouns and verbs and up and down.

However, the mailman, Mister Albertson, seemed to know all about it. I never expected that. He was a very handy guy with tools who was always talking with my dad about fixing things around the house. I remember the time when my mom and dad finally after much discussion and argument decided to add a porch on the back of our house. It was Mister Albertson who helped them every time they got in a bind and that was pretty often as I remember.

So, one day in November, as he pulled up in front of our house in his delivery truck with a load of local mail, I worked up the enormous courage to ask him the big question just as he was about to put the day's mail into our mailbox. He looked around carefully to be sure no one else was watching or listening, and then he whispered the big secret into my eager waiting ears. My jaw quickly dropped and my eyes popped wide open when I heard his magical words. What he said made so much common sense to me. I was amazed to say the least. I don't know why I hadn't thought of it myself because it was so obvious once I heard it. It was all there for me to see with my own two eyes. Here's exactly what he said to me for your consideration.

"He'll pull up and park the sleigh in your driveway, and then he'll proceed to pull out his trusty ladder which he will lean up against the house. Up the ladder he will go quickly with his bag of toys, and then he'll head down your chimney and out into your living room by way of your fireplace. His little helpers will follow along behind him carrying more gifts.

"It's as simple as that! Absolutely no secret tricks are involved as far as I know. Then, when he and his little helpers are finished delivering the gifts and toys into your living room, up the chimney they go and back down the ladder to their waiting sleigh and reindeer. They've performed this simple routine a million times or more for pitched roofs of every type. You don't have to worry about Santa pulling this off, because he's an expert at it to say the least. He's encountered and solved every single kind of problem you can think of when it comes to Christmas delivery."

With that major problem solved and out of my way, I looked for other problems that I might be able to help with even though I was confident that Santa already knew the answers. It's always good to be well prepared for the worst case. The design of our fireplace was the most obvious factor working against the old guy after the pitched roof and all the surrounding trees.

The chimney ran all the way from the living room floor straight up to the second floor and then a good distance above that. One day in November when everyone was outside doing their thing, I crawled into the bottom of the fireplace and looked straight up to see if I could see the sky from down there. Well, let me tell you that the chimney was not only really dirty, but it had only a very small opening at the top as far as I could tell. All I could see was pitch black…or was it black pitch? There definitely was no blue sky visible from down in the living room even at high noon. This obstacle did seem to present a serious problem!

If Santa was really as big as everyone said that he was, he was not only going to get his beautiful red suit all dirty in that filthy chimney of ours, but he was sure to get stuck up inside there with his fat bag of new clean toys. Even if he brought only the one toy I really wanted to get, it would never fit into that narrow chimney with all that soot and the narrow entry.

As it dawned on me just what a very serious limitation that grimy chimney of ours presented to him and to my grand plans for celebrating Christmas, I finally came to the only possible logical conclusion a thinking person could reach under the circumstances. My mom was big on logic and stuff like that so she would have been super proud of me at that moment in time.

There was no way that Santa was going to make it up or down our chimney on this Christmas!

Of course, I realized that this sensitive conclusion of fact was not a matter I could discuss directly with my parents. And my former nursery school teacher wasn't the brightest bulb in the town either. My aunts and uncles were out of the question, too, because they lived too far away to cope with the problem first hand. And before I presented the new question to the mailman, I figured out just who was the right person to ask even with the obvious risks involved.

This was definitely another big brother problem if there ever was one. Paul would know the answer to this tough one just like he knows everything else. After all, he must have had to deal with these difficulties over the past few years when I was too young to realize that these problems even existed. And, he was good at math, too, which would help with the size and shape problems. And he never complained about not getting the presents he wanted from Santa on Christmas. It was just a matter of catching him at the right time when he was in a good mood and ready for little brother questions. That wasn't always as easy as it sounds.

I might not have mentioned it because I just remembered it myself… or did I? My head still hurts a lot right now. Oh, well, here it is. Paul's real name is Jean-Paul, just like mine is Jean-Luc. But we all called him Paul as I said before because it was easier. For me it was a little different story. Some people called me Jean-Luc while others called me just plain Luc. It never really mattered much to me anyway. Oh, I'm going off on a tangent again. Sorry!

Well, back to Santa's house entry problems, which were really my problems when I think about it in detail. I was certain that I would have to do something nice for Paul to get his full cooperation in this matter. That's the way big brothers worked which I'm sure you already understand completely from your own life experience. When he realized what favor I had done for him, he would surely tell me without hesitation how to help Santa with this particular problem concerning our house.

Paul knew that I wanted a brand new bicycle for Christmas, and it was clearly my new bicycle that hung dangerously in the balance in this case. If Santa, or his elves for that matter, couldn't get the bike down the chimney in one piece and quickly because they didn't have all night to accomplish this feat, it would be another whole year on foot to school and back for me. This was a really sad and disturbing prospect for me. It was beginning to feel like my entire future was in the hands of that dirty old chimney and the soot inside. I had to win this battle!

I thought as hard and fast as I could and then I thought some more. There had to be a way to please Paul so that he would help me solve this problem without any hesitation or backlash. And most certainly, I wanted it to be my idea as far as the gift was concerned. If I left it for him to decide what I should do for him, I might learn to regret it for the rest of my life, and I would never see that brand new bicycle I had been dreaming about for almost a year.

All of a sudden, what I had to do for him before it was too late hit me like a flash out of the blue. It was a miracle as far as I was concerned. My dad and my big brother weren't back home yet, so I raced into the bedroom and put on my warm coat and boots and gloves, and then I slipped out into the garage without my mom noticing. This had to be my very own private secret.

That was one of the luckiest moments of my entire life so far! There it was standing faithfully right where I thought I would find it. That old fabulous snow shovel of ours! I knew that its days were numbered because my dad and the mailman were working on a machine that would blow the snow off of the sidewalk and the driveway, but they hadn't gotten it to work yet so the shovel still had a future as far as I was concerned. So, confidently I grabbed the shovel with loving care and went out the door and started to work on the driveway where a new coat of fresh fluffy snow had fallen overnight. So far, all was going well for me. A giant smile crossed my face.

I knew full well that my dad would tell Paul to shovel the driveway when they arrived home that evening. So, if I did the shoveling for my brother before that time came, he would certainly appreciate it very much. I would have earned my battle stripes, and I could go to Paul with my questions about Santa and his sleigh and our presents as a hero instead of as a dummy. I knew he would appreciate my efforts because I knew he had other things to do with the time.

Boy, was the shoveling ever hard work! The snow must have been six to eight inches deep out there. Just to be sure of my estimate I went inside and got a plastic ruler and stuffed it in the snow at the center of the driveway. Seven inches plus for sure! If I had had a camera at the time, I would have taken a picture to preserve the moment for all of history. To be sure my efforts would be obvious I started at the street end of the driveway and shoveled and shoveled and shoveled my way toward the garage with every calorie of energy I could generate with my scrawny little body.

After about what seemed like thirty to forty minutes to me, my mother came out of the house to see what the heck I was doing out by the front of the house. She must have heard me huffing and puffing and grunting with each shovel full of snow I was able to move off the driveway. Wow, was she ever surprised when she actually saw the mountain of snow I had already carried off the driveway all by myself. I think that she was really proud of me even though she didn't know why I was doing it in the first place. The mystery of my efforts made things even better for me.

She said that we had to go to the Timberline Tavern in a few minutes and that she needed me to help her put up the last of the Christmas decorations over there in the bar and restaurant. She assured me that dad and my big brother would be very proud of what I had done for them even though I hadn't even half finished the job yet. Wow, everything was going the right way for me.

So, while she watched my efforts, I shoveled enough snow off the driveway to clear the area all the way to the sidewalk and took the shovel back into the garage. As I came back out to get into mom's car, which was already parked on the other side of the street, I heard a big roar coming from down the street from the nearby intersection with the county road. The sound was very familiar, but I couldn't put a finger on it for a moment because my view was blocked by snow and parked cars.

Then, as I got into the car where my mom was waiting with a big smile, it hit me like a ton of bricks. The sound I heard was coming from the town snowplow! Reality was a very small town even for Alaska, and we didn't have access to a lot of the modern conveniences, but we did have a gigantic snowplow for clearing the streets after snow storms. And boy, let me tell you, the city fathers were really proud of that plow. It even appeared any time we would have a parade like on July 4th and the anniversary of Reality's founding. If we get time later and I can remember the details, I'll have to tell you the story on how we came to get it.

I realized that it was one of the city firemen driving the snowplow on this occasion. I could tell his identity from the red hat he was wearing. He was clearing the city streets of all the snow that had fallen the night before. I watched with great pride as he came past our house and the freshly shoveled driveway. He even waved at me from atop his perch as he went by. He would surely notice the fine job of shoveling I had done that afternoon on our driveway.

As we drove off for the Timberline Tavern, I did something I shouldn't have done. I looked back over my left shoulder one last time to admire my work of art. My mom must have observed the totally horrified look on my face because she immediately slammed on the brakes, and we slid to a stop in the middle of the block. At first she didn't utter a single word about what had just happened. She just looked at me and then glanced back down the street toward our house. The pain she saw on my face must have really hurt her as much as what I saw hurt me.

The city plow had pushed a huge pile of snow onto our driveway as it passed on down the street. Now, almost all of my hard work of shoveling was totally in vain! At that moment I must have started to shed a few tears because she pulled the car into the parking lot at the grocery store, and she told me as she was hugging me that she would tell my dad and my brother Paul what a wonderful job of shoveling I had done...before the snowplow came down the street and destroyed it.

Then, trying to suppress a smile that was breaking out all over her face, she told me that if I wanted to, I could shovel it again when we got back from the Timberline. Hearing those words felt like smashing into a brick wall. For the moment it seemed to me that Santa was going to have to solve his own problems without my help, at least this time anyway. After some reflection in my sadness I did see the latent humor in the situation, and I began to laugh, too. I could do all that work once again for sure and maybe still be a hero!

I think I told you that my mom worked part-time as a bartender at the Timberline Tavern. It was Christmas Eve and the place was going to close early for the holiday, something like eight o'clock in the evening. Sally was the person working behind the bar that afternoon as we came in the front door. I can remember her real well because she had lots of pretty freckles on her face. Blonde hair and freckles were her very own trademark! If you mentioned freckles, everyone thought of her first.

For some unexplained reason she would always poke me in the tummy and try to tickle me whenever I came over to the Timberline with my mom. I remember telling her in no uncertain terms that I was getting a little too old to be tickled in public where my friends might see it happening, but she said that in the State of Alaska it was okay to be tickled until I was eight years old. Oh, well, five more months and Sally wouldn't be tickling me any more. I could make it for five more months, but it wasn't going to be easy to do.

I helped my mom with the decorations as best I could under the circumstances. I was given the job of hanging little angels and elves from small pieces of Christmas trees that Sally and mom had attached to the wall and the ends of the bar. Making the decorations look good gave me some time to think about just how I was going to help Santa with our mutual problem. There had to be another way to do it, but we were running out of time.

The decorations I was hanging were for the Christmas Day Brunch. Sally told me that the people in Reality had a brunch every Christmas day and that this year the Timberline Tavern was hosting the event. She said that strictly speaking it really wasn't a brunch but that the people in town called it that anyway. There was another restaurant in Reality, but when they had brunch there, it was in the morning! Actually, I didn't really care much what they called it to tell you the truth.

The Timberline would open at five o'clock in the afternoon on Christmas day and everyone would bring over their leftovers, whatever that was. I soon learned that leftovers were the food people didn't eat at Christmas dinner. Sally said with a smile that they were really eating lunch because they all ate dinner so early on Christmas. I was really getting confused about the nomenclature to say the least. Brunch wasn't brunch, and dinner wasn't dinner. Or was it that dinner was really brunch, which then made brunch be dinner? At that moment I could have used a teacher or older brother to straighten me out.

Oh, well. That was Christmas day afternoon and early evening in my home town of Reality, Alaska. You couldn't always explain exactly what was going on, but it was usually great fun anyway. I just learned not to ask any questions or try thinking too much!

By the time I finally got home from the Timberline Tavern, I thought I had the answer to Santa's problem which, of course, was my problem, too. You remember exactly what it was, don't you? How was Santa going to get down the skinny, grimy chimney at our house with his bag of presents, especially when he was thought to be very fat and the chimney was…really very skinny? And the same goes for those chunky elves that worked with him. I've seen lots of pictures of them in books and movies, and they are a bit plump if I say so myself. Most of them were as wide as they were high! Not a pretty sight at all.

Well, you may not believe this after everything I've told you, but this whole thing was going to be easy for a change. I explained the gory details of my plan in great detail to my mom, and she responded that it was an elegant solution to a difficult problem. She was always using big words I never heard before on me to improve my limited personal vocabulary. I remember Sally looking really confused when mom would try them on her. And my dad would just shake his head and sometimes even scratch his head in response to her statements. I guess that she was just trying to get me a bigger and better vocabulary to use on my friends and the teachers in school when the time came. I appreciated her efforts to teach me, and there were plenty of occasions when I was able to use her training to my benefit.

Well, my final solution to the problem was really quite simple. Santa could just use the driveway for his landing instead of the pitched roof. All we had to do then was leave the garage door unlocked for him so that he could get into our house that way without having to haul out a ladder. Then, bringing in my new bike would be a piece of cake for him and the elves.

When I told my brother Paul about my plan, surprisingly he wasn't convinced at all. He said that Santa could make himself bigger or smaller any time he wanted to and that he could get down the chimney with ease regardless of how narrow the opening was. The same went for the elves, reindeer, and sleigh. As far as my bike was concerned, he didn't know whether that could change size on Santa's command or not.

I still thought that I was right and that I had the better idea no matter what anyone else said. Without fear, I bet my big brother Paul that Santa would have to come down on the driveway no matter what the circumstances were. We hadn't decided yet exactly what we were betting which was usually the way our bets went. Paul said he would think it over for a while and let me know before Christmas Eve exactly what was at stake for each of us. It was already Christmas Eve so I think he was just afraid to bet me on this one. I think he knew deep down inside that I was right about the driveway landing. I guess it would have been much too embarrassing for an older brother to lose an important bet like this to a younger brother especially after he had examined our peaked roof for the hundredth time.

Well, needless to say, but I'll just say it anyway. It snowed really heavily that Christmas Eve evening and into the morning! I could see the huge flakes falling toward the ground as I stared through my bedroom window. My bedroom was on the second floor so I was sure I would hear Santa and his sleigh if he landed on the roof above me. Well, actually, our attic would have separated me from Santa if he were on the roof, so I was tempted to go up the pull-down stairs and sleep up there just to be sure I didn't miss such a landing.

I remembered that dad had his sleeping bag stored up in the attic so I'd be warm enough for sure. From up in the attic I knew I could get a closer view of the action through the dormer windows, but my dad was one step ahead of me, as usual. Somehow he anticipated my backup plan, and he locked the attic door that night! I don't know how he knew of my plans because I didn't mention them to him at all. Sometimes dads can be mind readers; that's for sure. I learned that one the hard way!

Anyway, I must have dozed off during the night because the next thing I knew my brother was shaking me and screaming something about Santa Claus and his winning the bet we had made. I had to see things for myself so I leaped out of bed and flew down the stairs toward the living room as fast as I could go.

This was the big moment! And I had a crucial decision to make. Should I go out and look at the driveway like my brother wanted or should I go into the living room to see if Santa brought me anything? I froze for a moment as I considered the possible alternatives.

Heck! The driveway could wait. I ran full tilt into the living room, and there beside our Christmas tree sat the most beautiful sight I had ever seen. A brand new Schwinn bicycle! No note or anything, but I knew it was mine, and I knew that Santa had delivered it just for me. Just how he accomplished that feat would remain a mystery into the future.

That's when a terrible thought hit me! I had forgotten to leave any cookies under the tree for Santa and the elves. My mom had cooked… she said she baked them, at the Timberline Tavern when we were putting up the Christmas decorations, but I forgot them at the store. I remember how depressed I was. Still, Santa left the bike anyway, and I vowed that next year I would make up for my blunder. I had to redeem myself somehow. I wondered if the cookie error I had committed this year would hurt my chances for a good present next year.

As my heart alternately raced at the sight and feel of the bike and then slowed to a crawl as I wondered if Santa was offended, I noticed a package on the floor under the tree wrapped in Christmas paper with a big card taped to it. What could it be? I slowly moved over and read the label.

To: Jean-Luc. From: Mom and Dad.

Wow! It was a Christmas present from mom and dad. What could it be? It was only seconds before the wrapping was ripped off and the box top removed. The pleased and surprised look on my face must have said it all.

Skates! My first pair of real official ice skates!

As I must have told you, I had skates before, but they were wooden and had double runners so I wouldn't fall down so easily. These skates were the real thing! I loved my wooden skates, but it was time to put the double runners away for good. As I told you, dad was a lumberjack and loved to make things out of wood. And so when I was almost three years old, there they were waiting for me. Double runners for my third birthday it was!

But when I pulled the new skates out of the box, there was something else inside. It was a hockey jersey my mom had made for me, all folded up and with my name on the back. All it needed was the Pee Wee Lumberjack logo on the front, and I could wear it to the games.

I wanted to thank my parents, but I didn't see mom or dad anywhere around the living room at that moment. They must have heard the racket I made coming down the stairs. I didn't realize it at first, but they had come downstairs before me and were standing in the corner behind the tree watching me, hugging each other, and smiling at my antics. When I finally spotted them, I ran to where they were standing, and they each gave me a big hug. It was a moment I will never forget!

Then, the family sat down to a big breakfast of flapjacks, eggs, svidki, ham and sausage. I particularly liked the svidki. They were little cakes made by dropping some dough into a pan of hot cooking oil. After cooking for a minute or two, all you had to do was slap some jelly on one of them and stuff it right down. My brother Paul said you were only allowed one bite, and the object was to eat the whole thing at once sort of like a large snake swallowing a mouse. That's why I took the small ones first. I did suspect that mom made some really small ones for me so I could keep up with Paul who was focused on the larger ones.

I wanted to try out my new skates right away, so when breakfast was over I dragged the whole family down to the river. On the way out the door, Paul pointed to the driveway.

No sled marks!

I lost that bet.

Once at the river my mom helped me put on my new skates while my dad and Paul put on theirs. That's when I got another big surprise. My dad grabbed my hand and took me for my first short skate. *I could do it!* As I was standing there proud as a peacock, my brother handed me his present. *My first real hockey stick!*

In spite of losing the bet and leaving Santa without cookies, it was the best Christmas ever!

4

Valentine's Day

Will the spirit of love sneak up on my soul,
Like the tax man just because I was yawning?
Or will it honk its horn like a bus in the road
Because I was sleep walking in the morning?
Will it punch or kiss me on my shaven cheek
And keep me in sight as I'm soaring?
All I wanted was some free time with someone to love,
Not a place for my boat in an expensive mooring.

Geeze, I must have dozed off for quite a while because things have definitely changed. There is a very nice fresh bag of ice on my head, and I'm feeling much better than... Well, much better than before, indeed, whenever that was! Somehow, I've lost all sense of time along with everything else. I wonder how long I was asleep on this floor or whatever it is? Or did I just pass out? I must have been dreaming the whole time I was out because I was definitely walking around back in our house in Reality like nothing at all was wrong with me. Now, I don't even feel like rolling over or sitting up much less getting up. Standing up on my own is completely out of the question, that's for sure. I wish someone, actually anyone at all, would come over here to me and explain this all to me so I could understand it once and for all. Am I asking too much?

This last time as I remember I was floating softly in the clouds...yes, up in the clouds in the sky. I was happily dreaming about Santa and his elves. Before that it was my sister Danielle I was dreaming about of all people. Sure would have been nice to really talk with her when she called me on the telephone a while back. Boy, how I do miss Dani right now and the great advice and counsel she would give me all the time whether I needed it or not! I never really got to spend a lot of quality time with her before she grew up so fast and moved away to Barrow. You know where Barrow, Alaska is, don't you? From the confused look on your face I guess not. It's a really nice place and she loves it way up north.

Well, I was busy with my stuff, and she was busy with her stuff as all kids are. How fast your childhood goes by, and yet, when you are there, time seems to move so very slowly…just like a turtle in a pile of glue. My dad would say that that's something only Albert Einstein or his friends Schroedinger and Planck and Einstein could explain with any clarity! Dad never did go any further with his explanation. One of these days I'll find a quantum physics book and figure it all out for myself, but that will have to wait until I can get myself straightened out.

I remember wanting to grow up faster, much faster, so I could skate with the big kids and be big myself so I could knock them over with a hip check during an actual hockey game. In my mind I could do all the things those older kids could do on skates and much more with no problems at all. That was mostly because of the secret help I was receiving from my brother and sisters in all aspects of life. They always seemed to be teaching me something useful that I would need later on in my life. Now I can really appreciate what they did for me as the situations and problems become real. I was one lucky kid to say the least because most of my friends didn't seem to get all the great help I was getting!

But my friends were important, too. They were my first 'Peer Group' as my mom would say all the time. She said that peers were people you had access to of a status roughly equal to yours. That's when I ran into the very complex problem of figuring out exactly what my 'status' was so I could find my peers. Well, she sensed my problem and simplified things my saying that my peers were actually all my friends lumped into a single group, and they had a way of finding me. Some would help with some things and some would help with other things. Wow, that was a load off my mind for sure. I wouldn't have to spend all my valuable free time searching for advice and counsel from a bunch of strangers.

So, in the process of finding my peers and having them find me as I grew up, I really enjoyed sitting on the riverbank watching the bigger kids play ice hockey. I always had a favorite team, especially when Schultz started to play in those games. I knew I was better than him at just about everything, but he was big for his age and I was small for my age back then. And I somehow realized that he was someone I would always compete with but not in a friendly manner.

Naturally, I always rooted for the team he wasn't on, and usually I was rooting for the winner because Schultz was slow to react and always out of position on the important plays. I remember asking myself what Schultz would do in a given situation during the game and then doing the exact opposite when I was out there. That strategy usually worked out really well for me. He was the perfect negative example to learn from because he always seemed to do everything wrong!

I know that Dani didn't like Schultz much either, but she never said much about him at least when I was around to hear it. I guess she figured that he was my problem to deal with in the future and that all she should do then was help me prepare for it. Dani was two years older than I was so I always called her my 'big little sister'. She always helped me with all kinds of stuff, especially when girls were the topic of our conversation. And as it turned out in my youth, I really needed the help she gave me in that area because I had no idea what I was doing.

I was more than a little bit shy when I was a little kid. Well, I'm probably still that way now when it comes to dealing with girls and stuff like that. I spent most of my time in the winter months skating with the other boys in my neighborhood and playing in the woods with them in the summertime. When we couldn't skate because there was no ice, we would play 'hide and go seek' or a game something like dodge-ball, if you know what I mean. In these games someone was always designated as *IT*. If you were *IT*, it was your job either to find someone else and beat them back to the tree that we called home base or else in the case of dodge-ball, to hit them with the baseball-sized hard rubber ball we used before they could make it back into the circle where the game started.

Wow! You look pretty confused? I guess you were not the type of kid who belongs in my peer group. Let me explain so we can go on to more subtle things. It is important that you know the rules of any particular game before you start playing it. These are the games of life in one way or another and it's key that you learn to survive or bad things can occur.

If you are *IT* in hide and go seek, you have to count to ten while standing at the place designated as home base. You had to count aloud with your eyes closed…count slowly while the other kids hid as best they could. Then you had to find at least one of them and tag them before they got back to home base, which was usually a tree or a large rock or something similar that represented home base.

For dodge-ball everyone stood inside a circle drawn in the snow or dirt or with chalk on concrete. Each kid had a hole in the ground that would just hold a small rubber ball. A kid who was selected at random would roll the ball until it fell into a hole, and whosever's hole it fell into, that kid was *IT* for the game. We used other arrangements on concrete or snow.

When the ball fell into a hole, everyone else who wasn't *IT* ran out of the circle as fast as they could go. Then the object was to get back into the circle without being hit by the ball thrown by the kid who was *IT*. Pretty simple, huh? To say the least, you had to be pretty quick to survive in this game.

Well, I remember during one winter game of hide and seek when Dani came running up to me while I was hiding on the river bank. How did she find me so easily? That was a reasonable question. Heck, she was just about ten years old at the time! She was making a big commotion about something so I stood up out of my hiding place and then everyone in the game knew where I was hiding. It was my favorite hiding place, too, and now all the kids knew where to look for me.

I was exasperated to say the least especially when I discovered that Dani was there to remind me that I had to make a Valentine's Day card for school because tomorrow was the 14th of February. All I can remember is that the kids would never let me live that one down. Every year a bunch of them would query me about my Valentine's Day card and who it was for and whether I had it ready. Frankly, I got pretty tired of it, but I couldn't blame Dani. She meant well by what she did. And, remember, she was seeing things from a girl's perspective which I soon learned was usually much different from a boy's perspective most of the time. What a discovery! I certainly never forgot it after that.

Our first grade teacher, Mrs. Burkett, had plans for each kid in the class to make a Valentine card out of sheets of what she called construction paper. You were allowed to use scissors and glue to get the job done. Construction paper was just thicker paper of various colors and shades of colors. She said that we could write on the paper with a thick pen or cut letters out of another piece of paper and glue them on.

It didn't sound too difficult when I first thought about it, and it sounded like this might be fun.

I remember her in class saying that we were lucky to have the same number of boys and girls in our class. Lucky, for sure, because just a week before, a girl named Alice transferred into our class. Her parents had just moved to Reality from Washington. I was pretty good at geography so I decided to impress the newcomer with my knowledge. I asked her if it was the State of Washington or the Washington that was the city that was the capitol of our country. You can imagine my shock and surprise when she said it was Washington, Missouri! I guess I learned my lesson that time. The world was a big place especially for a little kid like me! I couldn't…I shouldn't make any assumptions even when the problem seemed simple and straight forward.

My teacher always counted herself as a member of our class so we had fifteen of each, boys and girls that is. Once the cards were made, each would be put into one of two bowls. One bowl was for cards from boys to girls and the other was for cards to boys from girls. Actually, the bowls looked a lot more like jars to me than bowls, but that's another story altogether. After the two jars…or bowls if you like, were filled with cards, each kid would pick a card out of the appropriate…container. Everything was being left to chance except when the last person picked.

That's when things got a little complicated. Cheating was pretty much out of the question because Mrs. Burkett took the bowls into the cloakroom and shuffled the cards…or so she said that's what she did. Then she put each bowl into a cardboard box so you couldn't see the size or color of the card you picked when you picked it. She obviously knew all the ropes because she had done this Valentine's thing with kids many times before.

But there was more to be sure. Mrs. Burkett was going to teach all of us to dance that Valentine's Day, too. She was dead set on it despite the looks on all the boys' faces when she told us. But the girls were another thing altogether to be sure. They were one hundred percent in favor of it. I guess dancing, at least in first grade, is what really separates boys from girls, at least in Reality, Alaska. The actual vote was a tie, but Mrs. Burkett said that as teacher she had the tie-breaking vote.

Now it's not that boys never danced at all in Reality. For instance, when you scored a goal in a hockey game, it was time to dance on your skates with all of your teammates who were on the ice with you. Now that was really fun to be sure! After I learned to skate well enough so that I wouldn't fall down all the time, I developed my own little dance that my dad said looked like an old fashioned Irish Jig. What he seemed to like a lot was the way I waved my hands in the air whether or not I was still holding my hockey stick.

As I remember, he used the word 'frantic' to describe what I did. I think it was all attributed more to my effort to keep from falling down than any mimicking of the Irish that I was actually doing. Frankly, to my knowledge I had never seen anyone dance an Irish Jig so how was I to know what the correct moves were for that dance? Now that I think about it a little more, that's probably still true to this day. One of these days when I have more free time and my memory comes back completely, I'll have to look into it in greater detail especially the part about how to do an Irish Jig. That might really be fun after all.

Well, forget my hockey dance at least for now. That was probably the farthest thing from Mrs. Burkett's mind at the time because she really didn't know much about the game. What she wanted to teach us was something totally different. It was a group dance that she called 'The Virginia Reel'. The first time she said the words all I could think of was going fishing at the lake with a rod and reel. You'd probably do the same thing if you heard her words for the first time.

When he went fishing, my dad would bring his favorite rod and reel with him. Come to think of it, there was a teacher in our school in Reality, as I remember, who looked a little like an actual sea bass. He had big bulging eyes and a set of ears that compared favorably with fish gills! I think he taught fifth grade as I recall, but I'm not sure right now. His last name should have been 'Bass', but the truth is that his name was Fisher. I'm not kidding. When I told my mom that he looked like a bass and his name was Fisher, she said that it was *ironic*. Right then and there I learned another big word with which to wow my friends and the other teachers at school. It just verified how smart my mom was.

Anyway, the name of the dance sounded funny to me, too, but not knowing anyone from Virginia at the time, I was at an impasse as to the meaning of it all. But, worse yet, we had to dance with girls in front of the whole school and our parents that Valentine's Day evening at what was called an assembly. My parents might understand my plight, but what about my own brother and sisters and my friends? Hopefully, even though they were older than me, my sisters were still too young to understand the gravity of the situation, but I was certain that they would all ask me for an explanation or something along those lines. It seemed to me at the time that my entire social future hung in the balance.

Well, to make a really long story as short as possible under the circumstances, my female partner for the first dance would be the unlucky girl who picked my Valentine card out of the bowl. Then, for the second dance, my partner would be the girl whose card I picked out of the other bowl. As you can see, there was no way out of it...no escape was available to me unless I didn't attend the festivities. But my mom and dad would never permit that even if I was on my death bed. Lady Luck would have her way with me no matter what!

Second dance! I was certain that I would never survive the first dance let alone be able to do it again on the very same day. This was child cruelty in its worst form for sure. For the first time in my life I could read the words on my gravestone as I stood there. 'He died from the Virginia Reel at such a young and tender age'. Now things were getting very complicated and serious to say the least! The pressure on me grew by the minute as I thought about my fate and the very short future I had left on this earth. How could I save myself from this?

Well, that's about the time Dani rode to my rescue. She was determined to help me with the first part of my problem, the Valentine's Day card I had to make for the drawing. Not only did she remind me while I was playing with my friends, but she continued to talk about it all the way home so I wouldn't forget. Forget? That wasn't in the realm of possibilities.

I was supposed to go skating at the lit public pond near city hall that night, but there was no way Dani would let that happen until I had met my obligation to society and particularly to all the girls in my class. All of my energies had to be focused on the card and only on the card. At the time my impending and ultimate doom seemed so near and so real to me!

I remember at the time wondering whether girls have stuff like Valentine Cards built into their DNA when they are born. Of course, back then, I didn't know what DNA was. Come to think of it, I still am not exactly sure what it is except that it determines some things about who we are based upon and who were our parents and their parents all the way back in time. My mom told me that it passes down family traits from parents to their children.

Now I began to seriously worry about my future! Would I grow up like my Uncle Jack? He was a nice person deep down inside, but I couldn't imagine drinking that much wine at one time! As I remember, he loved red wine more than white wine, but I really didn't know the difference. On several occasions he tried to explain the difference between the two to me, but I wasn't much into grapes with the one exception that I did enjoy grape juice. But that wasn't my current problem which needed to be solved immediately.

Well, I guess it's good to have a sister like Dani who reminds you of things that have to be done just in time to get them done. I mean things like birthdays, holidays and the like which boys tend to forget in everyday life. And Dani was a good sister to have around when it came to gentle and not so gentle reminders about such things. She wouldn't let me forget family members' birthdays, particularly hers! Getting her a present that she would like was always a big problem for me, but I always had plenty of time to think about it. Dani made sure of that, and she always provided plenty of clues so that I would find the right answer when I finally got around to getting it. And I always suspected that she fed the clues to my mom because she always seemed to know what Dani wanted on that special day.

When we got home that Valentine's Day Eve, which, of course, was on the 13th day of February, there was my mother standing in the doorway holding several big pieces of red construction paper for me. Right away I again easily deduced that my Mom and Dani were in cahoots in this matter. Mom always liked it when I used big words or new words so I spoke my thoughts aloud, and they both smiled with huge teacher-like grins. So, it certainly appeared that there was no way out for me on this one. I was going to have to make my Valentine card at home under their expert supervision and take it to school in the morning without fail.

The class teacher was sure to know right away that I got outside help on this project from both of them. Oh, well, my actual fate in this matter was sealed for the time being anyway. I decided that my best course of action under the circumstances was to throw myself into the Valentine card production project with great enthusiasm and get it all over with once and for all. Then I could let the chips fall where they may. That's exactly what I did for better or worse.

Both my mom and Dani insisted that the card had to be all red or have a lot of red in it and on it. That thought reminded me of one of my very favorite songs. It was 'Red' by Sammy Hagar, the Red Rocker. I began to hum the lyrics to myself.

I read that it's all black and white. Oh, the spectrum made a shade I like. Oh, those crimson rays of ruby bright. Ah, the Technicolor light.

Red! Red! I want red. There's no substitute for red. Red! Paint it red. Green ain't mean compared to red.

You don't know what it does to me. Yeah, that crimson sin intensity. I'm haunted by the mystery. Yeah! Yeah! The mystery of red, red, red.

Red! Red knocks 'em dead. Some like it hot-tah. I like it red!

That's all I could remember at the moment. At first I didn't understand why red was so important here. Then they declared that the heart on the card had to be big and red. I began to wonder whether the person getting the card could see anything if everything on the card was red in color? Could you use different shades of red?

Ah, hah! It finally dawned on me. It was the heart that was supposed to be red. Someone, probably Mom, once told me that the hearts inside our bodies were red in color. How did she know that? So, naturally, my next question was what in the world had a human organ to do with Valentine's Day or at least a Valentine's Day card? This was really confusing for a little kid.

Even at five plus years of age, maybe even earlier, I knew what a human organ was…pretty much anyway. I learned that from helping my dad and brother clean fish and chickens and stuff like that. They had organs, too, at least until we removed them from their poor dead bodies. When I realized what I was doing with that big knife, I began to feel sorry for all those poor animals. I guess that's why I don't go hunting or fishing anymore even if I could. I wouldn't want anyone cutting me up with a giant knife like that for sure and then eating my parts after frying them!

That was when they hit me with it like a ton of bricks! Mom said that the heart on the Valentine card was a symbol for…a symbol for love for the recepient.

Love? All of a sudden I felt like I was in way over my head. I had heard the word before, many times and in many contexts. My Mom taught me what the word context meant. But to use it…the word "LOVE" on a card that would be randomly given to a girl in my class by me, someone she could readily identify? I couldn't see it happening no matter how hard I looked. The word 'like' was about as far as I was willing to go at that point, and I wasn't really sure of that word. But what choice did I have? I was clearly outnumbered.

With Dani's verbal help I drew a near perfect heart on my very first try, and I cut it out of that red paper and pasted it on a heavy piece of white construction paper that Dani had picked out of the pile for me. What a relief it was to see the finished product. From the large number of sheets of paper my mom brought home for me to use in my attempts to carve out a heart, I guess she expected me to make a lot of mistakes right off the bat. I think I surprised her with my apparent drawing skills. I know that I surprised myself even more.

I was so proud of myself for a brief moment that I knew wouldn't last. Was I a budding famous artist from Alaska just beginning to create beautiful things for others to admire in art galleries? Just then Dani told me that I needed another heart, smaller this time, for the inside page of the card. She said it should have the same shape as the larger one. I faltered for a moment before I looked back at the perfection of the first heart I had drawn. And then I realized that it was so much bigger, too. This smaller heart for the inside would be a piece of cake! My confidence swelled.

That's when I learned what my friends meant when they used the phrase 'beginner's luck'. As I tried to reproduce the success represented by my first big heart, things turned really ugly. Mom shook her head as she inspected my first four or five tries, and she mumbled something about wishing she had a template I could use. I had no idea what a template was because she hadn't taught me that word yet so I just kept on trying my best because this was no time to start asking questions or backing down. I gritted my teeth and charged ahead.

Finally, on the last sheet of red construction paper my luck kicked in again. While I was cutting that last heart, I could swear that both Dani and Mom were holding their collective breath as my scissors cut away. You should have heard the gasps of joy when I held up the product of my work for their inspection. I tried to remain calm and just whispered that I knew I could do it all the time. Mom and Dani just looked at each other with the strangest smirks on their faces. Identical smirks at that! It must have been that DNA thing again or maybe just a girl thing. Who knows?

The only trouble was that I didn't get to celebrate my success for very long or at least as long as I wanted to. What more could anyone want from me now to prove my courage? Two hearts cut to perfection out of red construction paper! As I admired my work one more time, that's when my Mom broke the news to me. She said that I had to use the word *love* in a sentence inside the card. And she was firm on the requirement that these would be my words and not a quote from someone else! I guess she remembered how much I love rock lyrics… especially by Bob Dylan.

Love? There was that word haunting me again. Yikes! My friends would never let me live this one down no matter how much time went by. No matter to them that Mom and Dani made me do it. My mind began racing like a blur trying to find a way out. I was trapped like a rat with no Dad or big brother to save me! It was the most fearful moment I could remember in my life up to that point.

That's when serendipity struck! You know, it's the gift of finding valuable or agreeable things not sought for! We can thank my Mom again. I was hoping that someday I would get to use that word. The obvious answer leaped straight into my head as I turned around and glanced toward the door and thought about running away to save myself! There was my saving answer right in front of me on the kitchen floor…it was my pair of ice skates!

Quickly, I grabbed a pencil from off the table and wrote the sentence that was buzzing through my head down for all to see. I knew that my Dad and brother would approve immediately once they saw it. The eventual vote that evening was 3-2, and I won for sure. My Mom and Dani were so disappointed that I began to feel sorry for them. But I knew I would get over that feeling because I had done exactly what they told me to do. There were no violations of the Valentine's Day Rules as Paul, Dad and I understood them. I used the word 'love' in a sentence inside my Valentine's Day card as required! I had performed my duty without a flaw.

Why are you looking at me with that quizzical look? Is it my toothy smile that is bothering you so much? Oh, I see. You want to know what I wrote down inside the card that fulfilled my obligation, do you? Okay. Here it is for you to ponder.

I LOVE TO SKATE!

You seem sort of surprised. Well, it's true. I do love to skate! I'm not exaggerating or lying to you. Love is the right word for how I feel about skating. It was love at first glide!

Finally, I put my newly created card into an envelope that my dad brought home from the logging company and quickly sealed it before anyone could change their vote. I remember the great feeling of satisfaction that surged through me all that evening. I even slept with the card under my pillow so it wouldn't get lost or stolen. I didn't want some practical joker like my older brother making me go through this experience again, especially if there were a new set of revised rules to adhere to. I was taking no chances even with those who voted for me.

I would fight him to the death to keep the card until I could see my teacher nod as I slipped the envelope into the boys' Valentine jar and my obligation was fulfilled. I must have dreamed about a fight because I was sweating when I woke up the next morning. I immediately reached under my pillow and touched the card. What a relief. It was there and in one piece!

Oh, I forgot to tell you something else that is very interesting. I rummaged through a desk drawer and found another envelope and put some folded newspaper into it. Then, I put that envelope on my nearby dresser in plain view so everyone and anyone could see it who came into the room while I was asleep. It looked almost exactly like the envelope hiding under my pillow.

Sure enough, in the morning that second envelope was gone. My prediction had proven correct. You should have seen the look of disappointment on Paul's face when I failed to complain about the missing card at breakfast. As I headed for the door and my trip to school, the real card hidden under my coat, Paul leaped up and offered the purloined fake card to me. He actually thought that I had forgotten it. I just shrugged my shoulders and told him that I didn't need it anymore. I told him that he could have it as my Valentine's greeting to him. Then, I flashed the real card as I opened the front door. Once again, my older brother had been completely outwitted by none other than me! That victory felt so sweet to me.

That day at school was February 14th for sure. Valentine's Day in the flesh! There was no avoiding it. Plop! That was the sound of my well-guarded Valentine's Day card as it fell into the big jar from which the girls would pick. I remember my hand shaking as I dropped the card realizing that my whole life might be riding on the fate of that card and the person who received it. I tended to be a little overanxious in those days as you might imagine.

I was scared, all right, but since my name started with the letter 'R', I was one of the last boys to pick from the jar the girls put their cards into. I was secretly hoping that I would get Becky McCallister's card because she was the very cutest girl in our class. That was just my opinion, of course, and what did I know about girls anyway? She had red curly hair and green eyes to boot. Her Dad, Mickey McCallister, worked for my Dad at the logging company. They called him 'Big Mick', and if you saw him, you would know why. My dad once told me that Big Mick did the work of two men without even breaking a sweat. I was impressed.

But instead, I picked Claudette Bouchard's card and, would you believe it, Claudette picked mine! Was that irony again? Was Fate working for me or against me here? How was I supposed to know?

But there is an important fact that I didn't tell you, and I should have. In our school the first through third grades shared the same large classroom. This meant that while our Valentine's drawing proceeded, the ominous shadow cast by Schultz loomed from across the room. You see, my archenemy Schultz was a third grader but only by the skin of his teeth. Rumor had it that Schultz was being considered for what we called 'a layover'. That meant he might have to do third grade over again, and I would be facing another year with him leering at me, but from an even closer distance. The thought of two possible layovers gave me nightmares almost every night. What if he ended up in my class all the way through school? What had I done so wrong to deserve such a punishment?

However, that wasn't my first fear as I stared into Claudette's beautiful eyes. The awful truth was that Schultz considered Claudette to be *his girlfriend*! But, she whispered that she liked my card and said that she was looking forward to dancing the Virginia Reel with me. Wow, was I surprised to be sure! And when Schultz saw us together talking, laughing and smiling, was he ever mad. His face was red as a beet and at least as red as the heart in Claudette's Valentines card, and his ears had almost doubled in size, and they were really huge to start with. All of a sudden this Valentine's Day thing was turning out to be great fun for me.

Well, we spent the rest of the day learning to dance the Virginia Reel, and once our teacher was satisfied with our performance, it was time for cookies and milk. All of a sudden I felt like I was in seventh heaven. I had developed two new skills I never expected…as an artist and a dancer, and I nailed my biggest enemy by spending quality time with Claudette in class. Life was certainly very good. It got even better when Claudette told me that she thought Schultz was the most obnoxious kid in our school. I could only smile and agree by nodding my head. Schultz was seething with jealousy. I could feel it in the air when he came near us.

That night we put on a show for our families and friends. It was a total success. I can still see Dani's smiling face in the crowd as I was dancing the Virginia Reel with a big grin on my mug. Mom and dad seemed very pleased by the whole thing, too. Dani was just beaming with joy. Yes, sir, she was dancing right along with me right there in her seat. Proud as a peacock of her brother, she was, and I was proud of her, too. What a great sister!

I wish that big guy with the phone would come back. I would sure like to give Danielle a call! I want to thank her for all her love and help.

5
Me and Schultz

I have a friend whose older brother
had a very rough childhood. His father
of all people was an alcoholic, smoked
like a fiend, and was a bully to boot.
Although he never hit anyone, the
father was always threatening little
kids and women. That's a bully for you!

My Friend, Alfie

Here they come again! What do they want from me this time around? I wish I knew exactly who…or is it precisely *whom* they work for so I could lodge a complaint or two with their superiors each time they do this to me. And I don't see any means of identification on their shirts or jackets or hats for those that wear jackets and hats. When they look at me, can't they see that I'm deep in pain and suffering? It's pretty obvious that I need my rest to recover from this thing that happened to me…whatever it is. Since they are paying so much attention to me, you would think that they would have an idea of what happened. But, no, not one crumb of information for me, the obvious victim in these proceedings.

Move me over here? Move me over there? It just doesn't seem right or make any sense at all from any perspective you might choose at any particular time. You would think that they're trying to punish me for something that I've done, and I haven't done anything wrong, at least not as far as I can tell. But with my current memory of things, who knows? As I'm lying here do I assume that I was shot robbing a bank or run over by a railroad train? Of course, I might have been hurt while doing something good for my friends or country. Well, maybe it's something that I haven't done that I was supposed to do that gave rise to this condition? I have not a single clue as to what that is either. This is a real dilemma for sure!

With my small familiarity with the situation, only one fact stands out as obvious. I keep telling them that cool, clear ice...well, bags of cool, clear ice, are the only real answer to all of our current problems as far as I'm concerned, but no one seems to be listening to my pleadings as far as I can tell. They seem to have their tiny little minds or brains or whatever they're thinking or reasoning with made up already. Easy for them to do under the circumstances since they're not lying here on this table or floor! I'm the one enduring the pain and suffering and total humiliation for unknown reasons, and they just ignore me.

I know I keep repeating myself over and over and over, but what's this place we find ourselves in? Where in the world am I or are we for that matter, anyway? I've got to develop a new workable strategy and approach to deal with these lousy places and people. But it's hard to have the right answers when I don't know where I am or why I'm here in the first place. Oh, well, things can only get better.

Ah, they finally must have noticed me again probably because of my moaning and groaning and attempts to roll around which must seem pretty pathetic. Wow! Someone's coming over toward me right now as if I had just paged him! Now he stopped short, and he's pointing toward the door...well, actually at the doors over there. There are big flat double doors at the end of the room we're in. That's a fact! I can actually see them from down here when I roll my eyes as far to the left as possible. The fat guy is going down there, and, yes, he's pushing both of them open right now. I wonder where they lead to, if anywhere at all? It looks like a plain old dusty hallway from here just like the ones in my grade school back in Reality. That doesn't help me much right now because those hallways just led to other classrooms and storage closets.

It's probably the way to the kitchen because I smell an odor of food all of a sudden! Good grief! Ah, is that pot roast that I smell? My mom used to cook the greatest pot roast in the universe in our kitchen at home. You could smell it for miles up and down the streets around our neighborhood. Neighbors would line up outside our kitchen on the weekends just for a smell and maybe a lucky taste of some leftovers she would leave out on the window sill. They'd show up at our house almost every time whether they were invited to dinner or not. And it didn't matter which time of day or day of the week she made it.

My dad kept telling mom that she should open a restaurant of her own that specialized in pot roast cooking, but she was very loyal to her employer and didn't want the Timberline Tavern to lose all of its business. She would say that her job was just too much fun to give up and that running a restaurant was a very big responsibility and would require the whole family to get involved up to our necks. Secretly, I was glad because I didn't want to miss my hockey practices even in exchange for owning part of a real, live restaurant that specialized in pot roast. And my scrawny little neck was sure happy, too, because of reasons I can't verbalize right now.

Well, let's get back to the business at hand. It looks like I'm going to find out the answer to my biggest question first hand. Maybe all of my questions will finally be answered once that one is out of the way. Here they come right towards me, and here we go! I mean physically. They're wheeling me out of this big room that I've been in for God knows how long, but out to where? I hope there's food wherever we're going! I'm starving for sure!

Oh, Geez, we're shooting down a long hallway right to…a big elevator of all things! You know, it's just like one of those big freight elevators you see in gangster movies all the time. As I remember from those movies, they almost always go to the roof to get on a helicopter. The door's sliding open slowly, and in we go without any hesitation. Like I said I think we're going up, but I'm not sure just yet. Hey, we're moving, but it feels like we're going down.

Now we're stopping, and the door's opening very slowly once again. Here we go. Outside? We're outside the building! Holy cow! Finally, a little taste of fresh air for me for a change. What a relief! The cool air feels so very good on my face especially on my ears. It feels almost as good as the ice did.

What are those flashing lights? It isn't the cops, is it? I don't know how many times I've told them that I'm innocent, and I have a flawless alibi? Innocent of what and an alibi for when, I don't know just yet?

But, it will come to me sooner or later. It seems like they keep pursuing me wherever I go these days.

Wait! Nuts, it's an ambulance. How do I know it's an ambulance I'm in? Now I remember. That doctor fella said something about a hospital in my future. I can't remember his name or the name of the hospital. They're taking me to the hospital or at least I think so. Hey, I don't need no stinkin' hospital just yet. All I really need is a fresh bag of ice on my face and some food in my stomach. I never go to the hospital because it costs way too much. I feel a little woozy and my head hurts and my ribs are killing me, but that's no reason to go to the hospital, is it? Do I have enough insurance to cover this stuff? I can't remember.

Now, I'm inside the ambulance. Well, at least it's pretty nice in here. Lots of stuff is hanging from the side walls like tubes, wires, white clothes, and the works. There are two youngsters in here looking at me, smiling to beat the band. I'd smile back at them, but smiling hurts too much right now so I think I'll just wave a little. Hey, they both waved back at me at the same time and kept smiling. They surely must know just how I feel, a little fuzzy for sure.

I wonder if they're always this friendly to everyone they pick up? And they are acting like they know me. Ah, that's just to get me to relax. But they are very good at it for sure.

Well, things just got a little more complicated. One of them reached out and handed me a form to fill out, an insurance form of all things. Doesn't he know that I can't read this stuff or write very well? The print on the pages is way too small, and it moves with every bump in the road we hit with this vehicle. And, this is a very bumpy road we're on, for sure.

As I predicted, there it is; he's saying something about my insurance coverage being covered by my team. Insurance? My team? I already asked myself that very simple question. Do I have insurance? How would I know if I did? And what kind of insurance are they...is he talking about? I have no idea. Life insurance? What for? Do they think I'm ready to die? I hope not! Oh, my head's starting to hurt real bad again. Maybe I'm just thinking too much?

Ah, good! They must have figured it out for themselves. They're putting the form back in the cabinet up front. The last thing I need to do right now is fill out a form, especially when I don't know the answers to all the questions. Actually, I probably don't know the answer to any of the questions. Besides, right now I can't even tell for sure what the questions are. You'd think they would read them to me so I would have a little time to ponder them.

Ah, heck! There's that same old doctor in those same old clothes again! At least I think he's a doctor. I should really say that I believe that he's a physician because there are lots of doctors who are not physicians.

Where did he come from? He must have been hiding up front because I didn't see him get on the ambulance when we left. And, he's got a gigantic needle in his hand! That's not for me, is it? That's the biggest needle I've ever seen, and I've seen some pretty big ones. Back in Reality, when I was just a little, helpless kid, that dumb bully Schultz knocked me off my bike, and I flew right into a big old oak tree! Head first and I hit it dead center at that! When I finally woke up, that pretty lady who works in the clinic was holding a needle that looked even bigger than this one for sure. Well, it was at least as big as this one now staring me in the face.

As I remember, I started to scream just like they do all the time in the movies. You must have seen 'Jaws' and its sequels. All the girls in the movie did was scream all the time! Well, what do you expect from little kids? I remember the incident with Schultz and my bike as if it were yesterday. Slowly, as I watched, she put the needle down and then pointed to my scrawny little arm.

Oh, my God! That's when it hit me. She had already stuck the thing in my arm. No wonder my arm hurt almost as much as my head did. She stuck that thing straight into me when I wasn't looking! What the hell for? Did she put stuff into my arm or take stuff out of my arm? I don't know because my arm just hurt to beat the band. My dad would use the phrase 'to beat the band' whenever he wanted to emphasize something. I guess that's because bands are usually very loud?

When I look at or even think of an injection needle like that one, the very next thing that pops into my mind is that bully Schultz. It seems to want to tell me that Schultz might be responsible for this situation, too. My brother would always tell me to follow the clues when trying to solve a mystery. This big needle is certainly a clue and it points directly at Schultz!

And my new bike, the one I got for Christmas, where was it? That's all I could think about after I realized that the needle incident was over for now. But, the pain in my head made it hard for me to think very straight. But I finally realized that I would never make that mistake again…the mistake that I made with my bike. I don't think I told you about that yet? If I have, get ready to hear the story again because it's something I remember clearly and must learn from.

Well, here goes. Listen hard because maybe you can help me solve my problem once and for all.

I was riding my new bike down the sidewalk from school to our house like I always did. The grade school I went to was at one end of my home town of Reality and our house was way at the other end of town. So, then, instead of walking all the way, I could ride as long as there wasn't too much snow or heavy rain, which luckily was most of the time. But after a while I figured out where the snow had been cleared by the city so I could move ahead on my wheels.

I clearly remember that I was riding home from school on a very dark, cloudy day. It was three o'clock in the afternoon; that's when school got finished each day unless we had some special activities scheduled. I had to go home to get my skates and go to the river for practice. My mom and the teachers wouldn't let me bring my skates to school for some unexplained reason. For the life of me I could never understand why they did that to me? In this situation that silly rule of theirs was going to cost me big time as you will soon see.

Schultz and his cronies must have seen me coming along the street on my bike on that particular day. They didn't have much to do right after school so they just stood around looking for trouble. With their low grades you would think that they'd be home or at the library studying and trying to catch up to the rest of us. Schultz did have hockey practice, but it was a few hours later with the bigger kids.

Lots of times when I rode my bike, I kept my head down. One reason was to keep the cold air off my face during the winter. The other reason was that I was looking down at the chain on the bike to make sure that my pants didn't get caught in it. Nothing could be worse than having your pants caught in the chain of your bike, especially at high speed or in front of your friends…or enemies or anyone for that matter.

One of my friends, it was Alfie of all people, had a chain-guard on his bike like I think I already told you. How the rest of us envied him because of that. No way he would ever get his pants caught in the chain with that chain-guard on his bike. And when he locked up his bike, he made sure to lock up that chain-guard securely, too, so no one could steal it. It was bright red so stealing it probably wouldn't work, not even for Schultz and his gang. As it turned out, the chain-guard was almost more valuable than the bike itself.

I remember making a mental note to myself to be sure to write Santa and the elves and tell them that when they bring a bike to a kid for Christmas that it should always have a chain-guard attached. That would make all the mothers very happy because they wouldn't have to spend so much time and money repairing and replacing the cuffs of pants chewed up by the chains on their kids' bikes. And maybe they could bring me my own chain-guard next Christmas as one of my gifts.

Well, as usual, I came around the corner by the drug store, and as I looked down, Schultz and his bully friend, Fred, yelled some obscenities and threw snowballs at me which was par for the course. They missed as they usually did because they were terrible shots. As I remember, Fred threw snowballs like a girl…ah, no offense to girls, but throwing snowballs was a manly thing up in Reality in those days. But, anyway, I lost my balance because the sidewalk was uneven right there, and my bike started to skid! I can still feel the cold chill that skid sent up my spine at that moment. Somehow I knew something bad was about to happen.

In an attempt to save myself and my bike, I jumped off the sidewalk onto some ice on the street because I thought the street would be smoother. The bike…the tires lost their grip, and I flew off over the handlebars right into the big tree that grew directly in front of the drugstore window. I'll bet that all of the customers in the store were surprised to see me flying through the air right past them just then! After that I didn't remember a thing until I saw the big needle in the nurse's hand at the clinic.

That reminds me of a question. How did I get from the street to the clinic? Schultz certainly wouldn't have helped! Him and Fred must have hightailed it home immediately after seeing me airborne. After I woke up in the clinic I remember hearing my dad talking in the next room. He was talking to my mom and the doctor. He was saying something about going over to Schultz's house and beating the crap out of Schultz's father. Oh, boy, did I ever want to see that! But, unfortunately, my mother was there, too. At first, I thought she would help my dad put his coat on and send him right over to Schultz's place.

Not a chance! My mother stopped him and told him that I would have to learn to defend myself against *the little bastard*. Little? Schultz was at least four or five inches taller than me. Okay, maybe an inch or two? She told him that I would have to learn to fight my own battles! Now, that was a real bummer for me under the circumstances. What are fathers and big brothers for, I ask you? If they can't beat up the bullies that are messing with you, what good are they?

Gosh, I can remember that day so clearly. They put a big white bandage on my head. No stitches, though, none like the ones someone put on my head today when I was out cold. My friends heard about what happened through the grapevine and came to my house later to offer their sympathies. They wanted to form a gang and get Fred and Schultz when they weren't looking. They told me that they had a secret meeting after school to come up with a plan or two, but so far they weren't sure what to do. They realized that this revenge wasn't going to be easy.

But, you know, I realized that my mom was right as she always is. I had to stand on my own two feet…stand up for myself. I was small, but I was tough…for a small guy. And I was smart…smarter than your average bear as my older brother would say. And I would have to go to school like that…on my own, first grade it was. I had to walk into first grade with this big bandage on my head. Remember, Schultz was in third grade, and Fred was in second grade. Something had to be done to tip the scales of justice in my favor. At least our class met over in the corner away from the bigger kids. Thank God for that favor.

At first I asked myself the obvious question any kid in my situation would ask of himself. What would Clint Eastwood and Charles Bronson do to even this score? This would require some heavy thinking I could best accomplish before I went to sleep. I would start this search that very evening.

Anyway, somehow I survived the Schultz incident. But, I never forgot the details of the experience. I waited and watched carefully and quietly. It would take years, but I would get my revenge. I wanted to be like a tiger ready to pounce on his prey. Ah, well, more like a trapdoor spider than a tiger. I think I learned some details about trapdoor spiders back in school. I don't remember which grade I was in, but the teacher was big on trapdoor spiders for sure. It must have been sixth grade as I remember. I've never actually seen one in the flesh, as my mother would say, mind you, but the idea was good and the tactics were simple. Lay in wait for your victim. Bide your time because haste makes waste. Wait for the opportunity that would eventually come no matter how long you had to wait. See, it's easy and obvious when you think about it.

In the meantime I had to endure a continuing stream of barbs and jabs from Schultz and his gang of dedicated followers. But my teacher, when she saw my bandage and talked with my mother, she was more than ready for Schultz just as I was. She would make him stay after school an extra ten minutes every day for the rest of the time while I was wearing the bandage. She did it just to be sure that I could get home okay without having to fight off *the little bastard* and his friends.

My big brother Paul taught me not to call him a *big bastard*. That way I was less scared of him, and it was definitely more insulting. Paul said that it was a matter of semantics. Paul was good at using big words, too. Just in case, though, I kept the bandage on for an extra three weeks to remind the teacher to keep Schultz after school. It worked great, and he would get madder every day. The teacher could see his anger, and it justified her action to keep him after school. Revenge can be so sweet when you think about it. Schultz's punishment was just beginning!

I remember calling him a *little bastard* in front of my dad. My dad would call some of the people he worked for up in the woods *Bastards*. When my dad heard me use the name for the first time, he stopped me in my tracks and warned me about my language. He said such things were inappropriate for someone my age. I never did figure out what age had to do with calling Schultz a *little bastard*? Then I reminded my dad about what Schultz did. "Wasn't Schultz a bastard?" I said to him in my most serious tiny voice.

I'll never forget what happened next. My dad bent down and whispered to me, right into my ear.

"Son, you can call Schultz a bastard any time you want, but no one else! And, definitely don't do it when your mother is around…or your teacher. If those two aren't within hearing range, you can call Schultz *a rotten bastard* if you wish!"

Now that was really cool! That was really big for me to say the least. It was a major breakthrough. I could call Schultz a *rotten bastard*, and I was only beginning second grade. I'm not sure I could even spell the word back then. Even the teacher couldn't stop me now, I thought to myself. But, then, for reasons I'm sure you understand, I decided not to test out my theory at school. I would call him a bastard any time I wanted to, but not when mom or my teacher were anywhere nearby. That way I would keep my dad happy. I want to keep my allies on my side during this struggle which was the biggest in my life so far.

Well, the days turned into weeks, and my bandage finally came off for good and my head was fine, at least as far as I could tell. At least it was in better shape at that time than it is now. Not a trace of the collision with the tree trunk. The tree itself was fine, too, so we had both survived a terrible incident. The bandage had served its purpose, and it had also given me time to think about and carefully plan my revenge. I called it my 'thinking bandage'. You know, instead of a 'thinking cap'. But that didn't matter. I was waiting for my opportunity to appear. Then, guess what? It came!

It must have been the middle of March, and I was still in the last throes of first grade. I was down at the river skating with my big brother, Paul. There was nothing particularly unusual about that for sure. Like I said before, Paul would have beaten that Schultz to a pulp for me, but I took my mom's advice to heart. She was real good at understanding problems like this and the impacts of their solutions on both parties. It was most certainly up to me to learn how to defend myself just in case something like this problem happened again. I told Paul that I was waiting for the opportunity to strike back and to strike back with a vengeance. But I reminded him that if my plan didn't work out the way I expected it to, that I might need a little backup from him. He seemed to understand perfectly well.

I remember that I was preparing myself for the hockey rematch with Kaktovik. You remember, don't you? Maybe I forgot to tell you. The famous undefeated Reality Pee Wee Lumberjacks were about to hit the road. Well, the game was rescheduled by Coach Grimes, and it was a week before we were to again trek up to Kaktovik. We called it a road game. I didn't particularly like that name, but I couldn't come up with a better alternative so I kept my mouth shut.

So, there we were at the river with our skates and hockey sticks waiting for the rest of the Pee Wee Lumberjacks to show up when we spotted Schultz and his girlfriend coming along the road to skate on the river. Believe me, Schultz needed all the skating practice he could get.

Yeah, believe it or not, he had several so-called girlfriends, but this particular one wasn't much to brag about. Her name was Monica. Schultz used to carry his skates in a leather bag that he threw over his shoulder. As I remember, Schultz used to carry that bag just about everywhere he went even when he had nothing to carry in it. We used to refer to it as Schultz's 'purse'. That got a laugh from everyone, even my mom and my teacher. I overheard him telling the third grade teacher that he used it to carry his books and pencils so they let him take it wherever he went. I don't think I ever saw Schultz take a book or pencil out of his purse.

Well, on this particular day he was busy drooling over this girl Monica from the fourth grade when he wandered off trying to watch her skate. I think I can safely tell you that she was a horrible skater, but I never saw anyone trying to help her. Dani could have taught her quite a few things. Watching Monica stagger around on the ice for a few moments reminded me of just how great a skater Dani was. So, just as fate would have it, opportunity came to the patient trapdoor spider as it always does. That's me, of course, in case you forgot!

A couple of people from down-river had just finished a few hours of ice-fishing, and they were pulling their stuff onto the bank getting ready to go home. I said 'Hello' to them because they seemed very friendly and were smiling a lot. They were good about cleaning up the ice and stuffing snow into the hole to help it freeze again. There is nothing worse than skating along and hitting an open hole left by ice-fishermen. After some pleasant conversation and a few jokes, they left for home, and I thought I'd better start loosening up so I would be prepared when the rest of the team arrived. My brother, Paul, was a stickler for loosening up properly before practice or a game or any kind of athletic activity. He taught me just how to do it, and I'm sure it kept me from getting hurt all the time. I owe him many thanks for that. Many of the kids as well as their parents didn't realize just how important warming up properly is.

As I skated by the place where the visitors had been fishing through the ice, I saw something lying by the bank. When I got closer, I realized that it was a poor fish stuck completely out of the water. I thought I would go over and throw it in the hole in the ice, which wasn't frozen yet so that the poor fellow could swim away to be with the other fish and his family. I always tried to help the little animals when they got in trouble. The poor thing couldn't make it to the hole by itself. But, when I got there and picked him up, I realized that the poor fella was already dead.

I felt so sad at that moment. He was the cutest little fish I had ever seen up close. Just as I was about to bury his remains in the hole, I had an epiphany! *Epiphany* was my school teacher's favorite word. That's why I know what it means. She told me that it was a vision or an insight…whatever that means in any given situation. Well, I must have had exactly that right then and there. There was no other possible explanation. I picked up that poor fish again, gave it a kiss and carried it over to where Schultz had stashed his precious leather skate bag. He was around the bend not watching at the time so I proceeded to slip the poor fish, who I had named 'Trapdoor', into Schultz's leather bag. I dropped him right to the very bottom.

I sat there for a moment and said a little prayer for Trapdoor. It just seemed to me that we could have been such good friends if he had survived. My conscience tugged at me suggesting that Trapdoor might rather be under the ice with his friends, but I put myself in his place, a technique my mom often suggested to me in matters like this. Rather than just lie in the water, I knew I would rather help someone like me as my last act here on earth. It was really heavy thinking for a first grader to be doing.

We had our Pee Wee Lumberjacks' practice, and my brother and I went home afterwards. With all the excitement and activity, I completely forgot about the fish and my moves as a trapdoor spider. I forgot until the next day, that is. There I was at school going out to recess with my friends when it all came back to me in a flash. My new friend Trapdoor was doing his best for me.

Oh, yes, recess! That's where us kids got to take some well earned time off from the daily grind of learning to go outside and play as long as there wasn't a blizzard or thunderstorm or anything like that going on. Now, as Alfie and I walked by the room where the third and fourth graders were at the time, we both heard a blood-curdling scream from inside. It was coming from Schultz's girlfriend, Monica. She came running out of the room holding her favorite jacket at arm's length as she headed for the girls' bathroom in a panic.

The story I heard later was that Monica had placed her favorite jacket in Schultz's leather bag at the river and had forgotten to remove it when she went home. In the morning at school Schultz put the bag on the floor right next to the main radiator that was used to heat the classroom. The radiator was going full blast as it should trying its best to keep the classroom warm because it was quite cold outside that day. I couldn't have planned it any better by myself.

As you can easily imagine, after a night and day together with the dead fish in the bag, Monica's favorite jacket smelled like…well, you guessed it, fish. Dead fish! As you might imagine, Monica didn't speak to Schultz for weeks after that incident. That's what our spies in the third grade told me on the sly. And, Schultz, he had no idea how the fish got into his bag either. I'm sure he assumed that he jumped into the bag directly from the water. The only problem with that theory was that the water was frozen and Trapdoor wasn't big enough to break through the ice! Another lucky break for the trapdoor spider, although I must take some of the credit for recognizing and seizing the moment! Don't you agree?

But, as we stood outside the classroom, watching Monica sprint for the girls' room, Schultz saw me standing there, and I guess I couldn't resist laughing out loud at what I saw. It was the funniest moment in my life, up to that point, and I just couldn't hold my feelings back.

He gritted his teeth, pointed at me, and then yelled at me!

"You! Robespierre! Did you put that fish in my bag?"

As it turned out, I figured that this was one of those times when a good old-fashioned lie was in order. I just knew that my mother and father would both approve. Of course, my brother Paul and my sisters would be the first to agree. So, in self-defense, I just shrugged my shoulders with a smirk on my face that I just couldn't suppress, and shook my head 'no'. My plea was 'Not Guilty'. I really wanted to tell him that if I had thought of it, I would have done it!

In the next moment my entire life flashed quickly before me. I couldn't run, and I couldn't hide. All eyes were on me waiting for my reaction and response. If push came to shove, I would have to challenge the bastard. There was no doubt about that. Frozen in time and space, I waited for fate to deal the next card. Time slowed to a crawl. But I was again in luck. It was an ace or maybe even a joker!

Lucky for me, to say the least, Alfie was laughing and pointing even though he was in the dark on the whole thing. Actually, 'Lucky' isn't a strong enough word. Alfie, for some reason I'll never understand, thought Schultz was talking to him. He didn't particularly like Schultz either, and he had a reputation for pulling practical jokes. I'll explain that later.

So, Alfie just shrugged his shoulders and shook his head in unison with me…well, as I was doing the same, but he did it with a bit more emphasis and flair. It was a move that distracted Schultz completely. Actually, Schultz was easy to distract, but it was the timing that was perfect in this case.

It was absolutely perfect cover. Alfie always had the stupidest look on his face. It made Schultz forget about me just long enough for me to execute a quiet and unhurried escape down the hallway. I didn't want to miss recess!

Of course, in case you're wondering, this wasn't the incident where I made Schultz say *Uncle* three times. That came a little later as I remember. But Alfie somehow survived this close encounter with Schultz who never lived the incident down, particularly with Monica and her friends.

6

The Pee Wee Lumberjacks

For when the One Great Scorer comes,
To write against your name,
He marks not that you won or lost,
But how you played the game.

Grantland Rice
Alumnus Football

Here comes the really big, fat guy again! He's asking me something about an interview on television. Is he kidding? That certainly sent shockwaves through my system.

His comment seemed serious, and I began to wonder why anyone would want to interview me especially because of the condition I was in. Had I been in an accident of some kind? I sure couldn't remember it. Then my mind began to consider that I might have done something wrong. But I realized that no police officers were nearby, and my wrists were free of handcuffs. But my imagination wouldn't give up no matter how much I tried to relax.

What about my civil rights and my constitutional rights? Where's my defense lawyer anyway? I'm entitled to legal counsel for sure! Will they believe me when I tell them that I didn't know how old she was? Besides, who hit me in the head when I wasn't looking? I should be the one bringing the lawsuit here for sure! It isn't fair for them to accuse me of committing a crime when they weren't even there to see it or film it when it happened… whatever and whenever and wherever that was.

Now he's waving at someone back in the hallway. It's a guy in a uniform. Luckily, it's not a police uniform! And, better yet, it's definitely a hockey uniform. Hey, I remember that logo on his shirt. It's a tiger or panther or wildcat or something like that. I can't see his name, but his number is three. Number three! He must be a defenseman for sure. He's big enough to be one.

We defensemen wear mostly low numbers and high numbers. We leave the in-between numbers to the forwards and the goalies. Don't ask me why I know that. Don't even ask me why I think I even have a number. Like I think I said before, my favorite number has always been 53. At least as far as I can remember, it's been 53 on every hockey team I've ever played on.

Fifty-two cards in the deck and one for the joker!

As I think I already told you at least once, my brother Paul taught me that before I could even skate. 'Always leave room for the joker,' he would say. I still wonder why in the world he said that. But you know all this already, don't you? I know why…I tend to repeat myself over and over and over. I'll have to think about it so I can figure it out myself. Life can indeed be very confusing.

This number three is asking me if I remember him. Do I? Not really, but I must say that I've seen his face before. But I sure don't want to hurt his feelings because he looks pretty tough, and he sure seems totally convinced that he knows me. That's sort of embarrassing for me don't you think. So, what the heck! I'll just nod my head if I can do it. Ah, maybe not, but if it makes him happy, I'll do it. My skull still hurts quite a bit all around the edges. Maybe I can get him to tell me what put me in this condition.

But, for some reason this guy keeps smiling at me like a Cheshire cat. I remember now! It was in that book, *Alice's Adventures in Wonderland*. There was a cat that was always grinning, I think? I wonder why he's grinning at me that way? He looks just like that cat…except for the fur, of course.

Say, that's funny. I can't tell for sure if he's really a hockey player because he looks like he has all of his teeth! But, then again, I have all of my teeth…don't I? Well, most of them anyway. I can't feel my mouth very well right now, otherwise I would check and see if they are all still there. I'll do it next time I encounter a mirror and I'm sitting or standing upright like a regular human being.

"Yes," I finally whispered as best I could in answer to his question. He must have heard me because he's smiling at me again and nodding his head. Now he's even pointing at me and laughing.

"I have a present for you, Robber," he said, still grinning at me with a sneaky smile.

Robber? I think that I've heard that name before! It's one of those nicknames hockey players use for each other. Sure enough, Robber must come from my name, Robespierre. It's said with a long 'o'. Just like row in row your boat. My mom taught me that pronunciation stuff, too. She knew that knowledge of that kind would come in handy to me some day. It sure has helped me as far as I can remember.

Anyway, I wonder what his present for me is going to be? So many questions and so few answers! My head is spinning around just considering the possibilities. I hope it's another bag of ice for my head. The throbbing is still there, and I can feel the melted ice running down my face. It feels good, but the solid stuff would feel even better.

No, it's not more ice. He's holding it up in his hand for me to see. It's something small and black.

A puck! What do I need a puck for?

"It's *The Puck!*" he said loud and clear while continuing to grin like a cat. Actually, I would say that he's almost laughing out loud right now. What does he mean by *The Puck*? I've seen plenty of pucks before, so what's the big deal about this one? As I sort of remember, I have quite a few pucks of my own back at home in Reality. Personally, like I just said, I'd rather have another bag of ice for my aching head. I'll tell him that, and we'll see if he will go get another bag of the cold stuff for me. Now that bag of ice would be a real present that I would appreciate immediately.

Hey, somehow he's got the idea. This number three is no dummy for sure. He's yelling into the hallway back there. Ah, here it comes straight for me. I can feel the cold stuff already. Just what I needed! He's got a towel, and he's wiping the water off my face. It still stings up there, and my left eye isn't opening yet. I sure hope everything is okay. He's putting the new bag of nice cold ice on my swollen eye. Ah, the cool feeling is very good to be sure. I can't feel the pain nearly as much right now and that's very good for certain.

"I'll get the boys on the line and your defense partner and the goalie to autograph it for you," he whispered. "Hey, your defense partner?

Okay! That would be me all right!" That last bit of yelling really woke me up.

What boys on what line? Autograph the bag of ice or the puck? I don't see how they can do either one very easily nor why they would do it.

Now he wants to know if I want a cigar. A cigar? What the heck am I going to do with a cigar while I'm lying here on my back on this gurney or whatever? Besides, my dad always told me that smoking, especially cigars, shortens your wind and hurts your lungs. He told me it could probably shorten my life. And I certainly want to stay in shape no matter what. No cigars for me if I can help it! My dad would box my ears if he caught me doing that so leave me out.

I can remember him warning me about the evils of smoking right after the affair with the cigarettes. You remember me telling you about that, don't you? You know, the missing pack of cigarettes. Well, the funny thing was that every time I would catch him smoking a cigarette or a cigar, he would immediately say that it was bad for me and that it was a terrible habit. *Dirty and disgusting* were the words he would always use to describe smoking of any kind. If that's what he thought, why was he voluntarily doing it himself?

I also remember him telling me that he was going to stop smoking very soon, maybe even before the next week had come and gone. He said that he just wanted to use up the supply of cigarettes or cigars he had in stock so that they wouldn't be wasted. He was always big on not wasting things even if they were bad for him. He must have found out about my brother Paul and the cigarettes in the garage, but he never said anything about it directly to me and neither did Paul for that matter. There were just little hints, especially when he would take me to pee wee hockey practice. We would practice over behind the grade school building.

I was the smallest kid on the pee wee team when I first started to play. We practiced quite a lot, but our pee wee team didn't play many games against other teams because we were so far away from everywhere else...anywhere that might have a pee wee team for us to play, that is. When we would bring up the subject, our very excellent coach, Mister Grimes, told us that the nearest team we could possibly play against was way up in that town called Kaktovik and that he was trying his very best to schedule a game for us in the near future. It could be a home game or it could be a road game, he didn't say.

So, in the meantime we played a lot of what are called intra-squad games. I remember my dad and the coach sitting at the bar in the Timberline Tavern arguing about whether it was intra-squad or inter-squad. I couldn't spell either one back then so it didn't make much difference to me. I think my dad won that bet because the coach ended up buying the food and drinks that evening. If I remember, I'll have to ask dad about that bet next time I see him.

Our team was called the Reality Pee Wee Lumberjacks, and by all accounts that first year we were undefeated. Well, since we didn't have any real games for a while, I guess that the people in Reality expected us to be undefeated. So, in recognition, they hung one of our jerseys in the lobby of the city hall and another at the Timberline Tavern celebrating the fact that we hadn't lost. Actually, I think it was my mom who put the jersey up at the Timberline because that jersey had the number 53 on it. The bigger high school kids were sure mad as I remember, because they weren't undefeated. Far from it as I recall. They had to play some real games and quite a few of them were far away on the road. Unfortunately, they lost most of them. So, they weren't undefeated at all, and in theory, we Pee Wee Lumberjacks were undefeated. I just don't see why they were so darn mad. All they had to do was play better and win those games they lost. Then, they would have been undefeated, too. Then their jerseys would have been hanging all over town just like ours were!

Well, Mister Grimes after a lot of letters and phone calls finally scheduled a game with our big rivals in Kaktovik. I don't know why everyone called them our big rivals when we hadn't played a game yet?

But, I'll never forget it. Half the town of Reality drove up there for that first game just to see us actually play. We even had new uniforms for the big game. They were red, white and brown with our own logo on the front and our own numbers on the back. The moms didn't have time to sew our names on the back, which was just as well as far as I was concerned.

My new hockey shirt proved to be much too big to fit on my scrawny little back. I told Mister Grimes that I wanted to wear the jersey I got for Christmas or the one hanging on the wall in the Timberline Tavern, but he said he wanted the whole team to look the same. That way my fellow players and our fans could tell who we were when we got out on the ice. You mean our own townspeople didn't know who we were? I was really disappointed by that state of affairs.

That's when I first used the number fifty-three in actual game combat. It was my big brother who originally suggested it, as I told you before several times already. The coach didn't know about the sophisticated concept behind the number fifty-three except that he'd seen it on the wall at the Timberline. What I soon learned was that he had his heart set on me being number one because I was the smallest player on the team. But, luckily, my big brother Paul jumped up and down, and then my dad got into the act, too. He liked the idea of fifty-three, too. My dad, that is. He even made a special trip to the hardware store to get some extra cloth to make the number. That's what I call first class family support.

My mom cut patterns for the numbers five and three out of some cardboard and then cut the letters out of the cloth my dad brought home. The numbers were dark brown and my mom sewed them over the numbers on the jersey that had hung on the wall at the Timberline. They both assured me that my jersey would match those of my teammates. The numbers were a little big, and I remember the three wrapping around under my right armpit when I did a sharp turn.

But that turned out to be a good thing though, because when the goalie for Kaktovik swatted me with his stick during the game, the number sure softened the blow. But, I was still black and blue for a week where he hit me. Well, now that I think of it, he didn't exactly hit me during the game itself. But, that's another story altogether. Don't worry. I'll remember to tell you that one. You'll like it.

The game was scheduled for a Saturday, and the whole family drove up to Kaktovik with me that day. I guess they realized that I needed all the help I could get in my first real game. What really amazed me was the fact that even my sisters wanted to come to the game to see me play. Or at least they said so anyway. I've always wondered whether my mother twisted their arms or whether they just wanted to see the other boys in this new town. I may never know the answer to those questions. My sisters both have that knack for looking me right in the eyes and smiling just right. You know how it is with girls. Well, my sisters have a way of making me believe that everything they say to me is the absolute truth.

What the heck! It doesn't really matter, does it? No matter what the reason or cause, they were there the whole weekend to witness the… festivities. Yes, there's another one of my mother's favorite words. She always has been worried about my vocabulary. And I know what a vocabulary is. Mine is much bigger than anyone else on the Pee Wee Lumberjacks, that's for sure. And it's all because of my mom and her constant coaching. I could tell right away that she really enjoyed it when I tried to pronounce the word festivities.

Anyway, our once in a lifetime game against the Kaktovik Pee Wee Eskimos was finally here to be played. My very first real hockey game! As I think I said, the whole family piled into the old station wagon, and Paul and I sat in the very back. You know, in the seat that faces out the back window. Paul said that that would be a good place to talk about the game and my strategies. I really enjoyed those kinds of talks with brother Paul. Funny thing, my memory is touch and go right now, but I can remember those talks with Paul almost word for word. That's really weird! It's as if they are permanently written on my brain.

Kaktovik is between one hundred and two hundred miles from Reality depending on which way you went and how the weather and the road conditions were. Most of the roads were dirt and gravel as you got farther north. It was a nearly four, sometimes six hour drive winding through the Davidson Mountains up past Mount Michelson, then on down along the Hulahula River cutting east across the Alaskan North slope, then north to Kaktovik. You know what I'm talking about, don't you? Haven't you ever studied the subject of geography?

Kaktovik is really small. Paul said it was a village rather than a city. Actually, it's on an island! I'm not really sure why folks live up there? It's cold and barren to say the least. Winters can reach 56 degrees below zero. How's that for really cold? And there's not much to hide behind when that really cold wind starts to blow.

Dad says that there's not much in the way of logging work going on up there any time of the year. Some small lumber finishing mills along the coast is all they have. It's mostly Eskimos, and probably no more than five hundred people on the entire island if you count some of the people twice. Poor Schultz, I thought. I did tell you that Schultz and his family moved to Kaktovik, didn't I? Well, I'll fill you in on that soon. I realized immediately that it was somehow ironic that my first real game would be against my arch enemy Schultz!

Ah, the big fat guy just turned over the bag of ice resting on my head. That feels very good indeed. The cold stops the aching for a while, and that's good even though it's only a short while. If I could move my paralyzed arm, I could do it myself, but the old arm feels asleep right now. I can barely open and close my fist on my right hand, and it feels really weak. It hurts almost the same as when that goalie from Kaktovik hit me with his goalie stick.

Well, by starting early we got to Kaktovik early in the afternoon and had lunch at a place that looked a lot like the Timberline Tavern. We made good time because the weather was cooperative for a change and there was very little traffic. We were pretty much starving as Mom didn't bring quite enough snacks for the long trip. I remember my stomach growling something fierce when the usual breakfast didn't materialize. Luckily, the team had planned to meet and have lunch at that place that looked a lot like the Timberline Tavern. I think it was called the Kaktovik Inn, but it had a bar and tables inside just like the Timberline. It would have been a good bet to say that both places were designed by the same person.

Much to my great surprise there was a middle-aged man working behind the bar who immediately seemed to know my dad. He jumped up and down with enthusiasm and yelled 'Guy! Guy!' when he saw my dad come in the front door. Of course, that's no real surprise because my dad is named Guy. Guy Robespierre.

My dad has a middle name, too, but he didn't seem to like it that much. It was Francis. Or maybe it was Frances? Okay, it's still Francis. He hasn't changed it as far as I know. He told me that he thought it sounded like a girl's name so I never heard him admit to it being his name, not in public at least. But he often used the middle initial F. and told everyone his middle name was Frank.

For your information that bartender in Kaktovik was named Mike. My dad called him 'Big Mike'. He liked me right from the beginning. On that first visit he told me to call him 'Uncle Mike' which was fine with me. Uncle Mike was a really big man, must have been over six feet and four or five inches tall as far as I could tell. My dad told me that Uncle Mike or Big Mike, whichever you prefer, was the best logger in all of Alaska bar none. *Fall'em and haul'em!* Uncle Mike would say to my dad, and my dad enjoyed it because he smiled every time he heard the words.

There seem to be a lot of 'Big' names up in timberland. Big Mick, Big Mike, and there is even a Big Jeremy who works a timber barge on the river back home. But about three years ago a logging accident injured Uncle Mike's back pretty bad, and he couldn't do logging any more without suffering a great deal of pain. So, he married an Eskimo beauty, moved north, and bought the Kaktovik Inn after the accident. He really seemed to like being there and running the restaurant for a living.

Uncle Mike now owned the Kaktovik Inn free and clear of any and all debt, and he would give me and my dad free drinks every time we came to visit him. My dad, for his part, would always have a bottle or two of the Tennessee stuff I told you about for Uncle Mike. I would always get a soda in the deal, root beer being my favorite flavor. Then, if my brother Paul wasn't around, I would tell him later that I was drinking beer! It worked the first time, but he must have figured it out later. He would call my bluff and tell me where we could get some real beer without getting caught for being too young. I couldn't stand the gritty taste of real beer when I was a kid. It tasted so darn bitter that my face would get all shriveled up, and I would spit it out no matter where we were at the time. But, that's another story for another time.

As we were finishing our tasty lunch, the players from the Pee Wee Eskimos were coming in to the Kaktovik Inn fully dressed in their uniforms. I'm sure that they did it just to show off. So, now it was time for the Reality Pee Wee Lumberjacks to suit up for the game!

My Uncle Mike came with us to the game to cheer us on. They had an old barn near the main road just behind the Kaktovik Inn and next to it was a small lake. We changed into our uniforms in the old barn. To this day I can still remember how bad it smelled in there. And, boy was it ever cold, too, even colder than it normally was this time of year in Reality.

Of course, the lake next to the barn was named Lake Kaktovik. Those people loved that name 'Kaktovik'. I remember asking several of them who Mister Kaktovik was and how they would laugh and point at me whenever I posed that silly question. I never did get an answer to my question either. I guess it was some kind of local secret...very hush, hush at least with strangers like me.

The game must have been between Christmas and New Year's Day as my mind vaguely remembers because I recall the numerous pine trees still being decorated for the holidays. And some of the kids on the Kaktovik team had new store-bought skates, too. I remember how shiny and new they were. I still wonder where there was a store near Kaktovik at which new skates could be bought. Only one of the kids on our team had new skates to counter theirs with. Ours were still mostly homemade, but we could skate real good on them. That's what amazed the parents of the kids in Kaktovik. We were definitely much better skaters.

One problem we did have was that we only had ten kids on our team for this road game. One, Frank Malazone, as I think I told you before, was our only real goaltender by choice. He was a chubby kid, and he really couldn't skate very well, but he did have store-bought skates. You see, his parents were big fans of NHL goalies Jacques Plante and Glenn Hall so they went to Anchorage one weekend that summer and bought Frank a full set of goalie stuff. It was the real thing for sure!

They also bought him the best pair of skates Reality had ever seen. And he had his goalie mask painted by a real artist. When he got dressed in his uniform, pads, mask, skates and the rest, he was an impressive sight to say the least...as long as he was standing still. Well, at least until he got off the bench and started to skate out on the ice. But, since his family spent all that cash on his equipment, it would be a darn shame not to let him play.

What really counted with the coach and the parents in Reality was that his dad was the local butcher, and they all wanted Mister Malazone to be kept very happy. So they told him that little Frank was the star of our team, the next Glenn Hall or Jacques Plante. He must have believed them because after that he always brought lots of food along on our road trips even when hockey wasn't involved. As long as he was happy, the rest of our town was happy.

On this first hockey road trip for our pee wee team he brought a home-made grill and some hamburgers along with lots of cheese. He declared that we would have a barbeque after the game, before we left for home. I would try to tell my dad that Frank wasn't very good and that Alvin should really be our goalie, but my dad would stop me and tell me not to talk that way about Frank. He would say that Frank could prove to be our team's meal ticket. I guess he knew what he was doing, so I didn't say anything about Frank's goaltending when dad or any of the parents were around.

Alfie, Frank and I suited up together, and the talk between us was more like nervous chatter. The other kids were nervous and scared, too. Considering that this was our first time out of Reality, let alone for a hockey game against kids we had never met, on an island in a barren part of Alaska, with the temperature close to 15 degrees, and changing in a barn that smelled like dead fish, you probably can understand our plight. The only kid we knew was Schultz, and as much as I disliked him, to be truthful, I couldn't wait to see him in the flesh.

Just before the game on Lake Kaktovik began I remembered that it started snowing, real hard! The snowflakes seemed enormous, much bigger than one normally experiences in Realty even in the dead of winter. Every time the adults would get the snow cleared off the ice area set apart for the game, it would come down harder and harder. In the midst of this storm Coach Grimes came in and gave us our pre-game pep talk. He could sense how scared we all were, but he viewed the obstacle presented by the snow as good news. He told us that he wanted us to have great fun out there and not be worried about a thing.

My brother Paul came in and pulled me aside for a brief moment. He sat me down on a small bench that was located in the far corner of the barn. Wow, did it smell bad over there! Paul joked about the smell, and then he looked me right in the eyes as only he could. He told me how proud he was of me, and he said that I would have a great first real hockey game. He said that this would be only the first of many career games for me down the road. I was to relax, remember what my coaches and he taught me, trust my teammates no matter what, and above all…have great fun! His inspirational lecture produced quite a crowd of onlookers so he gave me a big hug in front of everyone and walked proudly out toward the now covered rink.

It was show time! We all got up and headed out of that smelly barn as a brisk wind began to blow again. Finally, we made our way down out onto the lake for the pre-game skate and warm up. Like I said, it wasn't a big lake, but the ice, once you found it, was very smooth. Some of the parents had just finished sweeping off the surface with big brooms for probably the tenth time as we arrived. As I looked around, I saw that there were at least a hundred people standing in the snow around the edge of the lake, and they all seemed to be watching our team, trying to assess how good we were. They were certainly all dressed for the weather.

That's when disaster struck! I remember looking at the people in the crowd as I stepped out onto the ice. That was a gigantic mistake. Before I knew it, I found myself flying through the air and landing on my butt in front of everyone! Next as might be expected came a huge cheer from the crowd. Someone had left one of those big brooms lying right along the path from the barn, and, of course, in the excitement of the moment I didn't see it lying there waiting for me. I tripped right over the handle, fell backwards trying to get my balance, and bang!

When I looked up, Alfie was bent over laughing hysterically. Fortunately for me, the Kaktovik team had not yet made its appearance on the ice, so my nemesis, Schultz, didn't see me hit the deck on my debut. That would have been very devastating to say the least.

I remembered what my big brother told me…to have fun above all else, so I popped back up on my skates like a bouncing rubber ball and just started skating around like mad. A few laps around our end of the little lake and my confidence returned completely and the adrenaline began to flow. My stick felt good in my hands. *Pass me the puck!* I thought. It was then that we realized that no one had remembered to bring the pucks from the car! All of a sudden there was an extended moment of silence across the rink.

That's when I heard my Uncle Mike yell at me from the crowd. I turned and there it was on the ice in front of me. He had a puck in his jacket pocket, and when he saw me looking around for one to practice with, he threw it out on the ice to me. That move really made me feel good!

Alfie and I started skating around, passing the puck and then shooting it at our defenseless goalie. Frank Malazone fell down hard a couple of times before he got his bearings. As I started to wind up for a big slap shot, I noticed that everyone on our team had stopped skating. They were looking over my shoulder across the lake. I stopped for a moment, and then I turned to see just what they were looking at.

That's when my heart leaped into my throat. It was the Kaktovik Pee Wee Eskimos! They looked so big compared to us. They came on the ice single-file dressed in yellow and brown uniforms…uniforms that all matched! Then came the real shocker. They had two goalies on their team!

But all of these things were secondary when compared to the one ominous sight that loomed from the middle of the line of players. There he was looking as nasty as ever. It was Schultz! As he stepped on to the ice, he looked up, and we made eye contact almost immediately. I froze! It was the one face I had hoped never to have to see again…except for that brief moment of melancholy I had experienced in the barn. But there it was right in front of me! And it was then that I realized that all the time I had spent with my big brother and my teammates practicing my hip check was finally going to pay off big time.

7

Hitting the Ice

In the darkness of life I stumble my way forward
Hopefully seeking the sun and the light that it brings.
But every inch becomes a mile through the dust and sand,
And I never seem to find that garden where the bird sings.

Finally, the biggest moment of my life so far had finally arrived. It was game time! I'd been waiting my whole life for this moment to come, and it was finally here. It had been lodged in the back of my mind since I can remember. My heart was pounding so hard and so fast I swore that I could see my Realty jersey moving in and out as I tried to stand quietly on our blue line with the rest of my teammates facing our opponents eye to eye.

Actually, the frozen lake didn't have blue lines painted on it, but there were two gigantic used truck tires sitting on either side near the edge of the ice as markers. And, believe it or not, the tires were freshly painted a bright blue for the occasion. The tires were laying flat in the snow, not standing on edge, if you know what I mean. That meant they were a little bit wide for the purpose of marking the locations of blue lines. Putting it another way, it meant that the blue lines were each several feet wide. So, immediately, I could imagine a difference of interpretation by an official linesman of an offside call depending on which team he was rooting for. This suspicion didn't help my confidence one bit as you might easily imagine.

On Kaktovik's side of the ice, instead of truck tires there were two large piles of rocks, which served the same purpose as blue line markers.

They were also painted with bright blue paint. What was most confusing to me though, was the fact that both the blue tires and the blue rocks also had yellow paint splashed all over them. I guess that it was just a hometown thing pulled off by the adults. The supposed blue lines were mostly yellow to match the home team's uniforms. Wow, I really began to appreciate what an uphill fight this was going to be for us.

Why they collectively picked yellow as their team color is a question I may never have an answer to no matter how long I think about it. It reminded me of a great movie I saw a while back where these robbers who didn't know each other for the most part were all given names by the gang leader based on colors. That way he must have figured, if one of them got caught during commission of the crime, he wouldn't be able to tell the cops who his partners were because he didn't know any of their real names. One of them was Mister Black, another one was Mister White, the next one was Mister Brown and another was Mister Green and so on.

One of them was given the name Mister Pink and did he ever complain about that choice of colors for his name! The big boss of the robbers in the movie…he looked a lot like Mister Malazone, told Mister Pink that he should be happy he didn't get named Mister Yellow! Looking at the yellow paint on the sidelines and then at the yellow in our opponents uniforms made me start to laugh out loud! I began to wonder whether any of these Kaktovik people had ever seen the movie. I wasn't really sure whether the town of Kaktovik even had a movie theater or television?

As I was standing there watching Schultz lumber around the ice on his shiny skates, I automatically went through the exercises Paul taught me to help me execute my devastating hip-check. I told you that Schultz's family was moving to Kaktovik, didn't I? I had no way of knowing whether they had completed their move, but well, he was playing on their team now. It was definitely his new home. Deep down inside I was really happy about this great turn of events. This would be my big chance to nail him for good in front of all the people in his new town…or most of them, anyway. And after that, he'd have a lot of trouble taking his revenge against me because I was living so far away from him.

Just then, the referee came up to me and asked me if I was the captain of our team. He was wearing a striped shirt just like a real referee, but I could see a couple of sweaters stuffed underneath that shirt, which was a good idea because it was really cold out on the ice.

Well, I looked around and told him that I didn't think that our team had a captain just yet. He just looked over at our bench where our coach was sitting trying to keep warm, and he pointed down at me with his finger. Our coach just nodded and the ref proceeded to grab me by the jersey while telling me that I'd make a fine captain for today's game. Then he dragged me over to where most of the adults were sitting to introduce me as the new captain of the Reality Pee Wee Lumberjacks! What a turn of events at the last minute! I had been at the right place at the right time as people often say about such things.

That was the first time I met Bjore Eriksson. He looked really snappy in his brown and yellow Kaktovik uniform. His jersey even had a 'C' sewn on it. I have to admit that I was both impressed and scared at the same time. The Kaktovik uniforms made their players look bigger than they actually were. Actually, much bigger! But, Bjore was friendly, and he took off his glove and shook hands with me without hesitation even though my uniform had no letter 'C' on it.

He even asked me my name while we were standing there! I think I stuttered just a little bit, but finally I got the 'Jean-Luc' out into the cold air. I told him that I was freezing to death just standing around so he would know that I was anxious to get the game started. He seemed to agree with my strategy.

Bjore was the first line center on their team, and I guessed that he was about two years older than I was, but I didn't ask. The referee whose name was Mister Lundgren told us that the people in the small wooden shed next to the lake had brought a portable record player, and that they were going to play the National Anthem on it before we began the game just like they did in the big leagues. I thought that was pretty neat for our first game.

Actually, he called the shed structure a 'booth', but I think he was being very kind to the home team. He told me to get the Pee Wee Lumberjacks lined up on our blue, ah…yellow line and have them take off their respective helmets once in line. I already knew that one should take off his hat…or helmet for the National Anthem so my first real job as captain was not a problem at all. So far, so good, as far as I could tell.

I was ecstatic to say the least! My first job as captain of the team successfully completed without a glitch! As I happily skated back toward what was to be our bench, I could see that all the eyes of my teammates were on me, and they were whispering the words! 'Captain Jean-Luc'! At least for a day, that is.

Anyway, it's a good thing that I didn't fall down, that's for sure, because there behind our bench stood my Uncle Mike waiting and watching. He was grinning from ear to ear and pointing at me. He had some sort of camera in his hands, and I think he took some pictures of me skating back to our bench. Actually, I'm sure of it because I've seen the pictures more than once, and he gave copies to my mom and dad. I must say that I looked good for my age in those shots! Heck! I just looked good for sure! My first game hadn't even started and I was being photographed.

When I reached the bench, all of our players grouped around me to hear what I had to say. I took a very deep breath before saying anything because I wanted to sound confident and in control of the situation. That was the captain's job. I wanted my teammates to sense my self-confidence whether or not it was actually there at the time. I told them what the referee had said about the National Anthem, and then I added something my big brother told me the night before. He was always way ahead of all of my problems.

"And when you're standing there on the line and the National Anthem is playing, stand up straight, don't fidget around. And, most important of all, look the opposing player directly across from you straight in the eyes. Give him your fiercest look! Don't blink! Don't smile! Just stare at him with your meanest face! And forget the fancy uniforms they may be wearing. Those are things that anyone can buy if they have enough money or someone to sew them. After we're through with this team, those uniforms will be dirty and torn and ready for the scrap heap!"

Then I added something of my own just like a cherry on top of a chocolate milkshake.

"And tell Schultz that he looks very good in the color yellow and that the color suits him perfectly!"

My Uncle Mike bent over laughing with a big roar, but I kept a serious look on my face. Even Coach Grimes was impressed with my remarks and challenge to our team. I didn't tell either of them that Paul had made me memorize most of my pre-game speech. But it must have worked, at least for the National Anthem. We skated out there and took our places on the imaginary line on our end of the ice. As I glanced down the row formed by our players, no one was smiling or looking beaten. I was impressed with the posture of each player, especially Alfie. And they were each staring with a menacing gaze across at the opposition looking even nastier than I could imagine. What a start! Was I a born leader? Only time would tell.

So I took my place at the end of the line, and as the first notes of the National Anthem filled the air, I conjured up my meanest look, which I had been practicing for days just for this situation, and cast it over the ice at the Kaktovik player standing directly across from me. It was only then that I realized that it was Schultz that I was glaring at! Wow! What a coincidence! How appropriate! From the look on his ugly face I could tell that my sudden ascendancy to team captain had permanently dented his fragile pride. He wasn't the captain of his team now nor had he ever been in Reality. Life was good and getting better with each moment.

The National Anthem was played and ended successfully, and it felt like I was in a living dream. All I could do was stare at Schultz and imagine ramming him at high speed with a hip-check. Suddenly, I heard my name echoing in the background, but for some reason I couldn't move. Then, out of nowhere, a sudden cold chill ran down my spine. It felt so real. I shook my head and turned to the right, and there right next to me stood Alfie! Now the cold chill made sense. He had just crammed a glove full of snow down the back of my jersey!

"Geez, Alfie!" I squeaked in a high-pitched voice. "Geez, Jean-Luc!" he replied calmly. "Heck, Luc, I have been calling you, and all you do is stand there frozen in space like a snowman. I know that it's pretty cold, but it's not *that* cold. Come on! Coach needs to speak with you before the puck drops."

I looked back over at Schultz, but by then he was gone. I don't think that he saw me freeze up, but what difference did it make?

As I skated over toward our team's bench, I heard my Uncle Mike yell out, "Hey, Luc, did ya have a nice chat with old Schultz out there, eh?" The people in the crowd began to laugh when they heard his comment. He must have told them about our mutual dislike for one another. I wasn't sure that was such a good idea.

"Sure did, Uncle Mike. I asked him exactly what words he wanted written on his tombstone?"

I said that? What was I thinking? I know that I didn't actually say those words directly to Schultz, but I had to say something cool to my Uncle Mike so he would be impressed. But that? And out loud for everyone to hear? Those fans would tell Schultz for sure. Oh, boy! I wondered what was going to happen now. I gritted my teeth and told myself to be ready for anything!

Coach Grimes gave us one last pre-game pep talk trying to build our confidence in ourselves and in each other, and we headed off for the face-off circle at center ice or what appeared to be a close resemblance to a face-off circle if you had a real good hockey imagination.

Did you ever have one of those situations where you were really excited for a certain day or event to come and the time really dragged while you waited for it to show up? You know, you can't sleep for hours or days or weeks. All you can think of and talk about to yourself and your close friends is that certain thing you are waiting for and exactly what you want to accomplish. And then, finally, the day and the moment arrives, and for some unexplained reason it doesn't feel that great any more. Well, this was one of those days and events.

I felt myself rapidly starting to lose my self-confidence. That was one thing Paul told me never to lose no matter what! And he really meant what he was saying when he said it. I needed to get my self-confidence back inside me and right then. Heck, I was the captain of our team now, the best defenseman on the team, and this was my very first real game! What a moment in my life! And, that's not to mention the fact that my entire family, more or less, was in the crowd to watch my every move! They would all know the result forever. I couldn't let them down by being unsure or lacking in confidence. How would I survive the ride home or the rest of my life if that happened to me in front of them?

I looked around at my teammates, and they were again real scared, too. The tough faces from the National Anthem were all gone now. Hey, I was their captain. I had to rally the troops again and fast before the puck dropped! I couldn't let them see or feel my own fear and uncertainty. I gritted my teeth again and prepared to breathe fire in front of them.

I skated up to each of my guys and tapped each of them firmly with my stick while I gave them a big smile and my most confident nod. It took everything I had to generate a believable smile, but it worked. I skated back to Frank who looked like a snowman crouched in the net and tapped his pads several times.

"You ready, Frank?" I asked still maintaining my confident smile and cloak of leadership.

"I guess I am," he mumbled back to me. "Those Kaktovik kids look so big! I have to admit that I'm a bit scared about this, Jean-Luc. You can call me a chicken, but it's exactly how I feel right now."

"Me, too," I replied, again relying on a strategy suggested to me by my big brother. I had to make sure that Frank didn't feel like he was alone. "But, Frank, we drove all the way up here to this godforsaken place to play this game, and we can't chicken out now at the most important moment! We've got to give it all we've got…and more. Remember, I'll be right here with you helping you every second to defend our goal. You just do the best you can and let the marbles fall where they may. I'll do the same. We have nothing to be afraid of except our own imaginary fear and nothing at all to lose. We win or lose this contest with them together…as a team! There is a famous saying for this kind of moment. *One for all and all for one!*"

I made up the marbles thing and the one for all on the spur of the moment, but Frank didn't notice that at all. I must admit that I stole the latter phrase from a book my mother was reading. She really liked those words, and so did I. Frank was just happy to have his teammates' support.

"Thanks a lot, Jean-Luc. I feel much better now, for sure. Now let's get the puck dropped because I'm freezing to death out here!"

As I lined up for the puck drop, a light snow again began to fall. Suddenly, the wind picked up with some serious gusts. The temperature was dropping as well, a sure sign that a storm was on the prowl and not very far off in the distance. I then remembered what my dad said on the way up to Kaktovik. He mentioned that the weather forecast called for snow, wind and dropping temperatures. Well, the weatherman was right on the money that particular time. The referee blew his whistle, put up his left hand, and dropped the puck with his right hand. We were on our way!

Bjore Eriksson won the face-off for the Kaktovik Eskimos and in a few seconds after two passes he was down across our blue…yellow line. My partner on defense was Timmy Daniels, and he was all over Bjore as he came across with the puck. Bjore faked to his right and then passed backhand to one of their forwards who was trailing him. As I moved up to check the puck carrier everything went black. Schultz had hit me from behind and knocked me down to the ice. I was seeing stars for a moment as the Kaktovik player with the puck skated by. When I was finally able to get up, Frank was on his back in the crease, and the puck was in the net. I thought for certain that Schultz would be sent off for interference or cross-checking, but the referee missed it all. Our coach was going ballistic on the sidelines while Schultz just stood over me and mumbled something. The best I could remember is that he mumbled 'punk' as he skated away.

I jumped to my feet as best I could and gathered my troops around me. This was no time to give up.

"Okay, guys. No big deal. Let's get one back for Reality, referee or no referee! Remember, these are Kaktovik's referees." This was my first 'shake-it-off' speech as captain of the team. But after the dirty hit by Schultz, my words flowed very naturally like I'd said them all before. Only time would tell how effective they would be and how I would get Schultz back.

The snow came down harder and harder, and the wind was even more ferocious than before. Whether it was my imagination or a head injury from Schultz's illegal hit I'll never know, but it seemed to be getting darker on the ice as well. We had to hurry if we wanted to even the score.

Hurry up, ref! Drop the puck already! I mumbled to myself. When play finally started again, we won the draw and I got the puck. Alfie exploded across center ice as we crossed the Kaktovik blue line, and I hit him with a quick pass as he split the defensemen. Straight to the net he headed with the puck. And their goalie froze! Their whole defense was caught off guard by our instant recovery. A quick wrist shot… top shelf, and the puck was in their net. Goal! My dreams were finally coming true.

Just as the puck settled into the bottom of the net, there came a bright flash of lightning. The loud crack of thunder that quickly followed almost knocked me to the ice, but I didn't feel a thing. My mind was celebrating my first point in a real game…an assist on Alfie's goal! The storm that had been brewing on the horizon all afternoon had finally arrived, but I was grinning from ear to ear and couldn't stop now for anything. Storm or no storm, I wanted to win!

The snow was falling heavier and faster than I'd ever seen before down in Reality. This was worse than the giant blizzard that hit Reality four or five years ago. Luckily, I was too small to shovel the driveway for that one. The entire makeshift hockey rink on Lake Kaktovik was filling up with the white stuff. Soon, we'd have to use snowboards instead of skates to get around. And how would we find the puck? As I stood in the middle of the ice paralyzed by the feats of nature and watching the other players hurry to cover, I suddenly found myself flying through the air, then sprawling on the snow-covered ice.

Was I hit by lightning? Could the fading rumble of the thunder have knocked me down? Or was it Schultz coming after me again… from behind, of course? At first I assumed it was Schultz so I started looking for his ugly face.

No, it was my defense partner, Timmy Daniels. There actually was a nearby bolt of lightning that struck the ground with a roar. Timmy saw it, let out a bloodcurdling scream, and turned to run for cover as best he could. But instead of getting off the ice to find safety, he ran smack dab into me as I stood there like a statute! I think he thought he was dead from the collision, too, because he just lay there on top of me shaking and at the same time mumbling something completely incoherent about heaven and hell. I tried to get up, but he grabbed onto me and wouldn't let go. He was really afraid, and he was hanging on for dear life!

As I turned my head toward the sidelines to look for help, I could see my dad, Uncle Mike, and the rest of the grownups making their way toward our pile on the ice. Then I felt someone tugging on Timmy and trying to console him. When I was finally able to roll over, I saw that it was Bjore Eriksson of the Kaktovik team who was talking to Timmy, calming him down about the storm.

Before I could get up on my own, I remember Bjore reaching down with his hand to help me up. He had a real stupid grin on his face, but he could tell that I liked it. He sure knew how to cheer a fellow up!

"That was a real nice play you made out here, Jean-Luc," he said chuckling out loud.

I can still remember those words I heard from my soon to be lifelong friend, but I was never sure what I did to deserve the compliment…if it was a compliment? Was it my pass to Alfie, or was it Schultz's dirty hit that did it? Or was he just referring to me acting as a human security blanket from the storm for Timmy? As I think I might have said, Bjore was about a year older than me and a few inches taller, and his voice was gentle and friendly.

"I can see that the two of you have met!" It was Uncle Mike's voice in the suddenly quiet air. "Maybe we should hustle over to the restaurant for some cocoa and cookies before the lightning hits us. It might be a little safer and a lot warmer over there and a lot more fun, too.

"The referee has called the game. I saw him running for his car, skates and all, as fast as he could go! I haven't seen lightning in a snowstorm like this in twenty or thirty years. Mother Nature has something special on her mind for us today! You boys will have to find out which is the better team some other time when Mother Nature is a little calmer and relaxed."

I just nodded my aching head because by this time my jaw was frozen shut for the time being. My dad grabbed me up from the ice, and Bjore picked up my stick, and we headed for the car, Timmy Daniels in tow and still in a daze. By now all of the other players and their parents were evacuating the scene at high speed, Schultz included. Bjore's dad was waiting for his son in the parking lot, and Timmy's dad met us with words of thanks halfway to the car.

As Bjore handed me my hockey stick and began to run over to his dad, I yelled, "Hey, you going to the inn for cocoa and cookies?"

Bjore stopped in his tracks and turned to answer. "Hot chocolate and cookies on a day like this? Wouldn't miss it for anything! See you there, Jean-Luc." Bjore's dad saw that we were getting along well, so he told Bjore to ride with Uncle Mike. He said that he and his friends would meet us at the inn.

On the way over to the Kaktovik Inn, I could hear Uncle Mike telling dad that we should stay over and not try to drive home through this horrific storm. He was very convincing from my point of view, and after some quick thoughts dad turned to me in the back seat and asked if I would like to stay overnight until the weather cleared up. I was finally warming up so I grunted what must have sounded like a 'yes'. Bjore slapped me enthusiastically on the back and smiled. He then pointed over at Timmy who was still in shock from the lightning strike.

"We may have to give your friend Timmy a cold shower!" said Bjore with a mischievous grin on his face. "Or, we could put him in the sauna for a while and then throw him into a snow bank after he's back to a more normal temperature. It does wonders for your courage and stamina."

That remark by Bjore snapped Timmy right out of his current malaise. His eyes popped wide open much to our instant relief.

"What? A cold shower? Fat chance! Not me at least! I'm okay! I'm just fine and dandy right now. The lightning bolt from above just surprised me. It was like a giant ball of fire coming out of the sky!"

With the heater in the car on full blast and everyone breathing heavily and talking, we were all warming up real fast. It was then that I realized why Timmy had that very strange look on his face. He looked at me and then looked down at his uniform. It had never happened to me, but I knew just what he was feeling without a word being said. When the lightning struck and the thunder rolled, Timmy had an accident of a biological nature. As he told me later, he had downed a little too much milk before the game in an attempt to calm his nerves.

"Don't worry! We'll have to get you boys out of those uniforms first thing after we get there," said Uncle Mike, who saw exactly what I saw. He had a huge smile on his face. "We have all of your street clothes in the trunk. You can change as soon as we get to the Inn."

Somehow, he must have figured out just what happened to Timmy and his uniform, but he never said a word about it directly. It would have been much too embarrassing for all of us to relive. Bjore also realized what happened as the car heated up and the odor began to swirl, but he looked straight ahead and didn't say a word about it. I wanted to laugh so badly, but Uncle Mike shook his head at me, and I figured he knew better how to handle this situation so I watched the scenery with a heightened interest along with Bjore.

The snow was really coming down hard by now, and I could barely see the road in front of us or behind us for that matter. Nevertheless, I felt quite confident with Uncle Mike doing the driving in this situation. Heck, he knew every curve and ditch in the territory. Then it dawned on me. I had forgotten something very important with all the hectic scrambling.

"Dad, where are they…Paul, mom and the girls? Did we leave them behind to be buried by the storm?" I asked sheepishly.

"They left to go to the Inn just as soon as the snow began to fall heavier. They needed Paul to drive them back. He has an emergency license just for this type of situation. Your mom didn't feel up to it under the circumstances. She's not real familiar with these roads and hills even under good driving conditions. By now, they're sipping hot cocoa and toasting their feet by the fire. We'll have you kids up there toasting yours, too, in a few minutes."

Wow, I felt relieved that they were most probably very safe. After a while we arrived at the Inn safe and sound in spite of the weather and its fury. The parking lot was full of cars to say the least. No doubt, everyone wanted some hot cocoa or coffee right now so I began to worry whether there would be any left for us. On the front porch of the Inn, mom stepped out and was waving while holding a steaming cup in her other hand. I was hoping that one was for me!

Mom handed me the beautiful cup, and we all went inside. It was so warm in there, and the smell of the embers and newly-made cookies filled the room. A big smile filled my face as I took my first sip of cocoa. Then I just shouted it out so everyone could hear!

"Hey, Bjore! Me and my family are staying the night here at the Inn until the storm passes. Far as I'm concerned, I don't care if we ever leave! This place is just like heaven as far as I'm concerned!"

So, as the story went, our pee wee hockey team was still undefeated. Oh, you still wonder how the goalie on the Kaktovik team hit me with his stick, don't you? Well, I had just gotten my skates on in the old barn, and I was heading out toward the ice on the lake when the kid in the Kaktovik goalie pads who was trying to skate to the ice in front of me, ran into Frank, who had just fallen on the ice in front of him.

The Kaktovik kid was all arms and legs as he was falling over the mass of Frank's body and equipment. In desperation he let go of his hockey stick, and it speared me right under my right arm. My whole side was black and blue for a week because of that. It was a good thing that we didn't actually play the entire game that day because the first time one of those kids would have run into me or hit me like Schultz did, I would have screamed and fallen over, I know it. Ah, but I sensed that the opportunity for my revenge would come some day pretty soon! And I just had to be patient because it would be a sweet revenge at that.

8

Back at the Inn

The sun will shine in my back door someday.
March winds will blow all my troubles away.
I wish I was a headlight on a north bound train.
I'd shine my light through cool Alaska rain.

I Know You Rider
Grateful Dead

The Inn was a very friendly and comfortable place with a huge fireplace in the center of the main room. It was obvious that this dominant feature had been in place for quite a while. What was most interesting about the structure was the fact that it had served the American armed forces during World War II as a barracks and mess facility along with weapons and ammunition storage. Kaktovik's strategic location with respect to the Bering Strait made the choice an easy one for the military commanders at the time. There were several large bronze plaques on the walls, which presented the history and heritage of the building to visitors. You could tell that the employees working at the Inn took good care of the displays because they were all very clean and shiny, and the visitors really enjoyed looking at them.

That's where I learned that the Eskimos called the strait 'Imakpik', and that there once could have been a land bridge between Russia and Alaska that allowed people to walk across and thus populate North and South America from the Asian continent. In geography class in school I learned that Cape Prince of Wales, Alaska, was the westernmost point on the North American continent. My teacher also told me the name of the Russian town directly across the strait, but I've forgotten that one as the years have rolled by. I'm going to have to look up the name when I get out of here because I shouldn't forget these things once I've learned them. Anyway, there's lots of history and geography up here to be studied and stored in my brain's memory bank if there's any undamaged space left up there.

But, as I remember, it was the bright flames of the fire dancing in the fireplace that were the first things I saw when I entered through the large double doors at the front of the building. Actually, those were probably the biggest doors I had ever seen or passed through in my short life. I recall my father bragging about the quality of the woodwork that went into their construction. The images of two large Alaskan bears were carved into the outside surfaces while the inside held carvings of ducks and geese in flight. It was absolutely beautiful to say the least. It was very easy to see that the military may have stored its tanks and armored personnel carriers inside there because there was lots of space in there and big doors to get in and out of.

We each took a drink out of the cup my mom had handed to me, and then we placed the empty cup on the bar hoping for a refill. The design of the building was quite different from the Timberline when it came to placement of the facilities. The Inn started with a bar to the left of the entry doors and a nice sit-down restaurant to the right, which I could tell immediately that my mom liked a lot. As for me, I couldn't wait to settle into one of the warm and comfy chairs near the sparkling fireplace with another cup of hot chocolate in my hands. Chills from the storm and dropping temperatures were still running up and down my skinny little spine like scared rabbits being chased by one of those bears on the doors.

Bjore, Timmy and I quickly changed out of our soggy uniforms in the men's room because our room upstairs wasn't ready for our occupancy just yet. Just getting my frozen arms and legs out of those damp and soggy clothes was one of the most wonderful feelings I've ever experienced in my life. Unfortunately, the hot showers we were dreaming of would have to wait until after dinner.

We returned to the area of the fireplace again and began the process of warming up toward room temperature as fast as we could. Uncle Mike quickly understood and hit us with another round of hot cocoa as we watched the other occupants from Reality try to decide whether to leave for home immediately or batten down the hatches and stay the night before the full intensity of the storm hit. From what I heard some of the parents say, this could be one of the worst storms ever experienced in Alaska! It seemed to me that the decision was obvious!

My dad was in the corner by the bar talking to some other parents who had journeyed up from Reality for the game to find out what they were going to do under the circumstances. Most were already packed up and ready for the ride home, as crazy as that sounds to me even now. I think my father was asking them to give it another thought before they set sail into the tempest. They all had chains and heavy-duty wipers on their rugged vehicles, but as I said, this storm had the potential to be the biggest they'd ever seen in these parts. Driving through the middle of it for hours on end seemed like a task to be avoided at all costs even to a little kid like me. I couldn't imagine what it would be like to get stuck out there with no help nearby.

Even though I was sitting quite a distance away, I could almost hear him politely suggesting that a warm dinner and a few drinks with polite conversation by the warm and friendly fire might be preferable to being stuck in a snowdrift in the middle of nowhere all night in a blizzard waiting for a snow plow to magically appear. I could just picture an alert Alaskan Huskie with a pint of whiskey attached to his collar furiously digging Timmy and Alfie's parents out of their cars in the snow and repeatedly barking out the words 'I told you so!'

How exciting an event this proved to be for me as I think back about it! This sudden and unexpected storm that almost everyone thought was terrible news turned out to have a huge silver lining at least for me and some of my friends. We took advantage of it. Here I find myself, on my first real long distance trip outside of my home in Reality, to go and play my first honest-to-goodness competitive hockey game, and now I get to spend the night at the house of the captain of the Kaktovik Eskimos! That was a total victory in itself.

I was speechless about my good fortune to say the least. Who would have ever imagined such a turn of events? The only thing that could have happened to make things better would have been a victory for our team in the game that afternoon. But, hey, we were still undefeated in games played, and I was now the new and first captain of our team also tied for the lead with scoring points totaling one! Right?

Once we had settled down into a relatively calm state for a few minutes, my mom came over to the fireplace to see how we youngsters were doing under the circumstances. She was real good at making everyone feel at home especially when we were away from our home in an unfamiliar place. I think that she was trying to set a good example for me, especially if I was going to be on the road in strange places playing ice hockey in my upcoming future life as we all hoped. She was most cordial to my newest friend as I knew she would be.

"Bjore, we've never been formally introduced. I'm Jean-Luc's mother. You and your family have been very understanding and hospitable to us, and I want to personally thank you for that hospitality and thoughtfulness. I just want to be sure that it's all right with your family for Jean-Luc to stay at your home this stormy evening. We don't want to impose upon you especially under the circumstances."

Mom already knew that it was all right because I saw her talking with Bjore's mom just a few minutes earlier. She was asking Bjore just to be polite to him. That's my mom for you. Also, I think that she was trying to teach me a social lesson here, too. I nodded and winked at her indicating that I got her point and would remember the lesson she was presenting to me so graphically. I was also an attentive student in my mom's social behavior training camp.

"Yes, ma'am," Bjore replied with a smile that told me that he had expected the question before it was verbalized. "I asked my mother for permission for him to stay the night just before I introduced her to Jean-Luc. She thought it was a really great idea. We have an extra room for visitors at our home, and I believe Jean-Luc will get a good night's sleep, storm or no storm. It will be much safer for him, too. I know that he'd rather stay with us than with his old friend Schultz!"

After we recovered from our serious laughing, we grabbed our travel bags, said goodbye to the others and met my dad and Bjore's dad by the front door of the Inn. My dad had some expected advice for me on how I should handle this situation.

"Now, Luc, you listen very carefully to everything Mr. Eriksson has to say to you and behave yourself. He'll drop you off back here in the morning, and hopefully the weather will have cleared up substantially for our drive back to Reality. This has really been quite a trip!"

I gave my dad a big hug and happily waved again to Paul, Dani, Seal, and my mom and hurried out to the station wagon that was waiting for me in the driveway. At first, the weather seemed to be getting even worse if that was possible as the winds picked up with strong gusts that blew small chunks of ice through the air. Then, as if on queue, the snowfall suddenly began to let up as we started down the road leaving the Inn for Bjore's house. Quickly, the driving became much easier for Bjore's dad which was quite a relief for all of us. Bjore commented that they didn't live far very from the Inn and that we would be there in their driveway in no time at all. It also helped considerably that the local snowplows had already cleared the main streets in Kaktovik. Now, that's what I call real timely efficiency.

During the drive all Bjore and I talked about was hockey, hockey and more hockey. We focused on our favorite teams and players and what it would be like to play together in the National Hockey League. Our favorite teams at the time were the Detroit Red Wings and the Chicago Blackhawks.

"The New York Rangers are one of my favorite teams, too," said Bjore after thinking about it for a minute or so. "Actually, I like all six of the original National Hockey League teams. Do you collect hockey cards? I did for a while, but it's hard to get them up here."

"You just wait, Jean-Luc," interjected Bjore's dad from the front seat of the car. "He has way more than just hockey cards in his personal collection. His entire room is full to the rafters with hockey stuff of all kinds. You are in for quite a treat when we get there! We moved here to Alaska from New York State about three years ago if my memory serves me right. When I was on the road traveling around to the big cities for my job, I visited quite a few places that were home to NHL teams and also home to major minor league teams. While I was in those places doing my thing, I made it a point to pick up something for Bjore's collection like cards, sticks, autographs, photos and jerseys among other things. I must be perfectly honest and admit that I had lots of fun collecting this stuff for him."

Boy, this visit to Bjore's home is really going to be great fun, I thought to myself. As I peered out the window near my seat, I wondered how much farther we had to go to actually get there. Just as I was pondering that question, we turned down a wide gravel road, and there dead ahead at the end of the road stood a remarkably beautiful two-story house.

"We're here!" Bjore said happily. "Grab your bag, and let's go upstairs right away. I can't wait to show you my room and my whole collection!"

Bjore's mom grabbed his arm before he could exit the car to give him a few words of motherly advice.

"Before you go running off into space, Bjore, you make sure that you hang up that damp uniform of yours by the washer and put your skates in the proper place in the garage so that your father can sharpen them when he gets the time so he doesn't have to do it at the last minute."

"Yes, mom," was Bjore's polite response. I helped Bjore with each of those chores, and soon we were heading up the stairs towards his room. Bjore's room was at the end of a long hall on the second floor, and on the recently painted walls were pictures of a bunch of professional hockey players and even some hockey sticks complete with autographs.

"Hey, Jean-Luc, do you think that you and I will ever get a chance to play in the actual NHL?"

"Absolutely! You can count on it, Bjore," I replied with a huge grin covering my face. He just nodded his head in agreement as he offered me a chair to sit on. I think it definitely was the answer he wanted to hear.

Bjore and I spent a good hour or more going through his extensive hockey collection. That's when I saw it! It was a copy of the New York Times sports section announcing the expansion of the National Hockey League to twelve teams from the original six. I immediately looked around to see if Bjore had a radio in his room. When I told him about the World War II vintage AM radio my uncle had given me, Bjore's eyes lit up like giant candles.

"Jean-Luc, you mean you can actually hear broadcasts of the games from the lower states all the way up here in Alaska?"

I was surprised that he thought it would be so hard to do, but then I remembered how surprised I was where I was first able to do it.

"Bjore, my dad told me that the radio waves from where they broadcast the games travel out into the sky and bounce off of...well off of electrons or something like that which are above the clouds in the earth's atmosphere. Well, I'm not sure what they bounce off of or why, but they do. We'll have to ask him when we get downstairs again. He told me that amateur radio people may sometimes talk to others all the way around the world if...if what he called 'atmospheric conditions' are right at the time. He knows all about this stuff he calls 'physics'.

"So, one night during a big storm down in Reality…sort of like the one we're having right now, I decided to experiment with my radio to see if I could pick up anything. To help me in my experiment my dad attached a long wire to the back of the radio, and then he ran the wire across the roof inside of our attic. He called it an 'antenna', and that it would help bring in the stations that were broadcasting. He said that we might have to rotate the antenna a bit if it didn't work the way it was. I spent a lot of time up there with him moving the wire around at different angles."

Bjore began carefully looking around his room as if he were sizing it up for a similar device in the future. I remember the look of excitement and anticipation in his eyes. He wanted to listen to the games that were on the air as much as I did. He urged me to keep on with my story, and to tell him every single little detail of what I did with my radio back in Reality.

"Well, Bjore, I started at one end of the radio dial and went slowly back and forth across all the available frequencies it gave me access to."

I remember telling him that we had to account for the different time zones the games were being played in, and that we were behind New York, Montreal, and Chicago by several hours. Most of the games began between seven and eight PM local time where the game was being played. We then took out some pencils and some paper and began computing just the right time to conduct the search. As we did this, I told Bjore of some of my most important discoveries.

"I would crank up the old AM radio and search and search all along the length of the dial. There were a lot of interesting things being broadcast that I wouldn't have expected. I found all kinds of preachers and quiz shows, mostly. Oh, once in a while I would get lucky and find some good music. In particular I found this great Chicago station… WLS it was called. They were playing what's called blues and rock'n roll music a lot. I liked it all very much, particularly the songs by Little Richard, Jimi Hendrix and Bob Dylan to name a few. I wrote the number down, you know, the frequency, so I could find it again.

"Then, I got really lucky! I heard a man's voice through the static, and of all things he was talking about a goaltender! I knew I was on to something big when I heard that. He identified the station as KMOX and soon I figured out that the signal was coming from Saint Louis down in the State of Missouri. Saint Louis had one of the new expansion teams, and the man was discussing whether the Blues were going to play Glenn Hall or Jacques Plante as their goaltender that night in a game against the Chicago Blackhawks.

"In my excitement I jumped up in the air so high that I hit the dial and lost the signal for quite a while. But I went back and kept searching relentlessly, and soon I hit the right place again, 1120 was the number on the dial of my radio. I put a piece of tape right there on the radio dial to mark the place so I wouldn't lose it again."

Bjore seemed to be hanging on every single word I said. I just wished that my memory was a little better as far as where all of the hockey stations were on the dial. It was all coming back, but very slowly.

"You know, Jean-Luc, my father once mentioned to me the possibility of getting a kit from a store in Anchorage and building a radio just like the one you're talking about. If I did that, I could learn how it works and maybe find the same station and some others just like you did. But, tell me, did you actually hear a game being broadcast on the station that night?"

I nodded vigorously and smiled in answer to his question. As I said, it was a game between the Chicago Blackhawks and the Saint Louis Blues. That's when I first heard about defenseman Bob Plager and center Red Berenson. Plager was a defenseman for the Blues, and Berenson was a center for them also. I could almost see them from the clear verbal description the announcer gave that night. His name was Dan Kelly. He said that Berenson wore number 7, and Plager wore number 5.

The signal was fading in and out so I missed some of the beginning action of the game, but I did get the best parts. First, Bob Plager got into a fistfight with a Blackhawk player named Duane Magnusson. Dan Kelly said Magnusson was a defenseman, too and had taken boxing lessons to improve his skills and that he liked to fight, but that didn't help him at all. Mister Kelly said that Plager hit Magnusson three or four times right in the nose.

I imagined myself punching Schultz just like that over and over again! Well, Magnusson was flat on the ice when the linesmen jumped in to stop the fight. I could hear the crowd screaming for more of the same even over the occasional bursts of static. It was only a short time later when Berenson scored a goal with a slap shot from the slot. Wow, was this ever fun!

I looked over at Bjore, and he was sitting still, staring at me. There were questions written all over his face.

"Who won? What was the score? Who was the winning goalie? Where was the game played?"

"The Blues won 5-2 at home before a sellout crowd, and Jacques Plante was the goalie that night."

Bjore's room was the coolest I'd ever seen in my short life. All he lacked to complete it was a radio like mine so that he could listen to the games as they were being played down in the NHL. I had a nice radio back in Reality that was for sure. I guess I was just lucky to have such a prize in my possession.

"Geez, Luc, I've got to get myself a radio like yours for this room. Do you think I can pick up those games way up here in Kaktovik?"

"I'm not really sure," I responded. "But, I don't see why it wouldn't work the same for you as it does for me. I could show you how to rig the antenna. And, better yet, Uncle Mike might know all about it. Dad told me that he was a Ham Radio person or something like that...whatever that is? We can ask him in the morning back at the Inn. I'm sure he'd be more than happy to help."

"You know, Luc, I've been thinking. We live up here in Alaska, and New York, Montreal, Chicago, Detroit, and Saint Louis seem so very far away. They just don't seem like real places in my world right now. Maybe, if I had a radio that worked like yours, that would change things for me immediately!"

"Oh, they're very real places, Bjore, We'll have our work cut out for us if we're gonna play in those towns in front of all those people. My older brother was explaining all the different leagues I would have to play in if I were to make the NHL. It was enough to make my head spin. At least he tried to explain it, but like I said, it was very complicated. Right now, we are considered Pee Wee players...as low as you can go on the hockey player spectrum as far as I can tell. I can't understand that right now because your team, the Kaktovik Eskimos, isn't what I would rank as Pee Wee. Then, after high school, there's what he calls the minors...I mean the juniors and then the minors...or college. It's a long trip, I'm sure, but if we work hard enough and refuse to give up, we can make it! We have to work our way up through the ranks, as my bother Paul always reminds me."

Bjore just rolled his eyes and shook his head.

"But, Luc, where are we gonna find all those leagues to play in? I mean, we don't get to travel much up here and neither do you. I don't believe that there are any teams or leagues like that around Northern Alaska. At least I'm sure there are none in Prudhoe Bay or Barrow that I have ever heard of. All the towns just have Pee Wees and high school leagues as far as I know."

I tried to remember exactly what Paul had told me.

"Paul says there are leagues and minor teams popping up all over the place. Some of them are not too far over the Canadian border. I think Paul even said that there was one in White Horse, and maybe even in Dawson. I know that Medicine Hat and Moose Jaw have teams."

Bjore just shrugged his shoulders.

"Medicine Hat? Moose Jaw? Luc, those towns are many miles away from Kaktovik and Reality. Even Dawson isn't that close. It would take days to get there from here by car. We'd probably get lost if we even tried to get to any of those places starting from here."

The room went quiet for quite a while as we were searching for a solution to our problem. I didn't know what to say to make things easier. But I knew that one day Bjore and I would be in those cities on whatever minor or junior or college team was there, and playing hockey, too, climbing up the ranks. I knew it! My brother, Paul, knew it, too. There was no doubt in my mind.

But, Bjore was looking disappointed. I had to say something positive and reassuring, but I was stumped for the moment. We both stared at the photos of our favorite hockey heroes hanging on the walls of Bjore's room. Just at that moment, Mister Eriksson's head popped through the door, a big smile on his face.

"Everything okay in here, boys? I thought I heard some yelling? It's getting late, I'm afraid. It's probably time for both of you to turn in for the evening."

"We're fine, Mister Eriksson. Me and Bjore were just sitting and talking about the day when we will play in the NHL and win the Stanley Cup!"

Mister Eriksson chuckled out loud when he heard my words.

"I have it from a very reliable source, Jean-Luc, that you two boys will indeed play in the NHL some day soon. Now, to further that moment, turn out the lights and get some sleep and rest. Even the biggest and strongest hockey players in the world need their rest so they can keep going against all odds."

As I got comfortable on my cot, I turned to look at Bjore across the room in his twin bed. He was smiling at that moment.

"See, Bjore," I whispered quietly, "I told you so. Even your dad knows that our day on the ice is coming!"

After the lights were out, there was still enough light for me to see a great poster of Gordie Howe that was on the wall near the foot of my cot. I didn't need much more inspiration than that to dream about the future.

9
Ice Fishing

Heroes come and heroes go through winter's never ending ice and snow.
How to succeed and how to win the game in play we don't always know.
Some are hailing from the north and some are rising from the south,
And all are waiting to hear those words from your mouth, 'It's a goal!'

In your life as you were living it did you ever experience one of those times where you just wanted to disappear into thin air? I mean just close your eyes real quick and open them and you would magically and instantly be somewhere else in space and time? You would have mastered time travel and space travel simultaneously without having to drive eighty-eight miles an hour in a modified DeLorean automobile. Boy, if there was ever a moment like that, ever in my little life here on earth, it was right there and then…actually right now. And how I wished it would happen to me at least this one time! I'll never forget it for as long as I live.

What happened was just 'fate' as my mom would say all the time when unexplained changes or events would occur. At times she was very melodramatic and Shakespearian in her words and behavior. It came from all of those books she read while she was waiting for me and my sisters and my brother to grow up. She would always refer to them as masterpieces. Maybe, deep down inside, she wanted to be an actress or a playwright or a movie director? And she would have been very good at any one of those chosen professions.

The fierce storm and what there was of the game had passed into recent history, but we hadn't left for home yet as planned. The adults decided that this would be a perfect time for some ice fishing of all things. That idea sounded to me like good news at first. I liked ice fishing very much when it comes to fishing so it was good news, wasn't it? What could possibly go wrong on a frozen lake or river? And the fish back in Reality would be completely safe as long as they stayed there.

There is a lot of irony in this story as my mom would also say. It all centered around the 'bike incident'. But in this version of that epic tale, it was *Me*, knocking Schultz off *his* bike! I don't think I started it, but the rumor mill ran the story all over and around town almost faster than it really happened and there were a few variations and modifications of the truth as you will see.

My mind and conscience instantly began communicating with each other as I pondered the situation and the facts. Boy, that's not what happened at all one of them would say to the other! The problem was... how am I going to get myself out of this one so far away from home? And by now before I could respond meaningfully I was a folk legend for tens of miles in all directions...a 'big time' hero in the eyes of all the other kids of Kaktovik, too! Wow, what a dilemma.

How come Schultz didn't say something to Bjore and snuff out this rumor before it could spread like wildfire? I mean, why didn't he tell Bjore what really happened that day back in Reality? He always seemed so proud of himself even though it was a sneak attack he and his friends pulled off. Could it be that he had developed a conscience all of a sudden? Nah... Now that's reaching far too far for someone like Schultz.

"Jean-Luc, are you coming with us or are you just going to stand there staring into outer space", Mr. Eriksson said as he leaned over the passenger seat and looked out the window at me. "I know that you like the wide open spaces, but there are better ways to enjoy them... especially around here."

"Er, ah, yes, sir. Um, I was just thinking about all those fish Bjore and I are going to have to clean this afternoon after you catch them. I feel so sorry for them with their bulging eyes and their fluttering gills and helpless tails flopping up and down screaming for help."

Just then my dad walked over to see what I was doing or not doing to slow things down so much.

"Son, you want to ride with Bjore and his dad, or run up to the lake with Uncle Mike, Paul and myself? The girls are staying behind this time. It's something about a big baking session at the Inn which, of course, will be in our favor. But, then you'll have to help us clean the fish as usual. I've already been warned about bringing our catch back to the Inn un-cleaned!"

"If it's okay with you and Uncle Mike, I'm gonna ride with Bjore, dad. There's something I want to tell, er, I mean talk to him about this morning. It's a kid thing if you know what I mean so you won't have to endure all of the gory details. It's all right with you and Paul and Uncle Mike, isn't it?"

My dad smiled. He was pleased that I would ask permission so politely. He was proud of his prodigy. But I could easily tell that he was very happy to avoid the details of our conversation.

"You know it is, Luc. You two have a grand old talk, and we'll see you at the lake! But, when we start fishing, we need some peace and quiet, so get your speeches done before we get to the lake so we have a chance to complete our mission out there. These are smart fish up here with excellent hearing skills in several languages. It's all a matter of evolution."

My stomach was all twisty-turvey. Or is that topsy-turvey? What's the difference? I felt lightheaded, too! Geeze, I just felt like something really bad was going to happen this day after things had gone so well for me. And it had Schultz written all over it, too! He was haunting me like a terrible ghost…or maybe a demon, and I couldn't figure out why this was all happening to me just now.

"Okay, boys! All aboard! Those fish are just waiting to be caught", Bjore's dad said with a loud roar designed to wake us all up, and me and Bjore piled into the back seat amongst the fishing poles, bait cans, tents and blankets to protect us from the cold winds whipping across the lake. I gotta tell ya, that terrible smell from the bait in those cans surely didn't help the way I was feeling, and with Mr. Eriksson's driving it would take everything I had to keep breakfast down in my stomach no matter how good it was! I guess that Bjore was used to it because he never mentioned the smell or the bumps or any upset in his stomach.

But, believe it or not, there was some good luck coming our way, too. The weather in Kaktovik had cleared up nicely and quickly from the previous day. Mr. Eriksson heard on the radio earlier that morning that the storm moved farther east than was expected, and that's why the weather was so clear and bright this morning. There was some fresh snow on the ground, but not nearly what could have fallen in the worst case had the center of the storm hit there. I don't even remember any thunder or loud winds last night after falling asleep like a log. Stuff like that usually wakes me up for sure, but I was out like a light for the whole night. Wow, it rhymes!

"So, Jean-Luc, what do you want to talk to me about this morning? I hope it's more about how we both will play in the NHL very soon. Hey, maybe even together on the same team! Imagine that! Is that what you want to talk about, Jean-Luc? That would be something we could write a book about, Luc! You and me on the same team on our way to winning the Stanley Cup! We would make everyone in the state of Alaska proud, wouldn't we Jean-Luc? Well, almost everybody."

All I could do was smile at Bjore. My mind was racing like no other time I can ever remember. All I could think of was what I was going to tell Bjore about the 'bike' incident because I just knew that the subject would come up sooner or later and it would be a lot better if he heard it from me first.

"Heck, Jean-Luc! You and me would be known by everyone as the famous almost brothers from Northern Alaska! Probably the first two ever to win the Stanley Cup! Now that would be something to write home about."

"Yeah, Bjore, that will be something, all right!" Then, possibly because of a strong pang of guilt that crept into my psyche, I turned to look out the back window of the car to see if Schultz was following behind us and listening to my every word. Of course, he wasn't, but I felt very relieved anyway by the empty road.

"Bjore", I started, "about the bike incident back in Reality. Ah, well, it really wasn't…"

Just at that moment Mr. Eriksson turned around to face us and without hesitation started going into his instructions for ice fishing on Lake Adaline. After about fifteen minutes of continuous lecture on the do's and don't, and what he wanted Bjore and I to do when we got to the lake, we turned down a dirt road with beautiful Lake Adaline sitting at the bottom of it. Just then Bjore responded.

"Yes, Dad, Luc and I get the whole picture. Okay, go ahead Luc. What were you going to say about the bike incident?"

The car came quickly to a stop before I could say another word. I knew that I had just missed my best opportunity to explain myself to my new friend. I wondered if I would get another chance.

"Out of the car, you two! We need to get out there and set up our spot before the rest of those slow pokes get here and ruin it for us. Bjore knows what I'm talking about. He's been through this before."

I turned to look up the hill and Mr. Eriksson was right. We were the first of the ice fishing crowd to reach Lake Adaline on this beautiful post-storm day. It was time to get out there and stake our claim!

Bjore and I cleared the ice and with a lot of help from the adults, we cut several holes in the deep ice. It was work, but it was really a lot of fun for both of us. Then we retrieved the bait and our picnic baskets out of the car and set up our windbreak. We were ready to go ice fishing.

Everyone finally had his bait under the ice in the cold waters of Lake Adaline, waiting for the first big one to bite. Now, they were all rubbing their hands together and looking at me, waiting to hear the detailed story of Schultz and the bicycle straight from the horse's mouth. This was to be my moment of truth. A chill ran up my spine as I realized what this meant for me and my future.

It was at that moment that my life seemed to flash before me. The story, or legend as Bjore called it, that had spread like wildfire, as far as I could tell, all over the north of Alaska, wasn't exactly the truth. Somehow, it got all jumbled up. Not by me, you understand, but I still had to decide on a course of action, and fast. Very soon, someone would ask about the incident and my reputation and honor would ride on the answer that I gave. And it seemed like a disaster for me either way.

You know how it is, don't you? The angel seeking truth standing on one of your shoulders and the devil himself standing on the other shoulder seeking the opposite. It was just like that right here and now. Glory and fame now, but the possibility of having to pay for the truth, sooner or later. I began to believe the truth was the best way to go just like my parents had always taught me. The facts were the facts for sure, and I shouldn't try to alter them.

But, on the other hand, when I compared the two, the real story wasn't nearly as good as the existing legend. If I told my friends and their parents the truth, it would destroy a wonderful fantasy concerning me that they carried with them. None of them, parents included, liked Schultz at all. That was a true fact. I could feel that they wished they were kids again and had the chance to go one on one with the big ogre and teach him a lesson or two with their fists. They all seemed so proud of me when the subject of my bicycle came up for discussion. How could I destroy that feeling of happiness and joy just to obey a rule? More than just my own reputation was at stake here. The happiness of the adults was at stake, too.

Well, just as I was about to spill my guts and ruin everything, a bit of very good luck came my way. Just up the ice from our fishing spot some of Mr. Eriksson's good friends began to set up a fishing hole, and Mr. Eriksson was eager to help them. He was also anxious to introduce my dad to his longtime friends, and I knew that they would have plenty of stories to exchange. Without thinking, Bjore and I volunteered to watch the poles and scream if anything hit the lines. It was my big chance.

Once we were alone, I told Bjore of my dilemma. He was very understanding. Just for the record, he said, I should tell him the true story, and then he would do his best to keep the legend intact. I agreed.

The first thing I remember remembering was that gigantic needle. I started to scream, but the nurse put it down and pointed to my scrawny little arm. I almost passed out. She had already stuck the thing into me. All I could tell Bjore was that it really hurt more than anything I had felt before. I could tell that his curiosity was aroused. Why was I being stuck with a needle?

Well, I went back to the beginning of the story. I was riding my new bike down the sidewalk from school to our house in Reality. The schoolhouse was on one end of Reality and our house was on the other as I already told you. So now, when there wasn't too much snow, I could ride to school on my bike instead of walking all that way. I was doing exactly that, riding home from school the day in question. It was about three o'clock in the afternoon. I was going home to get my skates so I could go to the river and practice with my teammates.

Schultz must have seen me coming, or maybe he just got lucky. I had my head down at the time. I was looking down at the chain to make sure my pants didn't get caught in it. Nothing could be worse than having your pants caught in the chain of your bike. One of my friends, Alfie is his name, had a chain guard on his bike. How the rest of us kids envied him. No way he could ever get his pants caught in the chain with that chain guard in place.

Well, I came around the corner by the drug store and as I looked down, Schultz and his bully friend, Fred, yelled at me and started throwing snowballs from a pile they had prepared. They missed, of course, because they were terrible shots, but I lost my balance anyway, and my bike started to skid out of control. In an attempt to save myself I jumped off the sidewalk onto some ice on the street. That was a very big mistake, but it was too late. The bike lost its grip on the ground, and I flew off right into the big tree that grew in front of the drug store. After that I didn't remember a thing until I saw the big needle in the nurse's hand.

Bjore almost fell off of the wooden box he was sitting on; he was laughing so hard he couldn't get up. I could feel my partially frozen face turning red as a frozen beet. I remember him telling me that my secret was safe with him for the rest of his life. You should have seen the look on his face when I told him that what he had heard was only the beginning of the story. My revenge was yet to come and sooner than I could have ever wished.

After about forty minutes, Bjore's dad came back and asked us to go get some water from Mister Peterson who lived in a farmhouse on the edge of the lake. Bjore knew the Petersons quite well, and he told me that he often went to their house for water and even occasionally for bait. But, what he liked the most were the Peterson's daughter, Colleen, and their German Sheppard who was called 'Bosco'. He said that he didn't have a clue about the dog's name, but that the big pooch was really friendly to him. He warned me that I should prepare to have my face licked by Bosco. It was the price I would have to pay for us to get the water.

It took us about ten minutes to get there, and after knocking on the front door it appeared that the family was out, or so we thought. As I turned away from the door, that's when I saw the prettiest girl I had ever seen. It was Colleen holding a leash to which Bosco was attached. After an introduction, Colleen asked me if I would take Bosco for a short walk so that he could do his business. She suggested that I take him to the garage in the back yard which was in the process of being built.

Bosco seemed to like me from the start, so we went around to the rear of the farmhouse while Bjore and Colleen retrieved the necessary water bottles from the cellar. Bosco helped pull me toward the garage, which obviously was one of his favorite hangouts. As he sniffed and pawed the earth near the entrance to the garage, I took the opportunity to peer inside. It was an oversized garage for sure. The newly poured concrete floor was covered with lumber, mostly 2x4s cut to become the support structure for the roof.

Bosco finished what he was doing and walked inside as if to give me the nickel tour. His tail was wagging, and he seemed truly proud of what his family was building. I think he had already chosen his favorite spots for hiding bones and taking naps. It was a great time and place to be a dog.

Well, after a brief inspection of the premises, Bosco seemed ready to head back to the main house when he suddenly tensed up and started to growl. As I looked up, I saw two figures standing in the doorway, and they weren't Colleen and Bjore. My greatest fears were soon realized. It was Schultz and one of his cronies. Bosco shot ahead and chased Schultz's companion out of the garage. I could hear barking and then high-pitched screams for help from the kid as he ran as fast as he could toward to lake. Bosco was doing his part.

But Schultz could have cared less. It was me that he was after, and he had my only means of escape blocked. I wanted to scream for help, but my pride wouldn't let me. The final showdown was finally here!

Schultz started by telling me that he had heard the false rumors I had spread, and that he was here to teach me who was the real boss. He pulled off his jacket and yelped at me that I should do the same. I guess that it was mostly out of fear, but I followed his orders in preparation for our upcoming fight.

"That stupid mutt can't help you now, Robespierre. Get ready to die or something close to it!"

I remembered what Paul had taught me about hockey fights. Get the helmet off first! But Schultz was wearing a stocking-cap type hat so that would have to do for a helmet. As I thought, he took a step forward and bent over to pick up a two foot long piece of 2x4! He was going to beat me with a 2x4! That's hardly a fair way to fight, I thought. At the same time I searched the floor for a similar weapon but none were near enough to me to be retrieved in time. I was in trouble!

Again, I thought of Paul's advice. 'Use your speed!' Schultz was slow, and I thought I might just lure him away from the door and wheel around him and get out. For sure, I would close the door behind me as I left.

What happened next took place in a split second so I will have to tell you in slow motion just like the replays on TV.

I faked to my left as if I were going up the middle of the ice. Just as I did, Bosco stepped in the door of the garage. He had a boy's coat in his mouth. Schultz didn't see him at first. Then I froze, pointed at Bosco long enough to distract Schultz, and then shot to my right toward a side wall of the structure.

Schultz wasn't going to let me get out, Bosco or no Bosco. His mistake was that he failed to look down! As he took a giant stride toward me, he stepped on a six foot 2x4 that was lying on top of and across another 2x4 just like a crude teeter-tauter. He came down hard on the end that was off the floor. After that, the physics was quite simple. The other end of the board came up off the floor with a vengeance and hit him just below his left eye! I could almost hear the birds in his head singing as he crumpled to the floor, out cold as they say on TV.

Other than Schultz himself, the pooch was my only witness, and I knew for sure that he wouldn't tell anyone what actually happened. As I stood over my fallen adversary wondering what to do next, Schultz's buddy came in the door looking for his coat. He saw the blossoming black eye on Schultz's face, and he was convinced that I had punched out his friend in hand-to-hand combat. I retrieved the coat from Bosco and gave it to him. He nodded with a half-smile as he backed quickly for the exit with one eye on Bosco.

"I'll wait on the porch until he can walk," he whispered. I never did learn his name. I guess he didn't want to tell me for fear that he would become a permanent part of the legend.

"Maybe you should call his parents to get him a ride home," I countered. He nodded and left. I thought I could see what I interpreted as a smile on Bosco's face. He also had something to brag about to his dog friends. There on the floor in front of him was the kid's hat. *An appropriate trophy for Bosco*, I thought. He certainly earned it, and the kid should be happy that he got his jacket back although I didn't get a chance to inspect it for holes and teeth marks.

As I walked toward the house, Colleen and Bjore met me. I pointed back toward the garage just as Schultz came staggering out the door with the world's biggest and newest shiner. Bjore went to help him, but Schultz was too proud to accept any help. But, that's when he did something completely unexpected. He shouted the word 'Uncle' three times up into the air as if he were talking directly to God! To this day I believe he said the mandatory three uncles to God so he wouldn't have to say them to me. It didn't matter, but this incident did remind me of something my Uncle Jack always said, especially when he was drinking heavily and telling stories from his past. 'Luck beats brains, any time!' I don't know if that's true, but it certainly applied in this case. Something to remember!

We finally got back to the lake with the water only to find the fishermen packing up their stuff. As it turned out, a big crack had appeared in the ice surface. It was nature's way of telling the fishermen to go home.

In the car on the way back, Bjore filled the adults in on the details of the Schultz incident...number two. They were all smiles, but I could tell that my dad had some questions he wanted to ask his heroic son but only in private. However, after a few minutes of accolades from Bjore, I guess he thought it better to let things ride. Needless to say, I was very happy with his decision.

10
Woodstock

I grabbed my guitar and made my way out the door
Without much to say except that I needed a place to play.
There on the farm with Lester's cows I met some pretty
People who just said 'Wow' and offered me comfort today.

This ambulance rides real nice and smooth whether it's going fast or slow. It's because these roads are so smooth and clear all the time. No big rocks or ice and snow or sloppy slush anywhere around here any time of year with few exceptions. Imagine that! Just lots of beautiful lush palm trees and flowers and tropical plants everywhere all of the time. Lots of beautiful birds and butterflies are always flying around and ducks floating in the water. And a nice and big warm ocean and gulfstream flowing right next door full of big fish and sailboats and lots of waves for surfers. My mom would call this arrangement a heat sink for sure.

In case you don't know what that is…it's something that tends to keep the temperature constant wherever it is. When the air gets too cold, it keeps it warmer. And when the air gets too warm, it keeps it cooler. Wow, it's almost like a heater and an air conditioner combined and both working in your favor! And it doesn't consume any electricity.

They say that the Everglades are just to the west of this place. Alligators and turtles and sea gulls and stuff like that live out there in the tall grass and weeds. There's lots and lots of water, and it's very warm almost all the time. If we were up in Alaska near Reality, we would be bumping up and down on the ice and the potholes in the dirt road not to mention plowing through your occasional snow drift somewhere on the side of a mountain.

Oh, yeah, we had some serious potholes up in the roads up near and around Reality for sure! It wasn't that the roads around the city were never fixed at all. In the summer the city workers were always working on the streets and bridges, in and near our town at least. My dad was always complaining about the amount of time he wasted on the way to and from work every day waiting while the traffic ahead of him was detoured or put on a one-way street to let the work crews do their thing. He said that Reality and vicinity was worse than Florida when the snowbirds from New York came south for the winter.

When I was a little kid, I would imagine flocks of these huge white-winged birds heading south to Florida from Brooklyn and Long Island to stay warm. Now I'm here, too, just like those infamous snowbirds! I know you're going to ask how I got here in the first place, but… well…I'm not sure right now, but things are getting clearer as time rolls past. And what is confusing is that I don't see any people with wings!

Oh, yes, we did have quite a few one-way streets up in Reality, believe it or not. Actually, you might call them alleys or gangways in the town you live in. They were very narrow and not well lit at night. You were lucky to get one car through especially when someone would try to sneak down the road going the wrong way which happened all the time. If you were traveling on those fabulous one-way streets you had to watch out very carefully all the time for traffic backing up in your direction. One little mistake could cost you an hour or two and a new radiator or fender.

With my new bike I was impervious to all the repairs and the potholes and crazy drivers and other existing obstacles. The way people drove their cars up there forced me to keep my bike on the sidewalks as much as possible if I wanted to live in one piece to see and celebrate my next birthday. That way, only the pedestrians were in trouble if something went wrong with a thoroughfare.

I tried to be very careful so that I wouldn't run any of them down, particularly the most vulnerable little old ladies. Well, except, that is, when a little brainless kid with a wagon would shoot out of a doorway without any warning. I almost caught my lunch that way several times, but fate always seemed to provide a way out for me. It was just a hazard you had to deal with all the time you were on your bike. Well, I'm sure that's not very interesting to you, but my birthday should be.

I remember my mom telling me about the day I was born. I'll bet that she wished she had been in a nice new ambulance like this, but instead she went to the hospital in my dad's pickup truck. It was May the 4th, 1970. I know because that's my birthday! At least that's what they told me. Back in those days I was a very clever little kid, and I knew the difference between the months.

Mom said I came into Reality a little early, but that I was still a big baby. I think she was referring to my size when I was born. At least I hope so. She told me that that particular May 4th was the coldest day in history for the town of Reality. For a day in May, that is. Maybe she just was confused, because my brother, Jean-Paul, was born on the coldest day ever recorded in Reality. He was born on the first of January 1967. It was fifty-six degrees below zero not counting the wind chill, whatever that is? Now don't get too excited because that was Fahrenheit, not Centigrade or Kelvin. She taught me the difference between all the temperature scales too so I could amaze my teachers and the other kids. On my birthday it was just seventeen below or so if I correctly remember what she said. But that's pretty good for early May for sure.

Mom once said that I was due to be born on Cinco de Mayo, which was a day later. Cinco de Mayo means the 5th of May and is important because it's the anniversary of the Mexican victory over the French more than a century ago. Why was that important? It was very complicated so stay with me.

Well, mom said that the first of May was called May Day, something about celebrating revolution. I had no idea what that was back then. She would talk about this man named Lenin or Lennon all the time. She called him Vladimir Ilyich Ulyanov, too. What I figured out for myself back then was that he was the guy who played a great guitar and sang for the Beatles. When I would tell her who he was, she would just laugh hysterically, but she would never tell me why. I know that she loved the music performed by the Beatles.

The second of May was the anniversary of my Uncle Jack's divorce. There was another event I didn't understand, but he would talk about it all the time in glowing terms as if it were a turning point in American history and personal freedom.

I particularly liked his former wife's name. It was *Godzilla*! Somehow I knew that Godzilla wasn't her real name, particularly because everyone would laugh and point at him when he mentioned her. I don't think he ever told me what her real name was. Now that I think about it, she would have been my aunt! Wow, I could just see her breathing fire all over the place and whipping that huge tail around knocking everything down. Hey, that breathing fire thing was not a bad idea when it's real cold, but it would have messed up the ice, too.

And then there was the third of May, which was the anniversary of the founding of the City of Reality. They always had a big parade and a party to celebrate the event. My Uncle Jack really liked that celebration because they had free beer. I would argue with the bartender about the fact that root beer should be free, too. After all, why would they call it root beer if it wasn't beer? I guess I wore him down so I drank free glass for free glass with Uncle Jack at the celebrations. The only difference was that after we were done, Uncle Jack couldn't walk very well, and I was just full and headed for the nearest bathroom.

So, you see, my birthday is one of five very important days at the beginning of May each year. Mom said it meant that I was destined to be a very important person, but she wasn't sure exactly how that would come to pass. I sure hope she was right! Uncle Jack's divorce was the only thing that really had me worried about the May sequence. What if Godzilla came back again? When I asked him, Uncle Jack explained she had been banished to Chicago as far as he knew so we would be safe as long as we avoided the place. Would she still be my aunt or would she be disguised as my girlfriend or future spouse or something worse? I hoped I would never have to face that situation in my real life.

My mom would call me *The Woodstock Baby* every once in a while, especially when it was raining outside. For the longest time I didn't know what she meant by that particular remark? Woodstock? *I'm not a bird, am I?* I would say that to myself when she would do it. Woodstock was a bird in a cartoon or comic strip, right? At least that's what I remember right now. How could I be confused with him? That thought would always make me check to be sure I wasn't growing any wings.

But, my mom was always nice to me so I didn't complain about it to her. For the longest time I just accepted the title as an honor of some sort. If it pleased her for that to be my nickname, I had to deal with it and make it my gift to her. Alfie and Paul would call me *Woody* every once in a while, but I let them know in no uncertain terms that only mom and dad could get away with that for very long without some form of serious retaliation.

It got to be so annoying that I even looked up Woodstock on the map when she told me it was a town in New York State. That place is pretty far from Reality so I still couldn't figure out what I had to do with the place. At least I wasn't a bird, not that being a bird would be so bad compared to being a town located somewhere in New York State. Hey, my good friend Ralph has a parrot, and it gets fed, has a house and can mess anywhere he wants as long as he hits the paper, and Ralph will clean it up without even being asked. If I tried that, I would get whooped real good!

Then one day when I least expected it, I finally found out what she meant by that nickname she had given me. My friend, Alfie, told me that Woodstock was a place in the lower forty-eight. I already knew that, and I let him know about it. I'm no dummy! The lower forty-eight is what we called the detached part of the United States, the part down lower on the map except for Hawaii. Alfie thought the forty-eight meant that there were that many towns down there. I had to point out that it was forty-eight states just like Alaska…maybe each one wasn't as big, but they had more people, usually less ice and snow, and far fewer moose than we did.

Alfie told me that Woodstock was where they had a big music concert in 1969. He said someone told him that it was where all the big kids and adults rolled in the mud and dirt for a week while they played great rock'n roll music all day and night. Now that really sounded like fun to me! Hey, Jimi Hendrix, The Doors, and more. A little messy and dirty, but super great fun nevertheless.

Alfie even said that he had a recording at home of some of the music from Woodstock. He even played some of it for me when his big brother wasn't home. Actually, the record belonged to Alfie's big brother, and I guess Alfie wasn't supposed to play it when he was by himself. I swore on a stack of Bibles ten feet high never to tell anyone about the incident. So, you keep your mouth shut about it or else!

My favorites were definitely the Grateful Dead, The Doors and Jimi Hendrix. I think that's who I heard on the record. Oh, I liked Crosby, Stills, Nash and Young, too, don't get me wrong. Or was it just Crosby, Stills and Nash? But I still didn't have a clue as to why she called me *The Woodstock Baby?*

It must have been a month later when Alfie asked his older brother Fred just what it meant that I was a Woodstock baby. I was there when he did it, too. Fred actually looked pretty dumb when you looked directly at him, but he actually was really smart sometimes. He had made it all the way to the sixth grade without failing, which in Reality was a mark of greatness to be sure. I remember swearing to try to follow in his footsteps no matter what.

Fred asked me when my birthday was and so I told him. The 4th of May of 1970. Fred definitely wasn't as dumb as he looked. He could count backwards, something I had yet to master to any extent. He said, *Let's see. May, April, March, Jan...ah, no, February, January, that's five. Now for the rest: December, November, October, September, August. That's five. But we can't count May, and we have only half of August. Almost nine. It computes!*

Computes? I wondered to myself. What computes? If I have to do all that thinking to make it to the sixth grade, I'm not so sure I'll make it all the way in the required time. There must be an easier way to solve this without directly asking Mom.

"That's how they make babies," he said point blank to me. He told me and Alfie that the adults rolled around in the mud for a while and then waited nine months, more or less, to see if a baby came out.

Came out? Came out of where? I was really very confused at the time. But now I know what he was talking about. It was such a mystery to me back then. So, I ran right home, and there was my dad sitting on the front porch smoking his pipe. I sat myself right down next to him, cleared my throat, rubbed my hands together and looked him directly in the eyes. I was as ready as I could be, but the correct words wouldn't come out of my mouth right away.

Finally, my dad asked me why I wasn't out playing with Alfie or one of my other friends. Before I could answer, our dog, Istahota, jumped up on me and licked me right in the face. It tickled something fierce. When he slobbered all over me, it made me forget what I was doing for a few seconds.

That's when my dad asked me if I knew where Istahota came from. Of course, I didn't. The pooch had been around as long as I could remember. My dad told me that they found him sitting on our front porch the day he and my mom brought me home from the clinic. I was only four days old then, he said, and Istahota couldn't have been much older than that.

My dad said his name means *gray eyes* in Lakota. The Lakota are Indians who lived near us, but that's about all I can remember about them right now. They were friendly and good athletes. I have sort of lost track of what I was talking about. But, it'll come to me sooner or later so hang in there. It must have been really important for me to forget like this.

Well, the ambulance has stopped once again, and they're opening the big doors in the back to take me out. This must be a hospital or a big clinic as far as I can tell. They're being real careful with me. That's a good thing. Hey, those people over there in the corner are pointing at me and waving. I'd wave back, but I'm too tired and weak right now, and my hands just don't want to work. But I did try to smile.

Oh, yeah, Woodstock! I almost forgot. Later that night at dinner I just caved in and casually asked my mom and dad why they said I was a *Woodstock Baby*. My mother started laughing really hard like I had just told her a really good joke and put her head down on the table, almost into her plate of food. Why was she laughing so hard? I started picturing the bird again, and believe it or not, I checked myself again to make sure I didn't have any feathers coming out anywhere!

My dad, for his part, tried to keep a straight face through all this. That was his usual style. He was tough, but he tried to avoid confrontation, especially with my mom. Then my mom looked up with the biggest smile on her face, pointed at my dad and told him it was his turn to tell me what that meant.

Boy, did my dad ever look dazed and confused. For a while I just sat there and looked at him, my eyes wide open waiting for an answer that might never come. That was the most confused I have ever seen my dad at any time before or since. He was not the kind of person to be confused very often. He usually knew what was going on before the rest of us, but this was obviously the exception to the rule. He was caught completely by surprise.

He just sat there, first looking at me, then taking a bite to eat, then looking at mom. The expression on his face never changed much. For a moment I thought I could almost see smoke rising from his head or at least from his ears. He was thinking really hard for sure! Then, like a military commander giving orders to his troops, he pointed over to the far wall where we had some things hanging as decorations.

"Do you know what that is, Son?" he said as he pointed to a little American flag that was draped across the wall. By little, I mean two or three feet high and wide, not one of those that fly from our flagpole at school. Those are real big for sure.

I was proud to say that I did know what it was. I told him it was our national flag, the American flag. I told him that we said the Pledge of Allegiance every morning in school to a huge flag like that. Then I stood up from the table and began to recite the Pledge of Allegiance for him just to prove it. I put my hand over my heart just like you're supposed to when you do the pledge.

You know what? For once, he just sat there quietly and listened to me say the whole thing. He didn't interrupt me once, not once. Now, that was truly unusual for my dad. When I finished and then looked at my mom, I thought I could see a tear forming in her eye. I'm not kidding. She was probably thinking that all that time I spent at school wasn't wasted after all. My recitation must have been perfect or nearly so because she had no corrections or suggestions for me. My chest swelled with great pride. I was in seventh heaven, whatever and wherever that is.

Once I was done with the Pledge of Allegiance, I just sat down in my chair, ready to start eating again thinking the incident was over. But my dad whispered something to my mom like *we'd better tell him,* so I waited for the big news. It dawned on me that I still didn't understand what the Woodstock reference meant but that could be resolved in the next few seconds.

"Well, Son, back in 1969, before you were born, your mom and I were down in the lower forty-eight and the eastern provinces of Canada visiting some of our friends and relatives. We were on a long vacation. While we were in Montreal, we heard about this big shindig, a concert that was supposed to last several days, going on down in the States, in a State called New York. It was at a place they called Woodstock. That was the name of the town. Lester's Farm was located nearby."

I'd heard of Lester's Farm before, but I didn't know why it was important right then.

"Were you rolling in the mud with the rest of the people?" I blurted out before I knew what happened and could stop myself. I was so embarrassed. I could feel the blood rushing to my face. I must have been red as a beet.

"Where did you get that from?" asked my mother with a look of concern on her face. I really surprised her.

I remembered the promise I made to Alfie not to squeal on him. But this wasn't squealing, it was my mom asking. So I told her the truth.

"From Alfie," I said in all seriousness. "And his older brother Fred told him all about it. I was right there when he told Alfie. The people got down in the mud and rolled around. That's what he told me. Honest, word for word. And he said sometimes babies come from rolling in the mud like that. He said that that's probably where I came from. I didn't know whether to believe him, but at the time and under the circumstances his argument sounded very convincing."

"It was raining all week, Jean-Luc," said my dad calmly. "And your mother and I went to listen to Jimi Hendrix play his guitar and sing a few songs. It was near the end of the concert, and he was playing the National Anthem."

"I know what that is, Dad. Our teacher has a record of the National Anthem, and the band on the record plays the National Anthem, and we sing along with it. I don't know all the words yet, but Alfie does. So, Jimi Hendrix played the National Anthem at the Woodstock concert! On our teacher's record, I don't think that it is Jimi Hendrix playing the National Anthem. It is some other band. I don't remember the name. But that doesn't really matter."

I hesitated to tell my parents that I had heard Jimi Hendrix on Fred's record. They didn't ask so I decided not to tell. Besides, my dad looked like he wanted to say more about Woodstock.

"So, Son, your mom and I thought about you just as this man, this Jimi Hendrix, was playing the National Anthem at Woodstock. And since we first thought about you then, that's why we call you *The Woodstock Baby*. We figured that you would have liked all that music performed there so the nickname was a natural selection for us under the circumstances."

Now it seemed so clear. Fred was absolutely wrong. Those people in the mud weren't smoking hay or grass or whatever it was and tearing their clothes off like he said. They were just listening to the National Anthem and thinking of their futures and those of their children. But my dad did say that we should keep that as a family secret. So I didn't tell Fred and Alfie that they were wrong about the whole thing. But I did tell Iskahota about the whole thing. I knew he wouldn't tell anyone. That's one of the reasons why dogs are your best friends, isn't it?

11

My First Funeral

He's either dead or
my watch has stopped.

Groucho Marx
A Day at the Races

Ah, I must have dozed off another time. After all, I still do need my rest every once in a while. It seems like they're rolling me over to some sort of medical device. Yes, it's the x-ray machine. How did I know that you might ask? I know that it's an x-ray machine, but I don't know just why I know…you know what I mean, don't you? My Uncle Jack would tell me that sometimes you know things without knowing why you know them in the first place. He told me that such things would happen to him a lot particularly when he was at the racetrack looking for a winning horse. He told me that there was this little voice living inside his head that he relied upon when he needed help making the right decision, especially when it involved money and important stuff like that. I guess that's the explanation as to why he's not very wealthy. At least that was my mom's conclusion.

He explained that small people who were called jockeys would ride horses they called race horses as fast as they could and try to beat all the other horses across a place called the finish line. At the same time people like him who were watching the race from the stands next to the track would bet their money on which one would win and which one would finish second and which one would finish third. Then, if you

137

guessed correctly, you would get back more money than you bet in the first place. I remember that I asked him what happened to your money if you guessed wrong. He just shook his head slowly and said that you lost all that money that you bet. I felt sorry for him when he said that because he had such a sad look on his face.

Wow! I liked the idea of winning more money a real lot, but what if you lost most or all of the time? There goes your hard-earned money down the drain, or in my case, there goes my hard-earned allowance down the same drain. I guess that's why they call it gambling. It's a high risk venture where your chances of losing exceed your chances of winning most or all of the time.

My Uncle Jack was a brave man for sure. He was fearless! Back then it seemed to me that he was risking his very own existence on the speed and endurance of a horse he didn't even know very well if at all. But, he somehow managed to survive that ordeal for months and years! He said that he survived partly because of this little voice in his head that told him which one of the horses to bet on. I remember thinking that the little voice must have come from his guardian angel up in heaven. At least that's what he told me. Or was it coming from one of the other guys lurking out there? You know what I'm talking about, don't you?

I clearly remember my mother telling me that Uncle Jack had something she called a gambling addiction. In school my teachers said that addicts were people who ate or drank things that were bad for them and that were usually illegal to have. My Uncle Jack sure enjoyed his beer quite a bit, but I'm sure that was legal because they served it in public at the restaurant where mom worked. And I've seen her open plenty of bottles of beer for people who were customers so that can't be it! I've got to think about this problem a little more.

Here he comes again…the guy with the real bright shiny thing on his head; I guess he's the doctor? He's pointing at my side, at my ribs or what's left of them! Now he's poking around my ribs with his fingers. Oh yeah, they hurt for sure! I could have told him that without all the poking and probing. These fellows aren't always the smartest guys in town.

Maybe something in there is broken? It sure feels that way. I must have fallen on my side or maybe something hard hit me there? I can't see it, but it just feels black and blue, for sure. You know what I mean, don't you? When somebody or something hits you in the ribs real hard, those ribs just feel black and blue even if you don't see them and even if they're not those colors. You don't have to see them with your eyes to know that! Black and blue is a feeling for sure.

I pretty much vividly remember all of the times I fell off my bike riding up in Reality. Actually, almost every time it was more like I flew off my bike into the air before I hit the ground. It was almost as if I was learning to fly. Someone real famous named Tom Petty once said that he was learning to fly, but he didn't have wings. And that coming down was the hardest thing!

One of the most memorable times was when my friends and I were playing a game we called Pony Express. This shouldn't be confused with the 'Schultz incident' which I described to you. The object of the game was for one of us to be carrying the mail for delivery at the fort or the outpost we established while the others chased him as if they were bandits or maybe the cops.

To win you had to get to the outpost or fort with the mail before they robbed you. It was like in all those cowboy movies I saw as a kid. That's where we learned the game except we had bikes instead of horses. This was a definite advantage for us because we didn't have to feed them or clean up after them. I most often favored thinking of my particular destination as a fort, while Alfie much preferred the term outpost. I never did figure out why.

Anyway, on this particular occasion, my friend Alfie was hot on my trail. I was pumping my bike faster than him, but I didn't see the hole in the ground coming up on me real fast. That was a very serious oversight on my part. As I remember, all I could do was fly through the air over my handlebars as I already said. When I finally landed, I hit a big rock…and the rock won the collision contest to be sure even though I had all the momentum. My mom taught me what momentum was in case you're wondering. It seems like rocks and trees were always out to get me even when they were sitting still and I'm flying towards them!

We didn't have one of these modern x-ray machines in Reality when I was a kid. Whenever I got black and blue as a kid, I just stayed that way until it healed by itself. Oh, I know that the x-ray machine can't cure the bruises, but it's nice to know that nothing is broken or bent out of shape under your skin where you can't see it clearly from the outside. And the x-ray itself didn't hurt at all.

I wondered exactly what an x-ray was since it was going to get so intimate with me physically so I politely asked the nurse for an explanation. She said that they were high-energy photons! Photons? And they were very high energy things at that! But she said that they were quite small clouds of energy and moved very fast. Small and fast! That was me playing hockey when I was…small and pretty fast. I guess it makes sense that we should come together. From that moment on I liked x-rays even though I'd never actually seen one in person. The nurse said that they were invisible so that solved that problem for me right away.

We didn't have a real hospital in Reality, at least not when I was a first and second-grader. I wonder if this place where I'm at now has a hospital? I heard the doctor saying something about taking me out in the ambulance somewhere for a scan of some kind. At least I think he's a doctor or something similar. As far as I know, I think that requires a hospital.

Oh, oh, I really don't like hospitals as I remember. Believe it or not, Kaktovik has a hospital; I remember that. But I liked our place much better. Everyone in Reality called it a clinic. I am sure that the men liked it because the nurse that worked there was very pretty. Even I noticed that right away. And she was real good friends with my mother, too. My dad was friends with her, too, especially when one of the men in his crew would get hurt. But I don't think my mom liked my dad being friends with her too much. That was hard to figure? She would say things about breaking dad's neck if he did something or other. What, I don't know, but mom was very serious for sure, and I'm sure she meant every word she said.

Come to think of it she was always kidding about breaking people's necks if they misbehaved. She didn't have to think about breaking my dad's neck. According to dad, almost every day a big rolling or falling log would come close to flattening him like a pancake when he was out on his job. We would all breathe a sigh of relief when we saw him pull into the driveway in that old Plymouth automobile of his. And when he worked up in the mountains or far away from Reality, then we really worried about him until he would call us in the evenings to tell us that he was okay because the angry logs had missed him. He was really brave!

Those big logs scared me a lot, too, even when I was far away from them. When he would take me over the bridge and up the side of the mountain with him toward where he worked, he would put me on this really big truck, right in the roof over the cab I was, so that I wouldn't get run over or get lost way up there. There was a steel cage attached to the truck up there on top. When he put me inside the steel cage, there was no way I could fall out and hit the ground unless the truck itself turned over. And at the same time I had a clear view of the whole forest flowing around me, too. That was much fun to say the least, but I often felt like a tiny little squirrel locked in a cage when I was up there. My brother would say that I looked more like a little rat!

Dad would bring a lunch bag along with him which contained some sandwiches and some pickles among other things. He liked those pickles quite a lot. And so did most of the men that worked with him. There was one kind of pickle that he called a dill pickle. He told me that he and his friends would eat them all the time when they were my age. They had sweet ones, regular ones and dill ones. To this day I really don't know what a dill pickle really is. Do they grow that way on the vine? And if you have a choice, why wouldn't you eat sweet pickles instead? I could never quite figure it out, and I don't think I ever did.

I guess because my dad liked them so much, I tried to eat my share of those crunchy dill pickles, too. I tried to eat all kinds of pickles all the time, mostly to get my energy up when it was sagging, but that approach didn't work too well at all. My stomach definitely didn't like an excess of dill pickles, and most of the time they made me feel sick. Not real sick like making me stay in bed or anything like that. My stomach would just feel funny and start churning and I felt like throwing up. There was one time when it got a little bit worse. I probably shouldn't tell you about this, but what the heck. We have plenty of time, don't we?

I remember the time I went to attend my grandfather's funeral. I was a first-grader at the time, and I was surprised when my mother told me that I was going to skip school to attend the ceremony for my grandfather. It was the first time I had missed a day of school ever in my life so it made a big impression on me to say the least. Several of my friends had skipped school on occasion, but they were sick with a disease called the flu. Our teacher kept asking us how we felt almost every day after that. I know that she was afraid that we might catch the flu from other kids. She didn't want the whole class to stay home sick. She had much too much stuff to teach us. So we all tried to stay healthy just for her.

Then one day when Schultz didn't show up for his third grade class, all of us first-graders cheered wildly, to ourselves of course. The big rumor that swept through our class was that Schultz had caught a rare variety of flu virus and that he might be sick for weeks to come! I know it sounds really cruel, but we were all hoping for a very long absence. My brother called it a protracted absence. Maybe it would be months… at least until school was out for summer vacation. We had our dreams! You can imagine the depression that set in when he was out for only two days total! We definitely felt cheated by Mother Nature and the germs on that one.

Well, I didn't know my grandfather very well, but he had lived in Reality almost all of his life. He was my father's father, if you understand what I mean. People often referred to him as a *Founding Father*. Later, I learned that his name was on a plaque down at city hall. Now that meant that he was pretty important as far as the history of the town goes. I was proud of him to be sure.

People said that he was one of the first trappers and fur traders in this area of Alaska. Well, unfortunately, one day he died, and then in several days we went to his funeral. Dad said that his father had died too young, and he was very sad despite the fact that he and his father didn't get along very well at all. I never knew exactly what the dispute between them consisted of because no one, not even Mom or Paul, would tell me anything about it. I guess that's why I never got to know him very well before he died. That was definitely my loss.

It was in the summertime so we went to the funeral at the Reality Memorial Gardens. The funeral home, which is what mom called the place where we met other family members and friends of my grandfather, and the cemetery were located just across the river from the main part of Reality. It was where all the people in Reality who died went after they died. Needless to say, the subject of actually dying was one that I was quite uneasy with. So, I was a little apprehensive about the whole thing, it being my first funeral ever.

First, there was a viewing of his body and then what my Mother called a memorial service. Even the mayor of Reality was there in the crowd to give a farewell speech about grandpa and his life. After the memorial service ended, we went over to the cemetery for the burial.

Well, there we were standing silently watching the adults lower this box called his casket into the ground. My dad was one of the pallbearers along with my older brother Paul. What bothered me the most at the time was knowing that my grandfather was inside the box all by himself. A man in a dark suit said something about my grandfather's soul and things like that and then they slowly lowered the box into a deep hole in the ground and then threw dirt into the hole. Like I said, it was the first actual funeral I had ever been to in my life and the experience sure changed the way I thought about life itself. It was certainly very heavy stuff for a five or six year old kid to absorb for the first time and all at once.

Anyway, from the scene conducted at the cemetery we retired to the Timberline Tavern for lunch. What a relief! I remember that I didn't see a smile on anyone's face at least until we were well over the bridge once again and back in the main part of our town of Reality. One thing was certainly for sure as I viewed the many different faces of the people in attendance. Everyone who attended the funeral was glad it was over and was also very hungry.

Pastrami sandwiches, cheese dip, potato chips and dill pickles were the main items on the menu at the Timberline that day. My mother had already reserved tables for all us, and we sat down to eat without any hesitation. As I said, everyone seemed quite relieved that the funeral was over and done with and there was lots of talking and such going on. For myself, I just remained pretty quiet and listened to the adults talk about old times and grandpa's long and productive life while he was here. My dad kept passing the pickles to me, and I was very hungry just like everyone else, so I kept chomping them down along with lots of cold milk. I was really thirsty; I remember that and the milk went down very easily along with many potato chips along for the ride. I must admit that everything tasted real good.

My dad and mom liked the Timberline Tavern a lot as I already told you several times. Don't get me wrong. I liked it a lot, too. It was a major meeting place for the people of Reality and visitors. My mom often said that the place had great sentimental value for her and dad. Not only did mom work there part-time, but she said that it's where she got to know dad before they were married. My dad told me that he came to the Timberline Tavern to eat lunch on his very first day in Reality. He said that his father came with him and that he introduced him to mom.

That was a big moment because my dad had just moved to Reality from Quebec, which is in Canada as you probably already know. I knew that he must have lived near Montreal because both he and his father were rabid Canadians' hockey fans. But as I found out later, you don't have to live near Montreal to be a Canadians' fan. They have a worldwide following among hockey fans.

Dad was proud of Canada where he was born for sure, and proud of being a new American, too. I remember him telling me about the day he came into the Timberline to tell my mother that he was now officially a citizen of the United States of America just like my mother was. He was both real happy and very sad at the same time, if you can actually feel that way. But my mom reminded him that he could still be a Canadians' fan even if he was an American citizen and after that all was well for dad. But, she told me that she did whisper to him that he'd better not say that too loud when he's in Toronto or Boston or places like that!

Later, he even told me that he hoped I was playing for the Canadians when I grew up. The first problem with that was that I probably would have to learn how to speak French. When I mentioned that to him, he told me to be sure that I learned Canadian French and not French French. Wow, was I ever confused! Were there two separate versions of French?

Well, he said that they were the same languages until the French Revolution. Then, the Revolution among other things caused a lot of slang to enter the language. I knew what slang was...after I mentioned it to my mom, and she explained the concept to me. Well, he said that the French spoken in Canada was the purer French. I couldn't argue with him, and mom just shrugged her shoulders when I told her what he said. To this day I'm not sure whether he was just kidding me about the language or he actually believed what he said. That's something I'll have to work on if I ever get to visit the City of Montreal.

So, it was on his very first day when he came into the Timberline Tavern for lunch that my dad first saw my mom. He told me that when he saw her for the first time, he thought to himself that mom had the prettiest blue eyes he had ever seen. And when she first smiled at him, he almost fell off the barstool he was sitting on. That was it for old dad. Every night he would come to the Timberline to court my mother. He told me that he didn't miss a day. I guess that my mom didn't mind at all because she never complained about it.

One day, when he came to the Timberline Tavern for lunch and to see my mom, there were men there from Juneau. My dad said they were part of a survey party, you know, the guys who figure out where the roads and buildings go before they are built. My dad said that the State of Alaska was building a new highway that would pass near Reality. Everyone in town was excited because they said that business would double or triple for the town, especially the mining and lumber work. A new mine was already being developed nearby in the mountains and a new modern lumber mill was planned. The people in the know said there would be more jobs and money for everyone in Reality to share.

It took quite a while to finish the projects that were in the planning stage then, over ten years, but I was happy because when they actually did get finished, my dad gave me an increase in my allowance, which at the time was only a dollar a week. It was hard for a kid to get by on a dollar a week even in those days.

Well, anyway, one of the men at the bar asked my dad if he was a *Frog*. I've never seen dad look like a frog or croak like a frog. At least I never think he has ever done it even on Halloween. And mom and my brother and sisters and the mailman or anyone else never mentioned such behavior. Based upon that information, I am sure my dad was never an actual frog.

So, to answer the question in a manner that came as a big surprise to me, my dad looked the man square in the eyes and said *Yes, I am!* Onlookers have told the story of what happened next with lots of pride.

What happened next is a little fuzzy, but they say…whoever they is, that the man whispered something nasty to my dad, but he whispered the words loud enough so that quite a few bystanders could hear. It must have been something very bad because my dad proceeded to go over and pick the man up off his stool and hit him in the stomach, real hard. They say the man had a real big stomach to boot. When the man got up off the floor and took a wild swing with his fist at dad, a swing that missed, of course, dad hit him once again and this time the fat guy flew right out of the front door of the Timberline Tavern backwards and landed on his butt. As far as anyone in Reality knows, that's the last time anyone has ever confused my dad, or any Robespierre for that matter, with a frog.

Anyway, there I was at lunch right after having seen them lower my grandfather into the ground and after eating many pickles, dill pickles, as fast as my dad could pass them to me, and slurping down milk and gobbling potato chips just as fast. Everyone seemed to be having fun talking to each other about my grandfather and his very successful life in Reality. It was pretty apparent that they were just really glad to have the whole funeral over with once and for all because it was so depressing standing out there in the graveyard and watching that box go into the ground carrying someone they loved inside of it.

Once the post-funeral brunch had run its course, we went out and got into my cousin Bill's brand new car. He was in town with my Aunt Lucille for the funeral, and he was so proud of his new possession. The car was a light blue in color as I remember, but I don't recall what make it was except that I think it was a Cadillac. They put me in the back seat with my aunt. My aunt remarked how much she liked the smell of a new car as she took a deep breath. My cousin and my dad rode up front. My mom was in our car with some friends of hers. We were all going to our house for dessert and coffee as if we hadn't already had enough to eat.

I guess it was that first bump by the bridge that actually did it to me. You know how you feel when you are riding a roller coaster and you get to the top of that really high part and you start looking down the tracks. When you finally start to go down, screaming as you go, your stomach stays behind at the top of the hill. At least mine always does when I do those rides. At times stomachs can be very smart, but it doesn't always work out well for the owner of the stomach.

So, when we hit that big bump, while going pretty fast I might add, my stomach started to tell me that something was very, very wrong. I tried to signal my dad concerning my new problem, but he wouldn't listen and neither would my cousin. They were too busy testing the speed and maneuverability of the new car, which my cousin said handled like a dream. They told me to hold on until we got to our house. That would turn out to be a big mistake for all of us!

My Aunt Lucille just stared at me and smiled like she always did. She said something about dill pickles, but the noise of the car on the gravel road drowned her out as my cousin picked up speed and began turning corners faster and faster.

Well, you know how that waiting thing goes when you are a little kid. My stomach was in no mood to wait for anything, so it just let go. It was awful. I puked all over the back seat of my cousin's brand new car! Half-chewed pastrami, potato chips, and, worst of all, pieces of dill pickle shot and poured all over the back seat of the car. I barfed, my cousin yelled, my aunt screamed, and my dad started laughing and quickly rolled down his window. By some stroke of luck I missed hitting my aunt who was rapidly shrinking into her side of the back seat. I don't think that my cousin Bill appreciated the joke very much because after that he never did talk about it. As I remember, I don't think he ever brought his car over to our house again. And he certainly never ever offered me a ride anywhere. I can hardly blame him.

Believe it or not, the worst part of this sequence of events was yet to come. After he stopped laughing hysterically, my dad told me in no uncertain terms that I was going to clean up the mess in my cousin's vehicle as soon as we got home. When my mother saw me, she said that my face was green, a sick looking yellow-green color to be exact! Later, after it was almost all over, she described my face as looking like a bowl of her favorite split pea soup. Ever since that incident I haven't been able to stomach split pea soup no matter who made it. I can't even look straight at a bowl of the stuff without my stomach rolling over. To this day even green tea, which is nothing like split pea soup and is supposed to be good for you, makes me a little bit queasy.

Mom just grabbed me without saying another word and took me inside to the shower. She made me throw all of my soggy clothes into the washing machine and then made me take a long, hot shower using lots of soap. Then, she gave me two tablespoons of some dark syrup out of a bottle and quickly put me to bed.

I didn't complain at all. It was my best means of escape. There was no way I wanted to face the awful task of cleaning out my cousin's car. My cousin had to do it. He got a little help from my dad, but not a lot according to my mother. My dad wanted me to be responsible for what I had done, but my mother stopped him dead in his tracks. My mom just winked at me as I crawled into bed, and I just stayed under the covers waiting for the mess to be cleaned up before I got up.

My dad promised my cousin that I would wash and wax his car for him the next time he visited Reality, but my cousin said something about not doing him any big favors. I could hear them talking because my bedroom door was open, and it was close to the living room. I couldn't quite figure out what my cousin meant by 'favors', but luckily he told my mom and dad that he had to leave and before long my aunt and cousin were headed out of town. The crisis was over…for the moment.

I never barfed in my dad's car. I made sure of that because I probably would have been dead meat had I done so. He loved his car very much. It was old, and he called it a beater in a very loving way. He said that all old cars that were still running were properly called beaters. I guess they must have gotten the name from an egg-beater. My mom had an old egg-beater; it made a funny noise when she used it, a noise just like the car made when my dad started it. The car was an old Plymouth with two doors. I think it was a 1961 model, but I don't remember right now. It doesn't really matter does it? You'll know a beater when you see one.

During the winter when it would snow a real lot, my dad would wait for the snowplow to go by our house before he could go to work. After I got to third grade, it was my job to shovel the driveway. I think I told you that stuff already? I would get up early and do the shoveling while he was eating breakfast with my mom and older brother. He would have oatmeal almost every day with lots and lots of raisins in the bowl. He said the raisins were good for your digestion. I could only agree with him on that. I didn't mind shoveling the driveway because I didn't particularly like the smell of cooked oatmeal. And if you let it sit for a while, the oatmeal would turn into rubber! I began to wonder if it did that in your stomach after you ate it?

Once he would get into his car, he would drive by the houses where his co-workers lived to see if they needed help to get to work with a push. My dad said that the Plymouth beater was as good as any four-wheel drive in existence. The people he pulled or pushed out of snowdrifts soon became believers, too. Everyone in Reality knew the car by sight.

Ah, my head is starting to hurt again. I'm just lying here on this gurney next to this x-ray machine, but nothing much has happened unless I dozed off there for a few minutes. The ice in the plastic bag on my eye has all melted and the water is leaking a little, and there's no one around to change the bag and give me some fresh ice. Never any help when I need it.

I can still hear them making all kinds of noise next door unless I'm imagining it. I could sure go for some of that Champagne right now, that Dom… something. The last name starts with the letter 'P'. Or even just a little water to drink would do. All of a sudden I'm really thirsty. Where is the guy in the uniform? He's got a three on his back as I remember, and his first name is Paul, I think? I can move my arm pretty good now, my right arm, that is.

Ouch! I touched my forehead, and it hurts like mad. My eye is all puffy and swollen shut. My forehead feels black and blue just like my ribs do. Is there any part of me that isn't broken yet?

Hey! What's this? It feels like stitches. Stitches in my forehead! I don't remember anyone doing that to me. I thread is so thick that I can almost count them. Two, four, seven, nine, eleven, twelve! Feels like twelve stitches in my head. Whoever or whatever hit me is gonna pay big time when I find out what happened. Any more stitches on my forehead, and I will be looking like the Frankenstein monster!

Ah, here comes that doctor again along with a couple of burly guys. They are pushing another flat thing that looks like a stretcher. Hey, they're picking me up and moving me over to it. Ah, it feels cooler and is softer, that's for sure. Here comes another bag of ice. Whoa, we're moving. They're rolling me out into the hallway. Wonder what's up?

12

Ridgeline

Photons fly through the air and into my eyes,
Yet, all I see with them are stormy skies.
And my brain is riddled with strange haunting dreams
That change my life into a nightmare it seems.

Lying here in this bed, at whatever hospital this is, sure feels nice. I sure would like to sleep because my head still aches, but that storm outside with all that thunder is making it tough to relax. Ah, the storms of South Florida. Hurricane season is what they talk about all the time down here. Not much in the way of menacing hurricanes up in Reality, Alaska, that's for sure. But we did have some strange thunderstorms up north especially in the early springtime.

The roar and clap of thunder would echo through the canyons of the mountain range on a regular basis. To me it always sounded like the drummer in a rock band playing a solo just for my entertainment. I always said it was someone like Alex Van Halen or the great drummer from the band Black Sabbath. My mother would always shake her head back and forth whenever I gave the thunder a name like that. But then she would break into a smile.

I can remember, and won't ever soon forget, that day back in May of 1981. I think that I was just about 12 years old at the time. Something like that anyway. There was still a lot of snow on the ground because we were still having snow-storms, although not nearly as many or as heavy as earlier in the year. Most years the big snows were over by April Fool's

Day so I would stash my sled safely in the back of the garage and break out my bike about then.

That particular night I awoke to the sound of distant thunder in the nearby mountains. Like I said, thunder was not really uncommon in Alaska, but this thunder sounded different from the usual thunder for some reason I couldn't put my finger on. It was deep sounding and seemed to rumble on forever and ever. This definitely wasn't my usual rock and roll drummer practicing for a gig.

Brilliant flashes of lightning lit up the entire sky, too! I was having real trouble sleeping anyway because I had a game coming up in the following afternoon, and I was a bit nervous about that as usual. I always seemed to have those crazy butterflies the day, and night, before an important game. I was not sure why this was happening to me? But for some strange and unexplained reason Paul always said it was good luck to have butterflies before the game but not during the game. The time you don't, he would say, was the time you didn't care enough to play your very, very best. Paul, always the wise one about such things for sure!

It stormed most of the night and I lay in bed watching the light flashes dart across the ceiling of my bedroom like dancing ghosts. The patterns were actually very entertaining and reminded me of our annual Fourth of July fireworks celebrations. Most of the bright colors of fireworks were missing, however, and the sound of the thunder didn't match the light at all.

But this time I knew exactly why. My mom told me that light travels much faster than sound. I had always wondered why they didn't travel together since they seemed to be partners. She told me I would see the light coming first and hear the sound later. It all depended on how far away the lightning strike was. My friends were in awe when I explained it to them in great detail. Physics is what my father called it. It felt good to feel smart, especially in front of your friends or the teacher!

I finally fell back asleep at 4:12 in the morning. I remember that time because of that darn clock radio with the bright red numbers that told the time to me. Every time I would wake in the middle of the night, I would be facing that silly clock! It just never failed no matter what. It had a battery backup so that the display would stay on even when we lost electrical power in Reality.

I rolled out of bed at 7:00 in the AM to the smell of food cooking downstairs in the kitchen. The morning seemed normal enough at first, except that something undefined felt out of place once I was up and moving around. It was Saturday morning and as usual Mom was busy in the kitchen fixing the usual Robespierre breakfast fare of oatmeal, flapjacks, eggs, svidki (my favorite), ham and sausage. That's one thing about us Robespierres; we loved to eat breakfast and eat a lot we certainly did! But I figured it was okay because I could run the fat off by skating a lot and riding my bike. I glanced down at my stomach just in case, but there was no immediate cause for alarm. I wasn't overweight like Frank and some of my other friends. That was a very comforting feeling to say the least. Dani and Seal seemed content enough playing by the fireplace as they usually did, but Paul was definitely on edge for some reason. He was staring out of the front window and then began to pace, back and forth again and again like our dog would when he wanted to go outside to do his business.

This, indeed, was strange behavior for my older brother. I also noticed that dad wasn't around anywhere. Maybe that was the reason for Paul's behavior? Did they have a fight, and dad left the house without him? I'd have to be careful so that Paul wouldn't get mad at me for asking about it.

"Paul!" I said a little too loudly. "Where's dad? It's Saturday morning and you, me and dad are supposed to head to the lake to practice before my game later this afternoon. The ice is still hard, but he told me that a warm front was coming in tonight and after that the lake ice would melt. I can't believe we can still skate out there this late in the year."

Paul didn't answer. He just kept looking out the front window while in deep meditation. Fresh snow had quietly fallen during the night. I was thinking how strange that was with all that thunder and lightning going on outside. This was a very strange year for the weather.

I walked over to the dining room table and grabbed a piece of sausage from one of the plates. Boy, it tasted good for sure! What a way to start a day, especially a Saturday. I wanted to grab a second one for myself, but I knew my mom wanted me to wait so I sat down next to her to wait my turn.

"Mom, is everything okay? Everyone seems so glum and down and out. I mean, dad isn't here like he usually is, and Paul is definitely acting a bit strange, eh? What's up that's causing this?"

She didn't respond to me immediately, and I realized that I was probably talking too much, as usual. Something was very wrong. So, finally I shut my mouth and waited for her to explain things on her own terms.

"The storm last night caused a fire at the mill up in the mountains," she said very quietly. "Your father along with his work crew had to head up to the ridgeline to assist in the fire-fighting efforts before the damage got too great. He left a few hours ago, and Paul is just worried, I guess. Your brother wanted to go along, too, but dad said he should wait here. If reinforcements were needed, Paul would get his chance to fight the blaze. Now all we can do is wait until someone calls to tell us what's going on."

That would explain it for sure. Paul and dad were real close when it came to working. About as close as me and Paul, you could say. That's not to say that dad and I weren't close. We were, but there is something about the oldest boy of a family and his relationship to his father. It's a special relationship that can get competitive as the oldest son grows up. At least that's what mom said to me, and I know that she definitely understands these things.

But, why was my brother acting so strangely on this particular morning? I mean, dad has gone up to the ridge at least a dozen times to take care of fires, crew fights, wildlife problems, and stuff like that and he never takes Paul at the beginning of the emergency or project. It's definitely a dad's job to assess the dangers first. What's so different about this day?

After a few minutes we all sat down at the table for our breakfasts, but the usual breakfast talk wasn't there at all. The girls were playing with their dolls and food at the table, which always got the best of mom, and Paul just sat quietly eating without looking up or saying a word to any of us. It seemed like he was just muttering something under his breath. This wasn't good! Here I had a huge game this afternoon against the team from Prudhoe Bay, the number one in our division. It would be our last chance to knock them down a peg or two. And, of all days, dad isn't here to motivate me, and Paul is lost in outer space. Unconsciously, I began to grit and grind my teeth. I knew that I would have to grow up and fast and that it wouldn't be easy.

The silence at the breakfast table was suddenly broken by the sound of the phone ringing off the hook. Mom literally jumped up and raced over to pick it up. She turned her head to look out the kitchen window so I couldn't hear what she was saying as she spoke. I could always read her face real well. I could tell if things were good or bad even when she tried to disguise her appearance. But she was smart enough to keep her face turned away from me.

I looked over at Paul, and he was staring right at her as if he knew what was being said over the phone. I started feeling very sick to my stomach as I read his face. He reflected a feeling that something very bad had happened up on the ridge. Mom hung up the phone and returned to the table. At least she was smiling, so a bit of tension in the room, for me anyway, was gone at least momentarily.

She told us that dad was all right, but more help was needed on the ridgeline to quell the fire. Reinforcements must be called up! That was what Paul and dad called the second wave of defense. She said he was sending a truck down to pick up some of the older boys and other men to help in removing timber and clearing more of the roadway so that the big timber front-loading trucks could get in.

Paul jumped up from the table and ran to his room as I followed in close pursuit. I wanted to help him get ready. Some day it would be my job to join the *Reinforcements*. As we reached his room, I decided to ask the big question that was bouncing around in my brain all morning.

"What about practice today, Paul? What should we do? Are they going to call off the game?"

He sat on the edge of his bed putting on his boots and knowingly smiled at me. It was just amazing. He always had the answers to my questions no matter what the situation or how difficult.

"You, Alfie and Frank can handle it. But most important of all, work on your hip checking with that Alfie kid today. The boys from Prudhoe Bay are fast and will use the boards for forward movement. That will be your chance to blast the kid coming down. Keep your eyes on his body movements and not so much on the puck. Stay on target and a bit low on the approach. You know the rest. You want to hit him on the waist as you're coming up. That way you will be left standing. He will be eating snow, and you won't get a tripping penalty in the process!"

He got up, grabbed his jacket from off the table. Then he hesitated and turned back toward me for one last shot.

"Jean-Luc, you're in charge when dad and I are gone. Remember that! Help our mom and our sisters whenever they need it. Soon, you will be an adult, and this is good practice for you. Make us proud of you!"

I nodded my head vigorously, but before I could speak to reassure him, we were interrupted. There was a knock at the front door. It was Mr. Malazone and Frank with the truck here to pick up Paul. Wow, I thought, even the butcher is heading up to the ridge for this one. This fire must be very serious because he was usually the last man called out on in this type of situation. Paul gave mom a big hug and a kiss. As Paul stood at the front door, he grabbed his favorite hockey stick that was leaning against the wall and handed to me.

"Here, use this in today's game. Remember, check, check, check! Don't let those suckers cross the blue line with the puck, not standing anyway! And remember to use the blueline special I taught you if you're on the power play. Keep the shot low like I showed you so that the forwards have a chance to tip it in past the goalie. Remember, shoot hard, skate hard and check hard!"

As the truck left for the ridgeline, Alfie showed up at the house. He must have smelled that breakfast was ready. That boy could eat, too! Maybe he was a Robespierre, and I didn't know it. Alfie schmoozed my mom to get a plate of food as he always did, and it worked as usual. That was something you never had to do with my mom to get fed. She would feed anything that was hungry and alive and in our kitchen. Between the Timberline and home, she fed more people than anyone in Reality bar none. And the food was always extremely good!

Frank and I sat by the fireplace as Alfie ate his breakfast, and we talked about this afternoon's game. Frank was a bit nervous about the situation and with good cause. Prudhoe led the division in goals, shots on goal, scoring chances, and just about ever other statistic you can mention or imagine. Those were statistics a goaltender really shouldn't think about on game day, but I seized the opportunity to make it a positive just like Paul would have had he been there.

"Frank, the more shots they take at you, the more you can stop. And the more you stop, the better is your save percentage. A high save percentage is surely any goalie's very best friend."

He seemed to like the idea as a smile broke out on his face, and he obviously started to relax.

"Bring'em on!" Frank shouted with all he had. "Lots of shots but no rebounds. You know that a rebound is the best pass in hockey, and I don't give rebounds to anyone! I heard Denis Potvin say that on the radio."

Frank and I continued our discussion of goaltending techniques. It was really important for goalies and defensemen to communicate well on and off the ice. Frank's voice had little high-pitch shrieks in it when he was excited which made it easy to recognize during a game even with a noisy crowd and the sounds of skates and sticks pounding the ice.

Alfie finally finished his second plate of chow, and soon we were off to the lake for practice. I had two sticks of my own, but it was my brother's stick that I wanted to test out for sure. I just knew I'd love it from the moment I laid my hands on it. Wouldn't he be proud if I got a hat-trick the first time I used it! That's three goals in the same game. Better yet, a natural hat-trick would do the trick even better. That's three consecutive goals by the same player! Wow! My mind was spinning with the possibilities that lay ahead.

I wasn't sure if any of the others guys, or Coach Grimes, would be there on account of the call-up for the fire up in the mountains. Practice on game day was an option and up to Coach Grimes, anyway. He would usually pick a few names to show up to work on skills they were lacking in. For me, I always practiced and always was on the ice before anyone else showed up. Paul was a main reason for that. Practice, practice, practice! He was my real coach.

We arrived at the lake early, and there was nobody there yet. My first thought was that our coach was up helping fight the fire on the ridgeline, too. We'd probably have to hold this game day practice on our own. So I seized the initiative. First, I made Frank shovel the snow off the area we used as a rink telling him that was a great way to loosen up, something he would have to do this afternoon before game-time anyway. He was all for it. The ice was still fine with the temperature in the low 20's.

I knew it would be up to me to cut back on Frank's workload in front of the net against Prudhoe Bay. Alfie already had his skates on, and he was stretching. Alfie, as aloof as he appeared, was very serious when it came to playing hockey. When our coach taught us something new, he was always the first on the team to pick it up. My big advantage over Alfie was that I had my brother Paul as an assistant coach. He taught me some of the more subtle techniques needed by a young defensemen well before anyone else learned them.

But Alfie was a fast skater with great hands and a nose for the puck. He particularly loved playing right wing even though he was left-handed. And he wasn't afraid to come back to play defense. I always appreciated his quickness on getting back to the defensive zone to help me out. We played on the same side of the ice usually, and we worked very well together. Several goals of Alfie's this season have my name on them for an assist. Alfie and I were a 'one-two' punch that was hard to beat as Paul would say! Paul would tell me to make the breakout pass and follow up for the rebound. Boy, that was really good advice.

Frank finally finished his shoveling with a smile. Alfie and I were stretched and already passing the puck back and forth. A bit of puck passing, then sprints, followed by more puck passing and more sprints. We also needed to work with Frank this morning. I knew that this was a great time for me to practice my ever-improving 'blue line special' just as Paul told me before he left. It was a slap shot from the blue line that Paul and I have been working on.

We would get dad to help by just standing there in net with me blasting pucks at him! He did that all the time when I was a tot, and there was no danger from my shots. I was just trying to get the puck all the way to the net. We let him wear a mask and pads now so he wouldn't get hurt because I was developing what Paul called a 'heavy' shot. Boy, how many kids would just love to do that to their old man?

I needed to work on my checking against Alfie, too. He, of course, had no clue as to that kind of practice, but he was certainly going to find out! The snow banks on the north side of the lake were big and soft so I could hit Alfie pretty hard and not make him too mad or get him injured.

Frank looked bored standing in front of the net, so I told Alfie it was pepper time! Alfie smiled, and we charged the net each with a puck. Right off the bat we caught Frank by surprise as we both got off blistering wrist shots at the same time. Talk about floundering! Frank butter-flied, both arms out stretched with his stick flying in the air, and then he fell straight backwards!

If I only had a camera to capture that one! Geez, the poor guy was stunned. After those shots I was laughing so hard that I skated right into the snow bank behind the goal as did Alfie! As I got up, I saw both pucks sitting inside the net.

SCORE! Frank just shouted 'Shut up you guys!' but then he started laughing to himself when he saw us buried in the snow.

We all regained our composure and began the one-on-one drill our coach stressed so much. Alfie would come down ice, and I would do my thing as he tried to get a shot off. I enjoyed this drill. I got to work on backward movements, agility and stick work not to mention some checking action! But I had to be careful because Alfie had some slick moves of his own. He liked to dip his shoulder and drag the puck with his rear skate whenever the defenseman got too close. Then he would shovel the puck ahead and break around his foe only to pick up the puck behind the defenseman and skate in on a surprised goalie.

Alfie experienced first hand my hip-checking action on this day. Down the ice he came moving the puck back and forth with each stride waiting for me to bite. Man, that Alfie could skate like the wind. Skating backwards as fast as I could, I kept my eyes on Alfie and that puck. My stick was out front and to the sides with every move Alfie made, but I didn't get too close.

At the spot where our blue-line would be on a regulation rink, here came my chance. Alfie dipped his shoulder and cut to the outside and then turned on the speed. I knew his next move would be to shift his weight and move into the slot to get the shot off. He never had the chance!

I shifted my body to a lower center of gravity, lowered my left shoulder with my eyes still on Alfie. I remembered Paul telling me to play the man and not the puck in this situation. 'Hold, hold, hold, wait…wait' I could hear Paul whisper. At just the right moment I lifted my upper body and shifted into his path bringing my left hip into Alfie's left hip.

BAM! Into the air and then down goes Alfie into the snow! His stick was tumbling end over end in the air. And the puck? I had the puck! I heard a loud hoot from behind me. Frank witnessed the whole thing and was banging his goalie stick on the ice. Then, he came skating over to see if Alfie was still alive. He was. Just had the wind knocked out him is all.

"Holy cow, Luc!" Frank yelled. "I've never seen you crack anyone that hard before. That was awesome. Where did you learn how to do that?"

I told Frank that my brother Paul was the source and that his hip-checking idol was Bob Plager of the St. Louis Blues.

We helped Alfie to his feet, and he brushed off the snow. Then, he proceeded to punch me in the arm! I laughed and asked him if he would care to try the one-on-one drill again. He just smiled sheepishly and declined. It was about time to head over to the Timberline Tavern for lunch and get an update on the fire and this afternoon's game. I probably didn't need to, but as we left, I reminded Alfie to keep his head up when he was buzzing down the ice!

The game was going to be held at our rink behind the school. The town's folk chipped in and made our rink really nice with new bleachers, lights and a concession stand with all proceeds from the games benefiting our school's hockey program. As much as I liked traveling to games, I really preferred playing at home. You didn't have to go far for a hot shower, and victories, and even the occasional loss, were celebrated at the Timberline just a mere two blocks from the rink.

Typically, the Saturday afternoon games at home were scheduled to start at 4:00 in the afternoon. Our team would meet at the Timberline at 1:00 for a team meeting, roster check and lunch. Pre-skate started at 3:30 with the puck drop at 4:00 as I said. It was now 12:30 so the three of us packed up our gear and began walking to the Timberline Tavern. My mom would be there, and I could find out what was going on with dad and Paul.

We arrived just as several of the other guys and their dads did. Mom, Dani and Seal were already there, but Dad and Paul were nowhere to be seen. Mr. Malazone was back from the ridgeline and was preparing the grill out back to cook up his 'World Famous Malazone Burgers'. These things were huge with the meat hanging over the edges of the bun! There was some kind of spice in there as well as chunks of onions. One of those was all I could eat, but Alfie, well, there was a different story. His record before a game was three Malazone Burgers with all the fixings! Hard to believe that boy could skate after consuming all of that food.

I asked my mom, "Any word from Dad and Paul?"

She said, "Yes, they called about an hour ago and said that the fire did more damage than was first thought. They're working as hard as they can so they can make the game this afternoon. Oh, Paul wanted to know how Alfie was feeling. Is he not feeling well, Luc?"

I just looked over at Alfie, smiled and said, "Oh, he's fine, Mom. Just fine!"

Coach Grimes came in, his face covered with black soot.

"Okay, fellas, gather round. I have this afternoon's game roster."

My heart was in my throat. How I wanted my name to be called to start on defense with the first line.

"Frank, you, of course, are in goal. Alfie and Alvin, you are our starting wings. Where is John Olsen? Right, you will start today at center. As for defense, let's go with Billy Mitchels and, ah, Jean-Luc. Go grab some burgers, and I will work on the other lines and let the rest of you know before the pre-game skate."

I got the starting call! Man, I was on cloud nine! Paul had to make this game. He deserved all the credit. And I wanted to show him my hip check in a real game situation.

13
My Friend Vladi

Sometimes the good things in life come to you from afar,
From across town or across country or even from a star.
Their faces and names are different, but their dreams are a match,
And they often race past your face trying to make their catch.

I haven't said much about one of my most interesting friends. His name is Vladi, and he came to Reality when he was a kid. I remember his story so well it's as if he were standing right here telling me the gory details. Even though I wasn't there, I can hear his father's words as clearly as if my father had spoken them.

"Vladi. Vladi, wake up, my son. Look out the window! These beautiful mountains below are going to be our new home. It's America, Vladi, America! Alaska! We are getting very close, Vladi. Wake up now. You have been sleeping for several hours. You must look, Vladi. This is a once in a lifetime chance to look at our new homeland for the first time as it spreads before us."

Alaskan Cargo Air flight 2430 gently banked to the right approximately an hour of flight time from the Fairbanks International Airport. Among the 75 passengers and crew on board, mostly oil executives and a crew of eight, were Serge Zhashnilov and his young son Vladislav. The Russian built Douglas DC-3 was flying at twenty-eight thousand feet, en route from Surgut, Russia on its way to Fairbanks, Alaska. The total trip would be a distance of fifty-eight hundred kilometers give or take a few kilometers. The stop to refuel in the northern Russian town of Tiksi on the coast of the Laptevas Sea was a welcome relief. There in the snow, they took on a group of additional passengers and some additional cargo consisting of fittings and valves on their way to the new Alaskan Pipeline which was under construction and that everyone was talking about.

"I was just dreaming like I always do, Papa", Vladi mumbled followed by a big relaxing yawn.

"And what were you dreaming about this time my dear son. Were you dreaming of your very new home, your many new friends you haven't yet met, and a new school where you will study and that awaits you in the future? Perhaps you were dreaming once again of playing ice hockey as you did so well back in Surgut."

"No, Papa. Actually, I was dreaming of my dear Momma and how I wish so much that she were going to America with us at this very moment. I do certainly miss her very, very much."

Serge Zhashnilov instantly felt his heart suddenly become heavy and tears began to form in his eyes, tears he could not hold back even in the presence of his son.

"Yes, Vladi, I too wish she were with us. But you know, Vladi, she is with us and will be with us always. She watches over both of us from high above in the heavens, keeping an eye on each of us, protecting us from danger and loving us every moment. You know this to be true, don't you, Vladi?"

Serge knew that it was a question he didn't need to ask.

"Yes, Papa. I know. Momma is a beautiful angel, and she loves us."

The young Russian boy so far from home for the first time in his life laid his tired head against the cold window and gazed out at the passing clouds and the snow covered mountains below. Tears, too, were forming in his young eyes as he realized just how much he missed his beloved mother.

Serge looked over at his son and noticed that his child's eyes were once again closed. How peacefully this boy could sleep, he thought to himself. It did make sense, though. The past few months had been a difficult time for his only son, and restful sleep provided a much needed escape from the harsh edges of reality. Serge hoped that this trip with all of its new experiences would provide a soft and mellow distraction to both their overwhelming senses of grief.

His eyes were growing heavy again so Serge Zhashnilov decided to sleep for the remainder of this flight. His thoughts and dreams were filled with images of what lay ahead and of what they had left behind. Was he making the right decision for his son and himself? He began to drift into a dream of his past.

"Serge! Serge, wake up! You'll be late for school!" his mother said in a somewhat loud voice as she nudged his shoulder.

"I'm awake, Momma. Tell me…is Pappa home? Does he know that I have again overslept?"

His mother gently ran her hands through Serge's hair.

"No, Serge. He didn't come home again last night. He went out with the men all night, again. But, you must hurry, Serge, and get ready for school before he comes home. You know how he is after he's been drinking all night long. He will be very, very angry with you and also with me, Serge. You hurry now, and I will prepare you a quick breakfast for you to take with you."

Serge sat on the edge of his bed rubbing his eyes. He fell back on the bed and stared up at the ceiling he knew so well.

What's the use of going to school, anyway, he thought to himself. His father made it clear that this would be his last year in the local school, and that he would be taking an apprentice position at the refinery working under him, just has he did with his father. Serge had no voice in this decision.

Gone would be the times spent with his many friends after school skating and playing hockey in the winter. His father didn't like hockey at all, and frowned at Serge every time he came home from the river.

"You should be working instead of playing that stupid game with your friends!" he would mumble under his alcoholic breath.

Gone, too, would be all things teenagers enjoy, though in Eastern Russia, at least in Surgut, anyway, there wasn't much to choose from. But, the point was very clear to Serge. At age sixteen, he didn't want to spend the rest of his life like his father and grandfather, wasting his life away working at the oil refinery all day long and drinking all night to try to forget the day. There had to be a much better life somewhere else on this vast planet.

"Serge"! His mother's voice was heard from the kitchen. "Your breakfast is packed. Are you ready to leave?"

Serge reluctantly picked up his trousers and shirt from the chair next to the bed and quickly put them on.

"Yes, Mama. I'm coming."

He gave his mother a loving hug and a soft kiss on her cheek as he grabbed the satchel full of breakfast food from the kitchen table.

"Serge, do not forget your knapsack with your school books!"

He looked at her, and she knew what he was feeling. She knew he was very unhappy. She just gave him a smile and handed him the knapsack.

The walk to school took about 20 minutes along the Ob River. In the winter, small areas of the river would freeze as long as the big oil tankers weren't running. Oh, how Serge and his friends would skate and play hockey for hours in the winter on those islands of ice!

As he walked along the river, Serge saw the two makeshift hockey goals up on the bank behind a clump of trees. As he continued to walk, he wondered to himself if he would ever have the time to play this wonderful game ever again.

A cold wind began to blow and Serge raised the collar of his jacket around his neck. Winter would be here soon enough, he thought, as he sat down to rest on a worn wooden bench overlooking the river.

From this vantage point he could see the bridge that connected Surgut with Nefteyugansk. The oil company discovered a large reserve of oil there just a couple of years ago, and it wasn't long before more was found all over the region. Serge's father would work there, as well, since there weren't many skilled refinery maintenance workers around, and they were certainly needed.

There was no doubt in Serge's mind that unless a miracle occurred and soon, he would spend his life here working as an oil refinery maintenance apprentice in Nefteyugansk and Surgut, Russia.

Ivan Zhashnilov, Serge's father, kept his promise. Serge didn't return to school that next year. As a matter of fact, at age sixteen in December of 1963, Serge and his father walked into the office of the Surgutoilco mid-river oil refinery and filled out the application for the maintenance apprentice position.

Working in the oil refining business, especially in the maintenance department, was demanding work, both physically and mentally. Over the years, this labor would take its toll on many of his fellow workers. Very little in the form of health care services were available to the workers in those days.

Ivan Zhashnilov's health began to fail him just two years after Serge began working for him. His health, actually, had been declining under the surface for some time. Years of physical labor, extremely cold winters, excess smoking, and a perpetual love for vodka had caught up with him.

"Papa? Are you O.K.? What is wrong with your leg? Why are you walking like that?"

Serge and his father were walking home from work when Serge noticed his father limping and favoring his left leg.

"There is nothing wrong with me or my leg. Now mind your own business. Open the door for your father!"

Serge opened the front door of their home and tried to help his father up the three stairs leading to the door.

"Stop that, boy!" his father bellowed. "I can do this myself! I do not need your help now or ever!"

This is the way it always was. Serge and his father never seemed to get along well in any situation.

Over the next several weeks, Ivan's health became even worse. He could no longer walk at all. It had been determined by the refinery health council that he had gangrene of the left lower extremity, severe in the foot, caused by diabetes likely secondary to his alcohol abuse. This was terrible news.

His mental status also became affected at the same time. He even had trouble recognizing his wife, Olga, to whom he'd been married more than twenty-five years. He no longer was able to work, and soon the benefits, which weren't much to begin with, ran out. There was nothing the health council could do to help him. Even if there were operations that might help, they would cost too much money and in Surgut, there wasn't a single skilled surgeon available to perform them.

Serge now found himself supporting his family. His mother and his father, who never showed him any respect, were now dependent on an eighteen year old young man for their survival.

Ivan Zhashnilov died in the summer of 1966 at home with his wife Olga by his bedside. Serge, sitting in a chair in the corner of the bedroom showing no emotion, got up and walked out the front door and headed to the river. It was a place that for three years he hadn't seen except during his walks to and from the refinery.

Once there he sat quietly on the bank and stared into the rippling water. Oil tankers slowly made their way up and down the river in front of him, but he hardly noticed them in his remorse.

'What was going to happen now?" he thought aloud to himself. "What am I supposed to do now that my father has passed?"

The answers did not come immediately.

The funeral for his father was a small and quiet event as most are in this Siberian region of Russia. A handful of people from the refinery, most were the men he worked with, and a few neighbors came to bid him a final farewell. Ivan never made any long lasting friends.

He was buried in an old cemetery where most with no money are laid to rest. As a matter of fact, nearly everyone that has died in Surgut over the past 200 years or more is probably buried there.

Nevertheless, Serge's position and status at the refinery were very good. He was a quick study and was given more responsibility than most apprentices. He was trusted by his supervisors and had excellent reviews each time one was given. He knew he needed to end his apprenticeship, and ask for a promotion so that he could make more money to support himself and his mother.

On his nineteenth birthday, Serge walked into the office of Mikhail Sidorov, the foreman of operations.

"Yes? Can I help you?" the woman at the desk asked.

"Is Mr. Sidorov in, please? I would like to speak with him for a moment, if I may. My name is Serge Zhashnilov. My father was...."

"Ah, yes. Please have a seat over there, and I will see if Mr. Sidorov can see you this morning".

Serge sat looking out of the window of this small dark office. The smell of crude oil filled the room as it always did.

Mr. Sidorov had only met Serge maybe twice before this eventful day. Once was when he and his dad came in to fill out the apprentice application which began Serge's employment. The other time was a brief encounter at his father's funeral.

Mikhail Sidorov had been in the oil and gas business his whole life as many growing up here have. He was a large man with rugged facial features and calloused hands and crooked fingers. He and Serge's father's relationship did go back to their childhood, and were both apprentices at roughly the same time. Ivan never saw the need to expand his career, but Mikhail did.

Mikhail Sidorov's younger brother, Alexander, would become the Mayor of Surgut in 1996.

"You can come in now. Mr. Sidorov is now ready to see you."

Serge, a bit nervous, entered his office. Mikhail was busy on the phone, but he extended his hand. They both shook enthusiastically, and then he motioned for Serge to take a seat on the padded chair in front of the desk.

Sitting there for what seemed to be hours was only about two minutes when the phone conversation was over.

"How are you doing, Serge? How is your mother? Are you getting along all right?"

"Yes, sir. I am doing well, and my mother, well she is holding up well, too, I suppose. She spends much of her time with her sister in Nefteyugansk, which is good for her. She doesn't do well alone, and with me working two shifts a day, her sister gives her companionship."

"I see. Working two shifts?" He sorted through a stack of papers and files pulling one file with Serge's name on it.

"You have been doing very well, I see, Serge. Attendance, productivity, everything is excellent. So, what can I do for you today, Serge?"

"Mr. Sidorov, sir. I have been an apprentice now for three years. I know the program is completed at four years, but with all the double shifts overtime and high marks from my supervisors, I thought it was time for me to move to something bigger. And, if I may be honest, sir, I'd like to make more money to support my mother and myself. I know this is asking much of you, Mr. Sidorov. But I would appreciate any consideration."

Leaning back in his high back chair, Mr. Sidorov smiled at Serge and began to laugh.

"You know, Serge. Your father and I go back to when we were just small boys here. You know that, Serge?"

Serge nodded.

"He was a good man, your father. A bit on the hard side, and he drank too much vodka. I can only imagine how he was at home. But, a good man and a good worker who spent all his years right here at this refinery. I never had any real trouble with him, and his men seemed not to as well.

Serge now leaning forward in his chair, again, nodded.

"That phone call I was taking as you came in? That was a recruitment officer for the new university in Tyumen. The Tyuman Industrial Institute it is called. He is calling the refineries and gas companies looking for prospective students to enroll in the first of its classes. He says they will sponsor a limited number of students for this. At the time, I didn't think of anyone. But now! But now, there is you, Serge. Would this be of interest to you, Serge?"

Serge sat back in the chair, his mind whirling.

" Sir, but I have no money and Tyumen is nearly 630km from Surgut. And, there is my mother, Mr. Sidorov".

"The question, Serge is, does this not interest you?"

"Of course, sir, it does, but…"

"You let me make some phone calls. Come back tomorrow after your morning shift. I will make this work for you, Serge. It is the least I can do for you and for your father".

With that said, both stood and Serge shook Mr. Sidorov's hand, turned and walked out of the office.

Tyumen Industrial Institute was established due to the manufacture growth and developing of natural resources in the Siberian region. Called the Ural Polytechnical Institute in 1956, and as more natural resources were being discovered by 1962, more than 700 students were trained as specialists in fuel, energy and construction.

Of course, none of this was known, nor made any difference, in what Serge's thoughts were. He was thinking of the possibilities, the future.

The walk home was filled with the 'what could be's'. Serge thought of his mother, his life.

When he arrived home, Serge found a note in the kitchen from his mother. *I will be staying, tonight, in Nefteyugansk. There is food in the ice box. I love you, Serge.'* It was signed, *Love Momma.*

As Serge sat at the kitchen table, staring at the note, he made a decision. If Mr. Sidorov could arrange for him to attend the institute, he would do it. No more working double shift at nominal pay. His mother would understand. It was for her benefit, as well, if he went to the university.

The next morning came soon enough. Serge, in hopes of good news, woke earlier than normal.

He reported to work as usual at 7:15 in the morning, and counted the hours until he would walk to Mr. Sidorov's office later that afternoon in hopes of news that would change his life forever.

"Good news, Serge! Come in, please, come in!"

Mr. Sidorov met Serge at the front door of the operations office.

"This should make you very happy, Serge, and I will do everything I can to make it so."

Serge walked and sat in the only chair in front of Mr. Sidorov's desk.

"I spoke with the registrar when you left yesterday. He did ask me many questions about you and your experience here. Of course, I told the truth, Serge, I had your file right here in front of me." He picked up a file and showed it to Serge.

"He has offered a position for you to attend. It is a four year study in gas and oil manufacturing. You will be away for that time, Serge. The university will provide housing, and we are offering to compensate any other costs, if, of course, you return here after graduating and work here."

Serge's mind was racing.

"This is an opportunity, Serge. I would not look at this twice."

"I will take this opportunity, Mr. Sidorov. Thank you very much. And I would be happy to return here and work for you and this refinery."

"Then it is done, Serge. I will complete all of the paperwork and notify you."

Serge stood, his right arm and hand extended.

"I must return to the captain and report for my next shift, Mr. Sidorov".

Mr. Sidorov shook Serge's hand.

"You take the remainder of this day off, Serge. I will notify the captain of this. You go home and share the wonderful news with your mother. She will be very pleased, and I am sure very proud of you, to hear of this".

Serge nodded, smiled and walked to the door with Mr. Sidorov walking besides him.

"You will do well, Serge. You will do well for yourself, your mother and your father."

The walk home seemed to take forever. Was this a dream? Could this possibly be true? And, the better question was, why?

The familiar bench was just ahead and Serge decided to sit for a moment to catch and gather his thoughts before returning home to tell his mother this news.

As he sat there, he noticed the two hockey goals behind the trees. Just maybe he would see the day when he would be out playing ice hockey again. This brought a wonderful feeling to his heart. He smiled, looked up to the sky and continued his walk home.

As Serge approached his home, he could see his mother in the kitchen preparing something.

"Momma! I have news to tell you. Come sit at the table and stop that work!"

"Serge, you are home so early, and I do not have dinner ready for you!"

"Momma. I spoke with Mr. Sidorov today."

Serge's mother looked at him with a hint of disapproval.

"Did you do something wrong, Serge? Is everything alright with your job. You know we need your work to pay the bills, Serge."

"Everything is better than alright, Momma. Mr. Sidorov has told me that I have been accepted to the new university in Tyumen. That the university will pay for my schooling and give me a place to stay while I attend the classes. And, he said….."

At that moment, his mother stood up and straightened her apron.

"Serge! Please slow down! I am confused. Accepted to the university? What university? Tyumen? That is so far away! A place to stay? Serge, what about your job? What about paying the bills?"

Serge was, for a moment, lost for words and sat down at the kitchen table.

"Momma, this is an opportunity. This opportunity will pay our bills and give you, and me, a better life.

Serge knew what his mother was thinking and was about to say. Since his father's death she has been so lonely. He was the only bright light in her life.

"Momma. I am doing this for us."

She walked over to where he was sitting, and brushed his hair with her hand.

"I am scared, Serge." That is all she said and walked back over the sink and continued what she was doing before he came in.

Over the next few weeks, Serge met regularly with Mr. Sidorov and the registrar of the university. Plans were made for Serge to attend.

His mother would move in and live with her sister in Nefteyugansk. Their house would be boarded up and not sold as per Mr. Sidorov's instructions.

"You will return and have this house again, Serge, for you and your mother."

It was all falling into place, though his mother was still not happy with this decision.

The day finally came. It was time to board the train to Tyumen. Practically the entire town of Surgut turned out. Refinery workers were there in their dirty, greasy overalls, the mayor was there and even the school band and students were there for the grand send off!

A total of twelve from Surgut, Nefteyugansk and from the gas field at Urengoy were ready to board a train that would change the lives, not only of these young men, but these small towns in the West Seberian Plain.

The year was 1968. Serge had been attending Tyumen Industrial Institute for two years, and had excelled in his studies.

He had been able to return to Surgut on several occasions to visit his mother and even to meet with Mr. Sidorov at the refinery.

His mother was doing actually very well living with her sister. She was smiling once again and in the summer months when the weather was warm she even had a beautiful flower garden growing.

This trip back to Surgut for the winter holiday break, Serge was bringing home someone special. He hadn't told his mother, at least not in great detail or in so many words, but Serge planned on marrying Nadia. He would make the announcement when he arrived.

Nadia works at the university in the registrar's office as a clerical assistant. She is tall and slender with long black hair and dark eyes. Serge first noticed her his first day at the university. It was hard not to! They have been seeing each other for about one year. They would meet every day when Serge was finished with his classes and would sit and talk for hours over coffee in the university student center.

They had a lot in common. Her family, too, was in the oil and gas refinery trade in Tyumen, and was an only child. They both shared dreams of a better life and planned on making those dreams come true, together. They were very much in love.

As the train pulled into the station in Surgut, Serge could see his mother and aunt waiting inside the small passenger building. Their faces peering out of the frosted window.

They ran out as soon as the train came to a stop.

"Serge, Serge!" his mother screamed as she ran towards him, practically slipping on the ice that had formed on the loading deck.

They embraced, laughing.

"Momma! It is so wonderful to see you. And Auntie, you too, as he embraced her as well.

The snow was beginning to fall heavier.

"Serge, Mr. Sidorov has sent a automobile for us to take us to Nefteyugansk. We must hurry as this weather will get worse."

"Yes, Momma. Momma? This is Nadia. The girl I have meet at the university. I have told you about her."

Serge's mother's eyes lit up and she began to smile.

"Nadia, you are so beautiful", touching her cheek and giving her a hug.

"Now, let us hurry to get home and warm! We have much to celebrate, eh, Serge?"

How could she possible know that there was something to celebrate?

The house was, indeed, warm and the smell of fresh baked bread filled the air.

"Now everyone take off your coats and place them here by the fire", Aunt Anna told everyone. "And sit, please sit and I will bring out tea and coffee."

It felt good to be home, Serge thought to himself, as he and Nadia sat on the couch holding hands and smiling into each other's eyes.

"So, my son. What news do you bring to me this visit?"

"Well, Momma, Aunt Anna. Nadia and I will be getting married", he said as he and Nadia both stood still holding hands.

Serge's mother raised her hands to her mouth and tears filled her eyes.

"Oh, Serge", she said. "I am so happy for you!" She stood and hugged them both.

Just then, Anna ran back into the room, tears in her eyes, too, with a bottle of wine.

"This calls for a big celebration!" as she raised the bottle and four glasses.

Two years had come and gone. And, in 1970, Serge graduated from the Tyumen Industrial Institute with honors. He received his degree in applied mechanics and transport operation in the oil and gas industry.

His mother, aunt and Mr. Sidorov, along with Nadia, and her parents, attended the ceremony.

Nadia and Serge were married in a small wedding in Surgut during that June of 1970. And, as promised, Serge returned to work for Mr. Sidorov at the Surgutoilco mid river oil refinery as the supervising foremen in transport operations.

His mother remained living with her sister, and Nadia and Serge moved into to the old house.

This new life of Serge's was truly a dream come true. His new position at the refinery, his specialized education and the increasing discovery of oil and gas in the Western Siberian Plain not only helped Serge support his mother, financially, but himself and Nadia as well.

The town of Surgut was also growing. The city experienced a growth in population and workers from all over Russia came there for employment.

Despite the long, brutal winters of Surgut, Serge for the first time in a long time was truly happy.

On a cold, winter day, February 6, 1971, Vladislav Zhashnilov was born. Though little Vladslav arrived a month early, he was a healthy and happy baby boy. His parents, Nadia and Serge, couldn't of been happier!

As Serge sat watching Nadia nurse Vladi, he thought to himself that he was going to be the father to Vladi he never had. There was no doubt in his mind that he was going to spend every free minute with his boy. Teach him, play with him and grow with him.

A warm and wonderful feeling came over Serge.

A short hospital stay was deemed necessary by the doctors since Vladi was born early. But, in a few more days and Nadia and his baby boy would be home.

Serge got up from the chair and walked over to Nadia, smiling. She was asleep with Vladi wrapped in blankets.

He bent down and kissed her and Vladi on the cheek and made his way home.

The walk home was cold, but Serge felt none of it. He was in his own world. A world of joy.

The new hospital was only a short distance from his home and the refinery. It was a familiar walk along the Ob River. One, Serge has made so many times before in his life. He stopped at the bench that has been there so many times for him in the past. He sat and his eyes caught the two hockey goals now on a small frozen area of the river. Three young boys were pulling them to bank as it began to get dark.

Soon, he and his son Vladi would be on that ice, together, skating and laughing.

"I'll teach him how to skate and play hockey!" he whispered to himself as he stood, pulled his hat down over his ears and continued his walk home.

"Come on, my little Vladi! Stand straight up and keep moving your feet! Skate to me, Vladi! That is very good, Vladi!"

At age three, Serge had his only son Vladi up and skating! His feet were so small and with no store around to buy skates, Serge had one of his mechanics at the refinery fasten and weld double steel runners on a small pair winter boots for Vladi to wear.

He seemed to be a natural skater, and by the age of four (1975), he was skating without help, and he was playing with boys older than he was and keeping up with them.

Nadia and Serge would watch him skate and play hockey with the other boys nearly every afternoon in the winter until it was dark. Sitting on the bench, talking and sipping coffee.

At night, Serge would sit with Vladi and read to him, and talk about playing hockey until the young boy's eyes would slowly close and he would fall asleep.

Life for Serge and his family was good. The refinery was operating at it's full potential. New pumping equipment had been installed, and the largest hydroelectric power stations were in full operation. Serge was now in management. No longer a small cold office on the loading docks. Instead, he had a new office in the main building complex. He served on many advisory boards that had been developed as the production of oil and gas in the region increased.

At age 28, he was one of the youngest, and busiest, managers in the oil industry in that part of Russia. But, as busy as he was, he always found the time to spend with his wife and son. He often thought of his father and the promise he made to himself that he wouldn't be like him. Serge Zhashnilov kept that promise to himself. He was not like his father.

In the summer of 1976, Serge's mother, still living with her sister, died from a heart attack while out working in her beloved garden. She was buried in a plot next to Ivan. After the funeral, Serge took Vladi to the bench on the river to try and answer the questions he asked about why his grandmamma died.

"You see, Vladi, it was time for her to go home. She was in her garden, which she called her home. And so, now, she is part of that garden. We live but a short time, and then we must move on to our reward. You will come to understand better as you grow older."

This was a confusing answer even to Serge, but what do you tell a five-year-old boy about the meaning of death?

"Papa? If I go to the garden, and I stand there and call her name, will I see grandmamma?"

"Well, Vladi, you just might see her, but know this. She is watching over you up from above, just like an angel. She will watch over both of us, and momma too, and protect us, Vladi. Of that you can be certain."

Vladi just smiled and looked up to the sky and waved. In the billowy cumulus clouds above he could almost see his mother's smiling face. He wished her one final farewell as tears rolled gently down his cheeks.

Summer quickly turned to winter. And this winter was one of the coldest on record in Surgut. Temperatures, at one point, reached minus sixty-one degrees Fahrenheit, and this was during an especially cold afternoon. Nobody went outside for fear of freezing, and the refinery was temporarily shut down as a precaution. Even the hydroelectric power stations were on limited output causing many homes in the region to be without power.

With this extreme weather came illness. The second week of January, in 1977, an influenza outbreak struck Surgut. Many in the town became gravely ill, and with the roads completely snowed in, reaching the hospital, even if there were medical staff there, was practically impossible.

Nadia Zhashnilov, after nearly two weeks of suffering, succumbed to this illness, along with eighty-six others in Surgut. She died at home with Serge and Vladi at her bedside.

Serge's world came crashing in around him. He felt lost, alone, confused and scared. He had lost his father, his mother and now his beloved wife, Nadia, all in a relatively short period of time. His life had been going so well, too. Why, he wondered, did all of this have to happen...at the same time.

"Papa? Did Momma have to go home, too?"

Vladi's question stood unanswered as Serge fell to his knees beside the bed, holding tightly to his son, the only one left to him. His son wept with his father as the frigid winds blew sadly outside their home..

Over the next year and a half, Serge tried his best to be both a father and a mother as well as a manager at the refinery. His Aunt Anna tried to help, but she was getting on in years, too. It wasn't easy for her to get around anymore, and her mind wasn't what it once was. Serge soon realized that he really couldn't leave Vladi with her for extended periods of time.

Mr. Sidorov was more than understanding, giving Serge a leave of absence every so often, but he was running a very large and productive oil refinery. It was only time until something had to be done.

Another year and then another rolled slowly into the past. It had been two and a half years since Nadia's death. Serge's life was finally stabilizing somewhat. At least on the surface it appeared that way. Work and his home life with Vladi were better. The winters, however, were as brutal as they ever have been, and the memory of Nadia during that time was something Serge couldn't forget. The church over the past year or so helped watch Vladi when he wasn't in school, which made it easier, if not better, for Serge and the refinery, and Serge and Vladi spent every minute together when he wasn't working. They took short travels in the Summer time, and skated in the winter time. Serge even got Vladi involved with the youth hockey group in Surgut, which brought some much needed joy to the both of them.

But, in late 1979, Serge came to the conclusion that he must do whatever it takes to make a better life for Vladi. Living and staying in Surgut was not part of the solution.

At one of his advisory board meetings, the topic of the relatively new Alyeska Pipeline came up. It had been discussed before at many meetings even before its completion in 1977.

Ever since back in 1968, when the Atlantic Richfield Company and Humble Oil and Refining Company announced a discovery well in Prudhoe Bay, word was that a new pipeline was going to be constructed from Prudhoe Bay at the north end of Alaska to the port of Valdez in the south.

Serge recalled how the professors at the university would talk about this, and what a task it would be to actually, on a multitude of levels, construct this pipeline, and what effect, if any, would that have on the oil production in the Western Siberian region. At this particular advisory board meeting, the talk was about employment opportunities being offered there, and the effects that that may pose on current production here.

Serge's mind was racing. Perhaps a new job there, in Alaska, working for an oil company would be the answer he sought. Surely, with his experience and education a position would be available for him. And, at the same time it would be a much better life for Vladi. Imagine, living in America!

That night as Serge read to Vladi, he stopped and put the book down.

"Vladi? How would you like to take a trip? A long trip to…America?"

"America, Papa?"

"Yes, Vladi. America. You see, there may be work for me there. A good job might be waiting there with an opportunity for us to live a better life than we have here."

Vladi looked at his father with sleepy eyes.

Serge smiled. "You go to sleep now, Vladi, my beautiful son. You sleep very well, and we will talk more tomorrow. Dream about a new life…a new beginning for both of us."

Vladi smiled back, and closed his eyes as he pulled the blankets up close.

Serge turned out the light and walked to the kitchen and sat at the table. "I will make some phone calls tomorrow", he thought. "What could it hurt?"

Turning off the lights in the house, he made his way to his bed. As he lay there, his eyes grew heavy. Thoughts of the future filled his mind. He fell asleep quickly.

"Papa! Papa! Wake up, Papa!"

Serge felt someone shaking his right shoulder. It was Vladi! Was everything all right? What had happened?

"It's Alaska, Papa! Look! The plane is landing in Alaska! We are here, Papa!"

14

Bowling Over Reality

When the first ball I threw gave me a seven-ten split,
I should have realized that maybe I should quit.
But I flexed my shoulders and continued to stand tall,
Never imagining for a moment that my next
throw would be a gutter ball.

It took me until the fifth grade to realize that there was more to the sports world than just my favorite, ice hockey. Oh, I knew enough about football, soccer and baseball as well as basketball, but these sports were meant for the lower 48 as far as kids in Reality were concerned. Then there was the mysterious game of curling, which we assumed to be solely for Canadians. Boy, was I wrong about that. Someone on TV said that even China did curling along with ping pong and other stuff like that. Did they have frozen rivers in China?

Curling just sounded too much like a girl's sport to me. You know what I mean, don't you? Something you do with your hair when you have nothing else to do during your spare time. Actually, once I went to see a curling match with Alfie and his dad at a town near the Canadian border. Unfortunately, I can't quite remember the name of the town right now. It sure took lots of practice and skill to compete with those fellows, but my friends would have laughed me out of town if they'd seen me practicing or playing with a broom instead of a hockey stick! Wow, was I bad at that for sure! So, I had to scratch the sport of curling off my list of other athletic activities once and for all. I would leave that game to one of my best group of friends, the Canadians. After all, they invented it, didn't they?

Then one day, at recess for certain, the rumor mill got cranked up to full speed, and we were all ears as usual. That means we were listening very closely or hard, whichever you prefer. My greatest fear was that we were going to enter a curling team in an upcoming tournament in a nearby town and that I would be one of Reality's first string curlers! I racked my brain for a multitude of excuses and any way to get out of it. Alas, thank goodness, I was wrong…as I usually am when it comes to interpreting rumors. There was no immediate need to fear curling just then.

But, it all started with Arnie's father. He, Arnie's father that is, was a construction supervisor. All Arnie could talk about was that he wanted to become an architect so he could design the big buildings his dad was building all over Alaska. Arnie's only problem was that his dad was out of town quite a bit of the time on building projects. At this particular time in my memory, his dad was in California doing a city hall. Needless to say, we kids were impressed with Arnie's dad. Those buildings served as monuments to his artistic and engineering skills.

Well, Arnie talked to his dad on the phone all the time which did help his obvious loneliness quite a bit. Lately, his dad was very excited about some new project that was slated to be built right here in Reality of all places. Arnie's dad told him that he would be bringing a new sport to Reality for the first time in its history. When I first heard those words issue from Arnie's lips, I remember that I immediately prayed that it wasn't a curling arena built on top of one of our hockey rinks.

For the longest time, Arnie refused to tell anyone exactly what the sport was that his father was referring to. I wasn't really convinced that his dad had even told him what it was. All we knew was that it was going to require a big new building and that said building would be less than a city block from our school! I wracked my brain over and over, but no answer came forth. That's when I realized that it was good to have a big brother. I was certain that Paul could figure it out or make Arnie squeal by applying a little pressure. But, as it turned out, it wasn't necessary at all. Other forces would come to our aid and yield the answer.

At recess that memorable day, Mister Carson, our gym teacher, walked up to us and out of a clear blue sky asked if we'd ever been…

bowling. Bowling? Visions of bowls filled with cereal and fruit danced through my head until he explained what he meant by bowling. According to him it was a game where you tried your very best to knock down ten bowling pins with a fairly large and heavy bowling ball thrown from a moderate distance down a bowling lane.

"Right up my alley!" I yelped before I could stop myself, and Mister Carson began laughing real hard while he slapped his sides and almost rolled on the floor in front of all of us. What had I said that was so funny? I scratched my head and shrugged my shoulders and waited for the answer to come.

"You've got it, Jean-Luc! It's a bowling alley! That was the best pun I've ever heard. You're a comic genius! I'm going to tell your parents to put you in the upcoming variety show at school."

That's all I needed to hear about my future as a comedian. I hustled straight to the library and asked Thelma, our really smart librarian, if we had any books on bowling so that I could get up to speed if you know what I mean. Is that another pun? Sure enough, they had one on the shelves so I checked it our before someone else got it. With a few little cloak and dagger moves Paul taught me, I stashed the book in my locker. I wanted to make sure that I was an expert on bowling at least as far as the other kids were concerned.

That afternoon I got the book safely home and then went immediately to my room to begin reading. Soon, I was conversant on gutter balls, a seven-ten split, a perfect 300 score and other basics of the game.

But that wasn't all that the rumor mill had cranked up. In addition to dedicating a new bowling alley building near our school, a grand festival of celebration was being planned, one that would include ice sculpturing and a full-fledged carnival! That statement right there tells you something about the efficiency of our local rumor mill. If the ice sculpturing were done outside a refrigerator, it would have to be held in the winter when the city fathers were sure it would be cold enough. However, the carnival people weren't stupid! They would only show up in the summertime so they wouldn't freeze to death.

Which one was it going to be, and how would we know? Even my own Uncle Jack was very skeptical, so he went right straight to the mayor to resolve the issue once and for all.

And, just in case you're keeping score, the mayor and the city council were the people we called 'The City Fathers' even though about half their number were women. That's Reality for you!

Well, Uncle Jack told me that the city fathers weren't exactly sure on just when the bowling alley building would be completed so the actual details of all the celebration plans were on hold. That was just as well with me because I had a plan of my own. Maybe I could talk Paul, my sisters, my dad and my mom into a little road trip to the nearest town with…, you guessed it, an actual bowling alley. That way we could check it out and practice some so we wouldn't look like amateurs in front of our friends when it came to bowling in Reality. Your athletic image was everything in Reality, so why risk it just because someone was building a new building? This plan would have to be hush-hush otherwise the whole town would migrate to the nearest alley, and it would be chaos for sure!

First, I had to decide whom to approach first with my plan. That answer was easy as you might imagine. It was Mom! She would be least likely to squeal on me if she thought it was a dumb idea. And the best time to do it was after she got off work at the Timberline. I decided to go with the plan that evening. She was off at 8 PM. There was no turning back now!

I met her as she was coming out of the front door of the Timberline. It was obvious that she could see that look on my face so she turned right around, and we sat down together in an empty booth in a far corner. Secrecy was paramount for sure. I explained my plan slowly and in great detail, and she liked it. She didn't quite get the secrecy element as much as I did, but she let that slide for the time being. She actually seemed excited by the prospects!

Our obvious first problem was where to go to find a bowling alley. She had three suggestions right off the bat. There was Fairbanks, then there was Nome, and finally there was Point Hope. I'd heard of the first two on many occasions, but where was Point Hope? Mom said it was a town in North Slope Borough. She said she thought the population was about five hundred people not counting dogs and cats.

Now came the geography lesson I needed. Point Hope was at the northwest end of the Lisburne Peninsula right on the Chukchi Sea. What was really interesting about the place was that it protruded out into the open sea, which brought the local whales close to the shore all the time.

Now it started to get deep. I remember my mother's intense love for history and geography. She told me that the first known recorded sighting of this cape was by two Russian explorers named Mikhail Vasiliev and Gleb Shishmaryov. The names of their daring ships were even worse yet if you can believe it! They were the *Otkrietie* and the *Blagonamierennie.* They named the headland they had discovered *Mys Golovnina* after a Russian Vice-Admiral, but, thankfully for me, it was given its present name by the Royal Navy in 1826. Only my good friend Vladi could handle these names with grace and some speed.

Then, mom bent forward and carefully whispered something almost unbelievable to me. She said that in 1958 the government wanted to set off a nuclear weapon about thirty miles from the village that was there at the time in an attempt to create a deep water artificial harbor! It was called Operation Chariot and would have actually involved more than one thermonuclear explosion to accomplish the task. Needless to say, the natives were restless and, luckily, the idea was killed.

With no further adieu, I decided that Fairbanks was the place to visit when it came to bowling alleys. I can still hear my mom laughing.

Fairbanks is, after all, one of Alaska's largest cities. She told me that she knew for certain that it had a ten-lane bowling alley up and running. With all those city people and ten lanes, no one from Reality not with us on the trip would see me practicing how to bowl. Of course, cameras would have to be banned, but to do that I had to negotiate with dad and Paul.

I asked mom if I could buy a bowling ball and shoes out of my allowance, but she told me not to be too hasty. Apparently, they have bowling balls you can use free of charge at the bowling alley, and the shoes can be rented cheap, too. Mom said she would take care of the latter for me so I wouldn't have to dip into my allowance. I was beginning to like this new sport or game or whatever it was, but I couldn't tell anyone just yet.

I'd never been to Fairbanks so I asked Mom what it was like. She told me that the location was sort of an accident. Back in 1901 a certain Captain E.T. Barnette was trying to establish a trading post at the spot where the Valdez-Eagle Trail crossed the Tanana River. The good Captain was aboard a steam boat named the Lavelle Young on the Chena River traveling to the above-mentioned place. Alas, he never made it! The Lavelle Young ran aground some seven miles up the river.

Smoke from the stranded steamer attracted a group of prospectors who met Barnette when he left the ship. Those men talked the Captain into changing his plans and setting up the trading post right there. So I found out the real reason why Fairbanks is where it is. Just to be complete, Mom told me that the city was named after Charles Fairbanks, a Republican senator from Indiana of all places. The man was even Vice-President of the United States in Teddy Roosevelt's second term. Wow, my friends and teachers were sure to be impressed when I told them!

So, eventually after much wrangling, I convinced some of the adults…ah, actually, my mother convinced a few parents that we should take a weekend trip to Fairbanks to check out the bowling alley. We took Valdi, my Russian born fellow pee wee teammate, with us in our car and set out early on a Saturday morning after a big breakfast. As the journey to Fairbanks unfolded, I worried less and less about being spotted learning how to bowl. The trip was relatively uneventful except for my chance encounter with the owner of the establishment. He was a former coach in the Canadian Junior League in Ontario and he was more than willing to explain the possible futures for 16 to 20 year old hockey players who wanted to reach the National Hockey League.

The only real problem I had was the fact that the adults always tagged us kids with classifications like 'Pee Wee', 'Midget', and 'Junior'. This alone was making the prospect of playing college hockey look ever so much better. His name was Mister Gilbert and he owned the Kegler Lanes bowling alley. For some unexplained reason the name Kegler always reminded me of my Uncle Jack's love of very large quantities of beer. But we'll get to that later.

Mister Gilbert explained that when we reached 16 years of age, Vladi and I should try to make our way into Major-Junior hockey in the Canadian Hockey League. He said that there were three leagues to shoot for. One was the Quebec Major Junior Hockey League operating mainly in Eastern Canada. Another was the Ontario Hockey League which included teams in Michigan and Pennsylvania. The third was the Western Hockey League which covered the Pacific Northwest in America and Canada.

He said that each team was currently limited to no more than four 16 year olds. I guess he could see our hopes drop from the expressions on our faces, so he changed the subject back to bowling. Vladi and I could worry about qualifying for the 'Juniors' when we got back to Reality.

Mister Gilbert told my mom and dad that he thought that a bowling alley in Reality would be a great thing. His idea was to have an annual tournament replete with traveling trophies for the winners and a big awards dinner. He pointed to the sizeable restaurant already operating inside his building.

Soon we donned our bowling shoes and the Kegler Lanes bowling shirts he presented to all of us as gifts, and we were on our way to our first bowling experience. I hope that you don't mind if I skip the gory details of my first three games, but honesty requires me to tell you that the results were pretty grim.

First of all, my bowling ball kept slipping right out of my hand. After clunking loudly on the floor, it then headed for the gutter, most times on the right side of the lane. I was sure that I could hear the ever present pin spotters laughing out loud back there behind the pins.

Secondly, my ball was quite heavy which required me to use two hands instead of one to carry it forward before throwing it. As I approached what I call the foul line, I could hear snickering from the other bowlers. How I wished I could hip check them when they were trying to throw their bowling balls.

But thirdly and worst of all, on a number of occasions I did knock down seven or eight pins which I thought was pretty good for a rank beginner like me. Yet, the pins left standing were on opposite sides of the lane. My mom told me that I had created the classic seven-ten split! This meant that I had a single shot to knock down two pins that looked like far away football goal posts.

'Just get one' my dad would shout. Good advice if you were a good bowler. Unfortunately, each time I encountered a seven-ten split, my ball would hit nothing as it rolled slowly between the two pins. Much to my humiliation, as the ball missed both pins everyone leaped up, shouted 'Field Goal', and threw their hands up like a football referee! With those words I knew when I was beaten. They would probably have to bowl in Reality without me.

Thankfully, after three games we had dinner with Mister Gilbert and then headed for home. I was never so glad to see my home town and then my skates and my hockey sticks!

15
Bad News

When the grimmest of the grim comes knocking at your door,
You must certainly begin to grit your teeth that much more.
The Reaper he is called and his blade is ever so tall
So you must keep your head pointed toward the sky or you will fall.

The truck bounced along Reality Ridge Road as the volunteers from town made their way up to the ridgeline. Despite the smoke pouring over them, the visibility slowly improved as the vehicle neared the crest of the ridge. Many aboard knew all too well what to expect to see once they got there.

Everyone who grows up in Reality, Alaska knows the drill from the very beginning. Major fires on the ridge are not uncommon events. Careless travelers and tourists start some with cigarettes and campfires; some are started by lightning and others are the result of strange acts of nature which cannot always be predicted or prevented. Regardless of how this one was started, it needed to be addressed immediately, and as usual the people of Reality were ready to respond.

Paul was sitting in the back of truck with Mr. Malazone and twelve other men and boys from town. Talk in the back of that truck was casual with some joke telling and laughter helping to lighten the mood. Nevertheless, Paul was not smiling and was silent. He was thinking about some comments his father made to him as he left the house earlier that morning. There was something about this call that was different from the others he had experienced. He couldn't explain his reasoning or conclusion to Paul. A feeling deep inside is sometimes hard to explain and understand. Paul clearly remembered his father telling him to be very careful if he was called up.

"Jean-Paul, you are mighty quiet this morning!" a boisterous voice yelled over the sound of the truck engine. It was a friendly and aggressive voice Paul recognized immediately.

"Yes, sir, Mr. Malazone. I'm all right. Just a little tired I guess. We were up late last night talking about Jean-Luc's important hockey game this afternoon. I was just doing some amateur coaching like I always do. It's really a great amount of fun for me, and I believe that Luc appreciates the attention and information. He's a really attentive student to say the least."

Jean-Paul knew that Mr. Malazone wasn't buying into that line even though what he said was true. But Paul reasoned that it was better than expressing his real, personal fears. Paul looked over and Vince Malazone, long time family friend, town butcher and long time resident of Reality just nodded his head, smiled and looked away. He seemed more worried than usual about this situation, too. Paul began to wonder whether his friend knew something about the situation that was facing them that the rest of the men didn't know.

The smoke started to get thicker again as the heavy smell of burnt timber made its presence known to the men in the truck. Soot now mixed freely with the lightly falling snow creating some strange patterns in the snow on the ground and in the air. Paul remembered seeing images in the cumulus clouds that hung over Reality in the summer and fall. This was similar, yet the colors were much different in this case. Paul wondered whether the numerous woodland animals that lived up here most of the year were confused by nature's strange way of painting of their environment. Hopefully, they took it as a warning.

As the truck negotiated a hairpin turn, Paul figured that they were about a mile or so from the mill that seemed to be the center of this activity. He carefully stood up to see just how close they were to the familiar buildings and all he could see was thick black and gray smoke in front of the truck tempered by a faint orange glow originating high atop the ridgeline. He fell back into his seat in the back of the truck frustrated at his inability to do anything right now to help the cause which seemed out of control. It was like sitting on the bench during a game when your team was being outplayed.

"Geez, Jean-Paul. You look as if you've seen a gigantic scary ghost!" joked Bobby Jackson as Paul sat down next to him. Bobby's dad was a timber leader on the project.

"Bobby, I have!" was Paul's stark reply. "More like an unexplained vision of…of something really bad…not evil, just very bad. I wonder if the ghosts of our forefathers are up here helping us quell the blaze? Maybe they are whispering advice into our ears? Maybe we just have to listen?"

Bobby just shrugged his shoulders as he thought about his grandfathers who both had lived in Reality and dealt with the hazards presented by its environment. He remembered their fire stories very clearly especially now. When out of control things like fires were happening, it was very scary. When the threat was over and the fire was out, the stories and memories were fun. Ironically, the men of Reality would sit around their fireplaces and relive the events.

It was around 10:45 AM when the truck carrying the men pulled into the loading yard next to the main sawmill. This was where the main office was located and the heavy equipment and trucks were stored. As Paul looked around before jumping off the back of the truck, he noticed that not many of the timber trucks were parked there in their usual places. It was common practice to move the trucks and timber haulers out of the loading area in case the fires spread rapidly down the hillside.

The scene was an especially eerie one, indeed. Gray ash covered everything and black smoke hung high in the air waiting to be drawn down into the valley below. Visibility was low again and the sound of crackling fire echoed in the distance. Behind all this lurked that ever-present orange glow high on the ridgeline. Paul couldn't help but compare it to one of those futuristic movies where the entire world was in ruin after a nuclear war.

"All right, everyone. Let's get lined up so that we can form teams. You know the routine", barked Jack Jackson, Bobby's dad, as he came around to the back of the truck, his walkie-talkie squawking with chatter from the men working the line.

"Vince, what in the world are you doing up here", Jackson said putting his hand on the shoulder of Reality, Alaska's very own butcher.

"Well, J.J., you know I never miss one of your bar-b-ques, and this one, well, is no exception! I might learn some tricks up here. I should have brought some frozen hamburger with me."

The entire group broke out in laughter and everyone's tension seemed to lessen. They could all envision a giant hamburger rolling through the woods, putting out the fire.

Jackson patted Vince Malazone's belly and said, "Yep, ole Vince, I can see that! You don't miss much! It's one less thing we have to worry about. Lunch!"

Vince Malazone was not the perfect picture of health. He stood about five foot five inches tall and was way overweight, but his heart was in the right place, and he was one of the kindest men you would ever want to meet.

"Gentleman," Jackson continued, "as grizzly as it looks around here, it's not as bad as it seems. Most of the fires on the ridge are under control, and the main road to the top has been ninety-eight percent cleared. We've got four teams up along the road seeing that we get the rest of the road cleared so that we can get you guys up there to remove the burnt and fallen timber, and to water down any hot spots that may be around. There is a fire team on top of the ridge, and they are putting out the last of the fires there. But, remember, our job is just as important as theirs was. If we screw up and leave enough fuel or hot spots, this could start up again, and we could be right here again tomorrow morning.

"Any questions so far?"

"Mr. Jackson," Paul asked, "where's my dad working?"

"Hey, Jean Paul, good to see you, son. Your old man is up on the ridgeline overseeing the fire team. I'll be sending you there with a couple of these other fellas in just a few minutes. I spoke to him just before you all pulled in, and he is just fine. He is tired, dirty and wet, but fine. He told me that what he needs most right now is a drink and a nap! Any other questions before I continue?"

Everyone looked around at each other and shook their heads.

"All right, then. Now remember that the ground along the road and up on the ridge…I should say, high on the ridge, is not in great shape. There are lots of fallen trees and a good amount of erosion from the run-off. One thing that helped us here with the fire was the amount of snow up there, but as it melted from the heat of the fire, it tore up the road something awful. But that's something we'll have to fix this spring.

"Needless to say, footing is not good so I am going to ask that only the sure-footed and in-shape guys head up on the ridge. The rest of you will tend to debris clearing at the lower levels, and once the road is totally cleared and secured we'll move the trucks further up to bring the timber down. Once those trucks return with timber, we'll have a team to unload them keeping whatever we can, and chipping the rest. Safety is the most important thing here today, men. Most of you have been through all this before, but please be extra careful and watch out for each other. Any questions?"

Again, the men looked at each other and shook their heads. Most began to head to the supply shed for helmets, axes, shovels, and the various other tools needed.

"Jean Paul, you all right?" asked Mr. Jackson quietly, his eyes fixed on Paul while putting his hand on Paul's shoulder. "You're looking a bit pale this morning. If you're worried about your dad, don't be. He is one of the finest, strongest and most reliable guys I know. He's probably got that fire by the horns as we stand here talking! You want me to raise him on the radio for you?"

"No, that's okay, Mr. Jackson. I'm fine, really. I guess I'm just a little tired is all. I'm worried about my brother's hockey game and about my dad. It's my fault. I've got to learn to focus on the problem at hand. Worrying doesn't solve anything!"

The snow was letting up, and the men were returning to the truck with their equipment. Paul looked up toward the ridgeline, and indeed the orange glow was now gone. Vince Malazone handed him a helmet, a rope and an axe.

"All right, men, I just got word that the fire on the ridge is out and the road up top is cleared. The crew up there had a bit of trouble with the continued run-off, but I have been advised that the road is stable enough for trucks to come up and come down. There will be a truck coming down with one of the crews that have been up there since early this morning. Once that truck gets here we will get a fresh bunch of you up there. Those going to the top, report to Guy Ropespierre. Most of you have worked with him in this type of operation. I'm sure you'll know what to do, and he will direct you to where he needs you."

Mr. Jackson was busy dividing the men into small teams and assigning a team leader as the first truck came down the road and pulled into the loading yard. Each crewmember that came off that truck was covered with thick black soot. Paul couldn't help but stare at each and every one of them. They looked beaten and worn. Most headed over to the office and sat down on the benches there, elbows propped up on their knees and hands over their faces. Their total exhaustion was felt by everyone.

Steve Grimes, the coach of the Reality hockey team, startled Jean-Paul.

"Your dad kind'a knew you would be down here, Jean-Paul. I would imagine Jackson will have you heading up to work with him. Your dad is quite a man. He dove right into the fray, and quicker than I could imagine, we had the thing under control."

"Oh, hey, Coach. That's exactly what Mr. Jackson told me as well. How long ago did you see my dad? I'd really like to see him when everything's done."

"About 45 minutes ago, I guess. He was working high on the ridge with a good team of guys. They pretty much, from what he told me anyway, had the blaze under control. They were still trying to figure out what started this mess."

"Coach, what about today's game? It's still on isn't it? I mean everyone will be heading to the Timberline to talk about the fire and get ready for the game. Big game at home, ya know?"

Coach Grimes chuckled and put his hand on Jean-Paul's shoulder.

"You don't have to remind me about today's game, Paul. Prudhoe Bay only comes to Reality twice a year, and we have a home reputation to hold up! You got your brother Luc ready? He's getting the start today. His game has definitely been improving, and I ascribe that mostly to you."

"Yes, sir, Coach. He's ready, and I am sure he's out on the ice already this morning. The lake was still frozen solid yesterday."

Coach Grimes smiled.

"Good to hear that, Paul. You know he thinks the world of you. And your old man, too, I suppose. All he does is talk about all the moves and skills you have taught him. I have no doubt in my mind that Jean-Luc will be a name to reckon with in the game of hockey. And soon, you can take over my job as coach."

Coach? Paul hadn't thought about that. What a concept!

Just then, Vince Malazone came up to the two of them, wiping his hands and face.

"Steve, we just got the call. The whole town is starting to head down to the Timberline, hungry and awaiting news about the fire and of the game today. Time we head down and let these young, fresh, energetic folks play up here for a while. They seem ready."

Vince's comment was a sign that the fire was subdued and only cleanup remained.

"Couldn't agree with you more there, Ole Vince. Let me grab my gear, and I will meet you at the truck."

With that said, Vince Malazone walked toward the parked trucks that were ready to head into town.

Coach Grimes turned and looked John-Paul in the eyes and said, "Look, Paul. I'll give it to ya straight, here. It ain't pretty up there on the ridge. Darn right dangerous now even though the fire is subdued. Watch yourself, work hard and safe and get your tail, and everyone up here down to that game this afternoon. We want everyone in one piece. I'll get the start delayed if need be. We want you all there to celebrate our victory."

"Yes, sir, Coach. I'll do my best. No shortcuts. But we all want to be at the rink."

"I know you will, John-Paul. I know you will."

John-Paul stood there, alone, watching as a dozen or so men boarded the truck. How he wished he were aboard, but knew that there was work to be done and that his fellow townspeople were counting on him. He realized that time was short because danger still lurked above him. He wondered whether he would be able to see his brother play in the big game. No matter. First things first! The safety of the town had highest priority for Paul.

Looking, again, to the ridgeline, a silence fell upon him.

Back at the Timberline, Paul's brother was having his own set of problems and doubts.

"Alfie! No more for you! Geez, we have probably the biggest game this year, and you're over here stuffing your face! You'll end up having lunch all over the bench like you did up in Winslow. That was awful! Even though it was just practice, you puked all over my best jersey… and I was in it!"

From the appearance of the plate in front of him, Alfie was breaking his own record of 'World Famous Malazone Burgers'. He stopped chewing for a moment and looked me straight in the eyes. He had that same silly grin on his face that I'd seen a thousand times before.

"Jean-Luc, I am well aware there is a big game today. One of our biggest! And it's very cold out there. My feet are nearly frozen from today's practice, and I am very hungry. Just sit down and give me your take on what, and how, you want to play these guys today. But, let me enjoy my food. I need fuel for speed. I need heavy fuel!"

Luc sat down across from Alfie. He searched his memory for where he had heard the term 'Heavy Fuel' before, but to no avail. His eyes were still staring at Alfie's plate. Pieces of bun and burger with gobs of ketchup smeared all over covered the dish. It wasn't a pretty sight.

"Alfie, I have a very good feeling about today's game. I really do! I mean, on home ice with the entire town here cheering us on! Prudhoe Bay would never have a turn out like this if we went up there. It's always so cold up there, I guess I don't blame them! Frank, as usual, needs a little help in goal, but with you and me, John, Alvin and Billy as the starting line, well, I think we can take it to 'em, fast and hard! Let's hit them hard before they even realize that the game is on!"

"It is an awesome first line, Luc, no doubts there", Alfie said as he stuffed the last morsel of burger in his mouth. "But, do you think we can hold them? I mean they are really fast, Luc. I've heard that they hit the hardest of any team around. I know we can strike first, but man, they are tough!"

Luc shook his head like his brother did in these situations.

"My brother Paul gave me a little inside scoop on how to control these guys. What we need to do is…."

Just at that moment, Coach Grimes sat down at the table.

"How you feeling, boys? I need you guys to play your very best today. With the fire and all, a win here today would be a very good thing. It would lift the morale of the town, and Lord knows we need it."

His face still covered with black soot only partially wiped off, Jean-Luc couldn't help but ask.

"Coach, how is everything up on the ridge? Really haven't heard much information at all, and I really want my Dad and brother to be here for the game."

"Talked to your brother, as a matter of fact, just before heading down here for lunch. Your dad seems to have a handle on things up there, and your brother was going to be with him. Just knowing you got the start, I am sure they will be down in plenty of time for the game. I want you guys to finish up with lunch, get your gear and meet with the rest of the team outside in about fifteen minutes. I want to get to the ice a bit early today."

Alfie and I nodded, smiled at each other and stood, making our way to where our gear was piled.

The game against Prudhoe Bay came and went like a blur. Funny, it seems like a million years ago, but it wasn't that long ago at all. If I close my eyes, I can still feel the cold against my face and the smell of the food at the new concession stand. I can still hear the crowd and see little kids running around.

That day was the best I, no, we, ever played. I can remember thinking to myself that afternoon that this was the day to shine! Nothing will go wrong, and we will make Reality proud. We didn't just live in a town somewhere up north; we lived in Reality, Alaska! There was no finer place on earth.

At game time the bleachers were packed, and rows of people from the small neighboring towns were even there standing where there were no seats. As I remember, the loudest roar ever greeted us as we took the ice. What a feeling it was! I never felt more energy coursing through my body than at that moment. Our whole team must have felt the same.

We won that game, indeed we did. The final score was 7-2 as I remember. It was my best day ever. I scored two goals and had three assists. Two of the assists were with Alfie, the other with Alvin. Alfie had the game winner with a slap shot from center ice with two seconds left in the first period. That goal made it 3-2. From then on we cruised with two goals in the second period and two in the third. Even Frankie had the game of his young life. Thirty-six shots on goal and only two made it in. One of them bounced off the post.

After Alfie's shot, the entire crowd jumped up and ran on to the ice, screaming and cheering! They weren't supposed to do that so we got a bench penalty, but we killed it off. It was just the first period!

Every once in a while I'd look into the crowd to find my Dad and Paul. Unfortunately, I couldn't see them anywhere. How could they not be here to enjoy this wonderful moment, I wondered.

Then, right at the end of the game, I saw Mr. Jackson talking with my mom. His hands were on her shoulders. I couldn't make out what he was saying. But my mom fell to her knees, her hands over her face. She was crying, and several other ladies gathered and knelt around her. Something was really wrong!

Just at that moment, Mr. Malazone told me to come with him. Frankie and Alfie were there, too. My head was spinning as we rushed across the ice.

It all happened so fast. In one moment we just won the biggest game of our lives. In the next moment I was swept away into a world of grief. My mom sat crying on the ice. I had never seen her cry like this before.

Accidents happen in the timber business. Tragedies happen as well. Most of the people who work in this business realize it every minute of every day. When tragedy happens, this town and its people try and put it behind them as soon as possible and move on. Tough in a way, I guess, but that is just the way it is. But I wasn't prepared for this. My knees buckled as I fell to the ice.

As it was told to me, there was a terrible accident on the ridge that afternoon.

The way the story went was, my dad, John-Paul and a couple of the other men were the last ones on the ridge. They were securing a stack of lumber with heavy steel bands, and making sure the wooden wedges were in place. These wedges were there to keep the logs from rolling much the way a rock or a piece of wood is sometimes placed behind a tire to keep a truck from rolling.

The ground had not been stable for the entire day as run off from water and snow had eroded much of it. As they just about finished, there was a loud snapping sound followed by a shifting of the entire stack of logs.

John-Paul pushed my father out of the way just as the stack came crashing down. Paul never made it to safety. He was killed instantly!

Life is strange. Some say fragile. One minute you're here, the next minute you're gone. I like to think I played that game for my brother John-Paul. That was his game, and our goals have his name on them.

My dad never was the same after that day. He blamed himself for what happened. Mom tried to help, but she had her own pain to deal with. He, in true Robespierre fashion, returned to the mill three days later. He said he couldn't just stay in the house and grieve for Paul. He needed to work to calm his mind.

My sisters seemed not to truly understand. They were older than me but too young, I guess. They asked a lot of questions that nobody could really answer. They just seemed unable to accept the situation, and continue being little girls. It was sad. I cried for them, too.

For me, I stayed to myself on most days, heading to the ice rink every day and skating until my feet were so tired that it hurt to even walk. I used Paul's stick each and every time I stepped onto that ice. Alfie, Frank and the rest of the guys, I think, knew I needed to be alone so they gave me some much needed space.

We are a strong family, and this is a strong town. In our own way, we both will survive and move on. I want to make my brother proud of me even though he isn't here to see it. But I do hope that he is watching from heaven.

I do miss my brother John-Paul.

16

Using My Head

It takes dynamite to get me up,
Too much of everything is just enough.
One more thing I just got to say,
I need a miracle every day!

I Need A Miracle
Grateful Dead

All of a sudden I'm lying on a table...or is it a bed or something similar. And all I see is the ceiling twirling above me like a horizontal Ferris wheel. Did you know that the Ferris wheel is named after George Washington Gale Ferris, Jr. But that thing up there should really be a merry-go-round, shouldn't it? If that's true, then Ferris wheels are just vertical merry-go-rounds. But a merry-go-round usually has horses or pigs or tigers or zebras on it. Oh, well. Next time I go to the circus I'll ask someone who knows about these things.

At least I believe it's the ceiling up there...if up is still up the way it used to be? Why is all this crazy stuff happening to me? What did I do... what evil act did I perform to deserve this kind of treatment and fate? I'd shrug my shoulders a bunch of times if that would help. Of course, in my physical condition as bad as it is, I really doubt that I could shrug these shoulders even a little bit up or down once.

As I lie here...or lay here, whichever is correct, a really strange thought has started bouncing around in my pea brain...and don't ask me what a pea brain is. Like mom always said, if you have to ask, then you've got one! And she was always right about such things. It was what she did. I wish she was here because I have a bunch of questions for her.

Why is it that nothing good accidentally happens to me every once in a while between the bad stuff that happens all the time? That is a good question from a philosophical point of view to say the least. But then I know what my brother would have said or asked or at least thought if he were here right now to help me.

"Give me an example of something good you want to happen to you besides living forever, punching out Schultz, or becoming a millionaire!"

Wow! The words that were flowing through my brain sounded very real…as if they came directly out of his mouth. Well, they must have at one time or another. His spirit must be here with me right now because he somehow knows that I miss him so very much and I am in serious need of his guidance and philosophy. He was my guiding light until that fateful day when he died so tragically and needlessly! And he still is my guiding light…or at least one of the brightest guiding lights in my life. His advice and counsel were always right on the money. If I had a younger brother to guide through life, I could never be so steady and correct as he always was. He built confidence in me with every word and action he directed toward me, and he set a perfect example that will live with me forever!

My mind again considered the question that the spirit of my brother posed. The answer came to me immediately as if he had stuffed it into my brain with the question.

"I want to see my sister Dani!"

I tried to gather what strength I had left to shout out the words for all…for anyone to hear. To my amazement I heard my voice echoing off that ceiling up there that I mentioned a minute or so ago, and the words seemed loud and clear!

Then, to my total amazement I heard a voice apparently answering my request.

"You don't have to shout, Jean-Luc. Your sister Dani is right here next to you. Just relax and say hello."

Was I dreaming all of this? I struggled for a moment and succeeded in forcing my eyes open. My view was blurry at first as you might expect, but much to my surprise the unknown voice was correct in what it said. There, smiling down at me was the beautiful face of my sister, Dani. Her bright blue eyes were shining with tears, and they seemed like happy tears if you know what I mean. My heart nearly leapt out of my chest as I studied her beautiful face. It was indeed a miracle!

And then to add to my new found joy I heard her beautiful voice whispering gently to me those words I will never forget.

"Jean-Luc, you are my hero! You are everyone's hero to say the least. You proved to the fans and the world just how brave and unselfish you are. You stormed the fort, cleared the wall and captured the castle and gave us what we wanted so badly. The Stanley Cup!"

I was stunned to say the very least. I needed to learn every last detail concerning what she had just said to me. So I smiled as best I could under the circumstances, and then whispered asking for her to help me sit up so that we could carry on a conversation. She heard me but executing my movement wasn't that easy. There were plenty of other people nearby because I could hear them clapping as I was lifted into a softly padded chair by two men with familiar faces who I would soon realize were two of my teammates. Wow, the chair was really relaxing, and I almost felt like a human again.

"Jean-Luc, the physicians told me that you may have what they called a concussion. They indicated that it should be temporary…by that they said you should be back to normal in about two weeks as long as you rest a lot. They told me that your recovery process is proceeding at a normal pace for this kind of injury."

I was stunned as you might imagine. But I was still in the dark as to how this might have happened. She could see the confusion in my sleepy eyes so she began to quiz me about what I had experienced and what I actually remembered. She quickly concluded that she had to walk me through the last forty-eight hours or so, but she wanted me to search my memories for the correct answers.

"Jean-Luc, do you remember that you were playing in the Stanley Cup Finals, and that yesterday was game 7, the final and deciding game?"

I swore to myself that I would be honest with Dani. I told her that I remembered being a hockey player as a child and having dreams of playing for the cup. That's the Stanley Cup. Every hockey playing kid in Reality did that. I also realized that the questions she was asking might have come from the physicians she had spoken with and that they might just be a test of my memory bank and whether it's still in one piece. I realized that the questions themselves might not be factual in nature. Saying that I was playing in the Stanley Cup Finals had very little chance of being true and was more likely a test of my current grasp of reality. Reality did seem like a hard thing to grasp.

So I told her that I didn't even remember how old I was or where I was as far as a city location goes. That moment was the first I recall actually trying to figure out my current age. Can you believe it? I was starting to very seriously worry about my damaged mental condition, and I could feel the warm perspiration running down my forehead as a result! This was mental sweat as opposed to physical sweat.

But there was certainly hope for me despite the uphill battle I was facing. Dani was here! I couldn't ask for a kinder and more loving helping hand just when I needed it. And as if it were waiting for her to appear before beginning to work, my voice started coming back. What a relief that was!

"Dani…it is so very good to see you!"

She smiled as I heard my words flow through the air in an almost normal tone. I could feel a smile starting to break out all over my face. Oh, it felt so very good to actually be really alive again!

"Dani, can you explain to me how it is that you find me in this awful condition? I remember almost nothing about the most recent events in my life except lying on this floor or bench or whatever it is in a completely helpless condition."

She smiled and planted a sweet kiss on my cheek. It felt so good and warm. I think my smile rushed back on my face again?

"Jean-Luc, do you know the name of your team?"

From the disappointed look on her face I could immediately tell that she knew the answer was 'no'. She paused for a moment as she let time roll back in her mind. She realized that I knew who she was immediately so she guessed that my childhood memories must be pretty fully intact. To confirm that conclusion she spoke the words she knew would provide an immediate answer to the question.

"Do you remember someone named Schultz?"

Wow! I must have lit up for her like a well-decorated Christmas tree. She obviously understood that the name Schultz was a four-letter word to me. I said several sentences I can't repeat here in polite company and in the process explained to her that I only remembered Schultz as a kid back in Reality. I slowly retold the infamous bicycle story and others including the black eye story all of which she took in very patiently.

Then she nodded her head and commenced to tell me what she was going to explain.

"Jean-Luc, I'm going to tell you what sequence of events put you on the floor as far as I know them, and we can see if that revives your memory. Stop me if you begin to remember what happened to you."

I nodded my head as best I could and waited for the long lost truth to finally be told to me by a source I could trust.

"As a child in Reality, you loved to play ice hockey, and your dedication to the sport certainly paid off for you. You excelled as a defenseman all the way up through high school and then you were signed to a profession contract and worked your way up to a team in San Antonio, Texas down in the lower forty-eight. From there someone else's bad luck turned into your good luck. A star defenseman on the Florida Panthers' National Hockey League Team got hurt and you were brought up to fill in just before the team entered the Stanley Cup Playoffs. We were all very excited."

Dani paused for a few seconds to allow me to absorb this information.

As I thought about what she said, I couldn't believe what I was hearing. But something about this story seemed true to life, yet I couldn't figure out why that was the case. And it wasn't because my beloved sister Dani was telling the story to me. I wanted to hear more so I kept my big mouth shut for a change.

"Your team played well and fought its way all the way to the Stanley Cup Finals and Game 7 of that championship series. And you played your way into one of the three pairs of regular defensemen with your tough play. Everyone was talking about what a great hip check you had. I was so very proud of you! But this is where the story gets even more interesting if that's even possible."

I could only agree with Dani. Of course, a victory in Game 7 would make things even better if only…if only I could remember the details of what happened. But her version of the story continued to amaze me.

"Jean-Luc, Game 7 went into overtime. Can you believe the tension and excitement this generated? The score was 2-2."

"Who were we playing?" I muttered under my excited breath.

"Why…The San Jose Sharks. That's the team Schultz plays for."

"Schultz?" I thought as my head began to fill with images of the past. The very idea of playing against my old nemesis must have freed up some of my memory. But I waved my hands in the air asking my sister to continue with her story.

"I was watching you every second, Jean-Luc. Your team was executing a line change, but you were down in the Sharks zone battling...you guessed it, Schultz for the puck. In the process you gained control and passed the puck back to your teammate, Bjore, who had just come off the bench."

Bjore was on the team with me! Wow!

"Just at the instant you passed the puck to Bjore, Schultz high-sticked you in the head knocking off your helmet right in front of the referee. The referee shot his hand into the air signaling that there would be a penalty on Schultz as soon as the Sharks managed touched the puck.

"You were falling to the ice as your teammate fired a shot towards the Sharks' goal. The shot was way wide, but that's where we got lucky... well, maybe not you so much. The puck hit you in the forehead or the side of your head as you were falling and deflected past the Sharks' goalie for the winning goal.

"YOU SCORED THE WINNING GOAL IN GAME 7 OF THE STANLEY CUP PLAYOFFS! And Schultz, of all people, made it possible! To top things off, the cheering section of fans behind your team's bench consisting mostly of loyal members of the Florida Panthers' Booster Club kept cheering and chanting your name for over twenty minutes!"

To say the least, I was stunned. Suddenly, I could see the look on Schultz's face as he saw what his high stick had done. Without me losing my helmet and falling to the ice, Bjore's shot would never have gone in. And when the puck hit me, it became MY SHOT!

Dani reached down and gave me a big hug. I sure felt a lot better now that I realized what had happened. I couldn't wait to get back to Reality, the one in Alaska, to tell all my friends the whole story.